"We can't kill this creature, ___ said. He lowered his voice to a whisper and leaned toward Borek. "If we kill it, we risk a curse falling upon the land."

"Says who?" The hunter turned to face Zimenes, folded his arms across his chest.

"The authorities," Zimenes said. He cringed inwardly at how effete that sounded. "The king himself."

"Bah," Borek waved his hand as though shooing one of the gnats that occasionally flitted about their heads. "They say that about all these monsters. I've killed my share, and I've yet to see crops wither or the women's teats dry up after." He nudged Zimenes. "It's just an animal. Does killing a hog bring down a curse from the heavens? What about a chicken?"

"This is different," he said. "It's... it's a magical beast."

"We'll see if it bleeds red like any other," Borek said. "Like any of us."

"You swore an oath—you signed a contract."

"And I will do my utmost to honor it," the hunter said. "But the king's cure is paramount—right?"

"Of course," Zimenes said. "But—"

"And if the king dies, and that son of his becomes king—would that not be its own sort of curse?"

Zimenes guffawed, then restrained his outburst. The hunter had a point.

"What's worse?" Borek continued. "Your king dying? And you losing your job, I might add? Or some vague threat of a pox upon the land?"

Zimenes folded his arms, stroked his beard, stared at the man's battered, mud-stained boots.

"The king's cure is paramount," Borek repeated.

Zimenes nodded. Met the hunter's stare.

"The king's cure is paramount," he said.

First Edition

# MIRRENWOOD
## A TALE OF THE UNICORN

Andrew Hallman

For RC,
with thanks for the inkle

# I

The boy clambered wearily over a slippery root that rose half his height. He was lost, delirious, despairing of ever seeing his home again. For days he'd been stumbling through the mazy tangle of the Mirrenwood.

Then, through the grasping, low-hanging branches, a glimmer. His head lifted. He scrambled toward the light, desperate for direction, for a way out. A way home.

He reached a clearing, and his breath left him. He ceased all movement. Barely a stone's throw away, a unicorn stood proud on a low rise, glowing spectrally in the moonlight. The creature's dark eyes gazed back over its shoulder, toward him. Its slender horn urged him onward. Beckoned the boy to follow.

"Ahem." The king's cough startled Zimenes out of his reverie.

The physician stirred and straightened in his chair, inhaled deeply. The living, breathing vision of the rampant unicorn, white mane rippling, flattened into a brocade of azure and vert and sable and indigo silks, highlighted with threads spun from pure silver and gold. The enormous tapestry filled his vision. It dominated the throne room, where the king now insisted on passing his days, and his nights, on a narrow couch. The simple wooden throne waited, empty, behind the king, lost in the shadows.

Zimenes turned from the boy in the lower corner of the tapestry, turned from the distant past, to the waking king, in the present moment. To his patient, and friend. He'd arrived for his morning visit to find the king sleeping, for a change, his breathing regular, the creases in his forehead smoothed away. He'd taken a seat at the king's side, let the man rest.

"You're here." The king's voice quavered.

Zimenes reached for his friend's fair hand with his own much darker hand, but the king recoiled, fear occluded his limpid blue eyes, and he tucked his hands under the heavy blanket that covered him from chin to toes. The disease that steadily gnawed at his patient from the inside lately plagued his mind with the melancholic delusion that his entire body was made of blown glass. He now believed that the slightest touch by another, or even a too-swift movement of his own, might cause his corporeal container to chip, or crack, or even shatter completely into a thousand pieces.

"So are you, my lord," Zimenes answered, as he retracted his hand, leaned back into his chair. He thought he could discern a faint smile through the king's flowing white beard and mustache.

"That joke," the king said, "is not very funny."

"Sire."

"But I want you to keep making it, please."

Zimenes smiled. A glimpse of his old friend, Adalmund. Hiding in that fragile container, somewhere. The man the lost boy in the tapestry had grown to become. The man he had been for nearly three decades before falling prey to this wasting disease. A disease whose cure eluded Zimenes, who was not only the king's friend, but also—and more importantly now—the king's physician. Master Eireneaus had died only five months before, elevating Zimenes from apprentice to Master, leaving him in sole charge of the king's health. In that time, Adalmund's condition had not improved. If anything, Zimenes had to admit, his patient's state had worsened, despite the various palliatives and medicaments he continued to administer, strictly following the regimens and protocols Eirenaeus had bequeathed to him.

Believing his body made of glass, the king had lately refused to allow his attendants to shave him, or to cut his hair, or to trim his fingernails or his toenails. Premature aging, a symptom of the wasting sickness, had leached color and vitality from his blond hair and beard, leaving it a wispy white. Combined with his unkempt state, the king had taken on an elderly aspect that pained his physician. At thirty-eight, Zimenes was only seven years younger than his patient. Though to look at them now, one would suppose the difference to be that of a full generation. Or even two.

The king would not even allow his physician to bleed him anymore.

Zimenes placed his palms on his knees, rose to standing, stretched his arms overhead, arched his back as though he were splayed on the disused rack buried in the deepest dungeon of the castle, a room that only rarely housed prisoners in this time of peace and plenty. A slight groan of intermingled pain and pleasure escaped him.

"I will open the curtains," Zimenes said as he moved toward the tall windows.

"No," King Adalmund said, his voice a hollow husk. "Please don't."

Zimenes halted for a moment, then continued. "As your physician, I insist. You need light. The morning air is sure to be refreshing."

"The light shears right through me," Adalmund said. "It sears me at my core."

"Nothing can penetrate those heavy blankets," Zimenes said. The king had taken to wearing heavy flannel pajamas, a quilted robe, shearling slippers, and draping himself under thick woolen blankets whether sleeping or awake. Which wasn't the worst course in the chill of winter, but now that spring had come to Averonne, he was overheating, and sweating. The dim air in the cavernous throne room had grown stale, and torpid.

"I must open one," Zimenes said, "lest I fall asleep."

He threw back the heavy velvet curtain, and a shaft of morning sunlight struck the floor in the center of the throne room. Outside, in the courtyard, several faces turned toward the movement in the window, hands lifted and fingers pointed toward the figure framed there, toward Zimenes. The people were desperate for news of their ailing king, praying for the slightest hint of an improvement, despairing that his illness was tightening its bony grasp on their beloved leader. Zimenes turned from the window.

King Adalmund had raised his hand to shield his eyes, which he had clamped closed.

"It burns," he whispered. "I close my eyes and still the light leaks in."

"Today you must stand," Zimenes said. He crossed from the window to the king's side. "Enough of this, sire. You must come to the window. Your people wish to see you."

The king shook his head, eyes still closed, though the wrinkles at the corners smoothed somewhat, and he lowered his hand.

Zimenes returned to the king's side.

"What say you, sire?" he whispered soothingly. "Let's shake off these heavy shrouds, and allow the clear light of day to chase away the shadows clouding our minds, the morning breeze to stir our appetite. Let's stand on our own two feet today. I will help you rise."

The king opened his eyes into a squint. "I feel so—" he began. Zimenes waited as his friend searched for the right word. "So weak."

Zimenes kept his shoulders from slumping, kept his grin from melting away, as he stared down into his king's face. How had this great man been reduced to this? How had Zimenes allowed this vile disease to take such firm control of his most important patient?

There was a cure. The ancient authorities—Socoridides, Nagel, Gallibulus the Younger—described the remedy, and the more modern practitioners in the Imperial City of Gothenburg—renowned doctors of physic such as d'Aubusson and Kuhnrath—were in agreement as to its efficacy. However much their prescriptions varied, there was one ingredient common to all their recipes: the powdered horn of a unicorn. A hope, however remote.

Zimenes fell to his knees at the king's side. Clasped his hands together at the fringe of the king's banquette, as though in prayer.

"Sire," he breathed. "I beg you. Open the Mirrenwood. Grant your subjects license to hunt the unicorn."

A delicate weight touched the crown of Zimenes' head. The king's palm.

"You know I cannot permit that," the king said. "The unicorn graces this hall, as it once graced me with his presence. My shield, my banners, my pennons, they all bear his likeness. The unicorn is why my people follow me. It's why they call me king."

"That's hardly why, sire," Zimenes said, head still bowed. "They love you because you and your father unified the strongholds and repelled the northern barbarians. They love you because you protect the meekest among them and you keep the lords and landowners in check." Zimenes lifted his head. "That"—he pointed toward the tapestry—"is mere myth-making."

"He revealed himself to me," the king said, his voice little more than a papery rustle. "When I was lost."

"I know."

"I was starving, despairing of ever seeing my family again."

The words and their order were intimately familiar to Zimenes, from countless tellings.

"I was going to die. I was sure of it."

"Yes."

"More sure than I am now, with my physician kneeling at my side, looking as though he needed some of his own medicine to loosen his bowels."

Zimenes chuckled.

"Rise, friend." The frail pressure left his head. Zimenes' knees crackled as he straightened them.

The king lay on a narrow couch with many cushions. He shifted his weight to his elbows, struggled to lift and straighten himself. Wary of touching him, Zimenes helped arrange the bolsters so that he sat upright. The effort left the king breathing heavily. He smiled wanly at his physician.

"My postmaster tells me he delivered a letter to my queen in her cloister," the king said.

At the far end of the hall, the small door inset into the heavy double doors opened, and a young man stepped through, closed the door softly behind him. He wore white fur trimmed in gilt and an ermine cap pulled down snug over his close-cropped blond hair. He refused to trim his equally blond facial hair, though at his nineteen years the scraggly wisps did not yet form a proper beard, or mustache. From across the hall, it simply looked as though it had been a few days since the young man had last dunked his head in the washbasin.

Prince Carlès, the king's son and heir, come to chase him away. The prince slumped into a cushioned chair beneath the tapestry, dangled one leg over the armrest. Though Zimenes had assured the prince that his father's disease was not contagious, he nonetheless kept a generous distance between them. He did not wish to disturb his father's rest, he would say. Zimenes knew the prince's bored demeanor often belied a suspicious attention—especially when he was attending his father.

"A letter from you," the king continued, reclaiming Zimenes' attention.

"It is true, sire," the physician said.

The king waited patiently. Despite his frailty, King Adalmund's silences could demand more than his questions.

"I simply expressed that if she wished to see you again," Zimenes said, "now might be an opportune moment. As you seem to be convalescing—"

"Don't lie to me, physician," the king said. "Eirenaeus would never honey the truth."

He softened the admonishment by resting his papery palm—as warm and yet insubstantial as sunlight—on Zimenes' hand. What if he were to clasp that hand roughly in his again, as when they were younger men, with the same firm grip, and haul this man to his feet as though he had done nothing more than stumble momentarily? To show Adalmund that he was not, in fact, made of glass, but forged of a much sturdier stuff, the same as any man? Certainly, sturdier stuff than had been used to fabricate Zimenes. Standing next to the reclining king, he felt himself made of little more than fabric, and fabrications. Out of whole cloth.

"So that time has come," the king whispered. "The time for farewells and amens."

Adalmund turned his head toward the tapestry. Zimenes watched the king's gaze settle first on the boy, lower, *sinister*, then follow the diagonal bend upward through the trees toward the magical, mythical beast above, *dexter*.

"I expressly forbade you to write to her," the king said.

"Sire."

"Have you heard from her?"

"It's too soon—" Zimenes began, but the king rocked his head side to side against the pillow.

"I mean, ever," Adalmund said. "In all these years."

Zimenes stared at the king. They so rarely spoke of the queen. Lately, they rarely spoke of anything other than the king's symptoms, remedies, and possible cures. But even before he had fallen ill, she was a topic they rarely touched. Even after the queen had departed, Zimenes had only once asked Adalmund why she'd left, to which he simply said, "She had to follow her calling." A wholly unsatisfactory answer.

"Why would I be so privileged?" Zimenes asked.

Had he written to her over the years? Yes. Countless times. Only to crumple and burn each letter in his fireplace. A decadent waste of fine parchment. Every single one, until this most recent.

Unsurprisingly, the queen had never replied to any of his unsent missives.

"I should like to hear some news of her," the king said, voice soft. His hand trembled on Zimenes'. "To know whether she is... if she is well."

"I haven't heard from her, sire."

The king swallowed, with effort.

"I, too, have written to her, in recent days," the king said. "I asked that she refrain from visiting, so long as I am ill."

"She is the queen," Zimenes said. "She will do as she pleases."

Adalmund turned his head from the tapestry, closed his eyes, and smiled. A grunting chuckle turned into a cough that lifted Carlès from his chair, until his father quieted. Zimenes removed his hand from under his friend's palm, pulled a pouch from his pocket, gently placed a honeyed lozenge on the king's tongue to suppress the catarrh and soothe the throat.

After sucking on the pill for a few moments, Adalmund said, "I would hate for Tesse to see me like this."

"Then allow us to seek the cure," Zimenes said. "Open the Mirrenwood. It's our only chance. Master Eirenaeus—"

"Let me meditate upon it."

"Sire. It's been months now of meditation, deliberation, consultation."

"It's not as simple as you suppose," Adalmund said. "There are...considerations. Complications."

The king closed his eyes, and a sigh escaped his lips. He seemed to have drifted into sleep again, as he so often did. These days, the simple acts of speaking to his physician and adjusting his position on the couch were quite enough to exhaust him.

Zimenes glanced across the room, toward Prince Carlès. The young man pared his fingernails with a slim ornamental dagger.

Directly above the prince, the poor boy in the lower left corner of the tapestry, scrambling over the gnarled tree root. The root ran along the lower fringe, connected to a yew tree that towered high above the boy, dominating the right margin of the design, rising to the hill in the upper corner where the unicorn stood, glowing. This same tree's sprawling branches clawed after the unicorn, shielded from any evil by a silver aura. Standing on his hind legs, *regardant*, the unicorn's visible eye, black, gazed back over his shoulder in the boy's direction, but his ivory horn pointed toward a clearing in the trees, toward a break in the border, toward the way out of the Mirrenwood. The way home.

"Do you ever feel, Zim, as though you, too, are wasting away? Attending to me like this?"

Zimenes lowered his gaze back to his patient. He smiled and shook his head. "No, sire."

"This illness keeps me prisoner here. Yet you—"

"Since I came to this country twenty years ago, my destiny has been tied to yours, sire," Zimenes said. "And I have no regrets on that score."

The king breathed in, breathed out.

"Would she come, I wonder?" he asked. "If she thought I were...."

There was, of course, only one "she" the king ever referred to. Only one woman in his life, though she'd been absent from the court nigh on ten years.

"Your guess is as good as mine, sire."

Prince Carlès stood and crossed the hall, came to stand several paces from the foot of his father's couch.

"I beg you, sire," Zimenes said, aware that his time had come to an end, "consider your humble subject's plea."

Carlès tilted his head toward the door. Zimenes nodded and turned from his friend. The prince and the physician walked the length of the hall, tapestry on their left, windows on their right, empty throne behind.

"I don't like you filling my father's head with these fantasy cures," Carlès said as they walked. He kept his voice hushed.

Zimenes stopped, turned toward the prince, who sighed and reluctantly turned back to face him. Regretting that he had said anything, Zimenes supposed, because now he would have to spend more time in the physician's presence, would feel obliged to at least pretend to listen to whatever he had to say. The lad was callow. Jealous of his father's favor. Suspicious of Zimenes' foreign accent and sun-ripened skin.

"I will not suggest it again," Zimenes said. He did not match the prince's quiet tones, but spoke aloud. He did not mind whether King Adalmund overheard him. He had stressed many times to the king that the unicorn horn represented their last hope for a cure. "If your father would rather perish than hunt the unicorn, that is his choice."

*And who am I to say that it is not the correct choice?* Zimenes thought. He had not been the one to see the unicorn. The king always spoke of his encounter with the creature in the most reverential tones. It had been a spiritual experience, a formative experience unlike any other. "A greater day than the birth of my son," the king had told Zimenes late one night, after many cups. "Greater even than the day I first met Tesse. That creature was even more beautiful than she, so infused with the divine...."

Carlès turned from Zimenes and continued on across the hall. Zimenes resumed walking as well, leather slippers shuffling over the flagstones. The prince waited for him at the door, hand on the latch.

"A clever ploy, this unicorn nonsense," Carlès said. "Absolves you of producing an actual cure, doesn't it?"

"A moot point, as your father won't open the Mirrenwood. He won't allow the hunt."

"As though such a beast even exists," Carlès whispered.

"Ask your father," Zimenes said, "whether what he saw was real."

"A vision, *in extremis*," the prince said, grip tightening on the latch. "In that feverish state, one can see all manner of things. And now you tell him that there is a cure for his malady, if only this fantasy ingredient could be acquired. Rubbish."

"All the authorities—" Zimenes began.

"Spare me your authorities," Carlès spat. "Don't forget, I grew up hearing all the after-supper stories, too. You're no physician. You've never been anything more than a camp cook with a knack for being in the right place, at the right time."

His voice grew louder, echoed down the hall. He quieted, gathered his composure, returned his voice to a whisper, a breath.

"Your days here are numbered, charlatan. It pains me to say it, because those days are so tied to the thread that binds my poor father to life. But if I were as clever and self-serving as you, I'd make myself scarce before that thread severs."

"I am all too aware that I have yet to produce a cure," Zimenes said. "I am equally frustrated. Equally disgusted, with myself. Do you think that you can call me any name I haven't already called myself? Charlatan. Mountebank. Medicaster. Prestidigitator."

"I have a simpler one," the prince said. "Fraud."

"That too." Zimenes held the prince's eyes in his own. He accepted his responsibility. Acknowledged his failure. Swallowed his guilt. But he would not blink, would not avert his gaze.

The prince glanced away, toward his hand on the door latch, shook his head. "I don't know why he trusts you so," he said, not for the first time.

"I am his friend. I would be yours as well."

"Hah!" The prince's shoulders shook. "In all these years, you've never spoken a word of encouragement to me. Never a kind word about me to my father."

"I've never uttered a word about you to your father."

"Exactly," the prince turned sharply back toward Zimenes. "But you always spoke so glowingly of my sister. Perhaps you supposed I wouldn't notice."

"Vialle was my pupil," Zimenes said, surprised at the depth of the prince's anger, the breadth of his suspicion. He wondered if Carlès, too, had come under the sway of the profound melancholia that had settled over the throne room. "As heir, and as a man, you had more important things to learn than the ancient authorities' opinions on recondite arguments and philosophical abstractions."

"Save your big words for someone more easily impressed," Carlès said. He threw the door latch with a booming metallic clank, and his countenance brightened with a smile. "Time for our public faces."

He waited, smilingly—his teeth white, even, perfect—for Zimenes to match his smile with a grimace, then, finally, a grin. Only then did the prince pull open the door.

The king's attendants and those who sought audience waited in the antechamber, and their faces lifted, their eyes studied the physician's face, for any trace of hope, for any hint of despair. They rose to their feet, questioningly sought out his eyes, hungrily tugged at the fabric of his robe. His grin felt like slowly setting plaster, as he fought to maintain it.

Prince Carlès beckoned for one of the courtiers to come inside, an earl or possibly a duke; Zimenes recognized the man but could not remember his title.

"Two more only, for a few minutes each," Zimenes admonished the prince as he pushed through the crowd, which let out a collective groan. "The king needs his rest."

"Yes, of course—physician." Carlès leaned with irony on the final word.

Zimenes strode rapidly from the Great Hall, across the courtyard. He knew he shouldn't let the prince bother him so. The boy had his father's best interests at heart, Zimenes believed. And was probably scared of what the future might hold for him. All understandable.

*That boy sure knows how to boil my blood, though,* he thought. He could feel it in the flush of his face—a warmth that, fortunately, his complexion hid from the public.

He would scour his books, yet again, for any hint of a cure that might not involve this prohibited ingredient. He had been through them all—even those that had arrived in recent weeks from far corners of the Empire—and all he had managed to come up with were palliatives and suppressants.

First, he must check with the postmaster. To see if any further books awaited him. Or any correspondence.

As he passed the gatehouse, more faces lifted in his direction, nudged neighbors, turned bodies to face him: laborers, craftsmen, merchants, beggars, all gathered outside the iron gate. Just as the courtiers had, these men and women also eagerly searched his face for any sign, for any news.

He again pressed his lips together, stretched the corners of his mouth into a smile that he did not feel internally. Even without the callow lad's barbs, Zimenes almost never felt like smiling these days. These past months. Years, even. Possibly since the queen's departure. Strange how an absence could pall more than a presence. That removing someone could shroud the entire castle with her shadow.

One gaunt figure called out, through the bars, "Doctor! What news?"

Zimenes raised his hand in acknowledgement. "Same as yesterday," he said.

"Same as yesterday!" the man said. "Same as yesterday! That's all we ever get from this one!"

As Zimenes entered the office, in the shadow of the gatehouse, another man cried, "Is he a doctor, or a parrot?"

This drew some laughs, but then a string of condemnations and curses, followed by a few buffets and shoves. It could not be good luck to anger the king's physician. For now, most of the people supported him. He knew that the populace's mood, the attitude of the courtiers, could swing from protective to hostile in a heartbeat—or rather, in the cessation of such. Very soon those curses might be aimed in his direction. Those curses, and much worse.

"Good doctor," the postmaster's assistant said. "On time as ever."

Zimenes took from him a packet of correspondence. He didn't dare scan the envelopes, the wax seals, the handwriting—not yet. Back in the privacy of his chambers. He did not want the people to take his disappointment as a reflection of his recent meeting with the king. Disappointment, or possibly his elation, though he held onto no real hope for that.

"A book as well." The assistant handed him a small leather-bound volume. *On the Rhinoceronte, the Oliphant, the Unicorn, and other Horned Beasts, Illustrated with Over One Dozen Cuts*, by one Lord Meyrick, only a few decades old. Perhaps of some use, should the king change his mind.

Zimenes' chambers were located in a small cylindrical tower at the south end of the courtyard, away from the hurly burly of the petitioners at the gate, the hustle of the market beyond the castle walls. As instructed, his apprentice, Claude, had a welcoming two-log fire going in the hearth. Zimenes removed his robe and sat before the flames in his high wing-backed chair. Set the book aside on a small table, crowded with unopened envelopes, several previous days' worth of mail, correspondence with physicians in other lands. He would get to these letters in the afternoon.

He held the fresh envelopes in his hands. It was a torture not to flip though the letters, not to inspect the handwriting of the addresses, the returns, the wax seals. But putting off his inspection also maintained the possibility he might hold this letter, might hold the spirit of this person, in his clammy palms. Only by looking would he confirm that the one letter he truly sought was, indeed, not there. It wasn't. It wouldn't be. It never was. But he wouldn't be certain until he looked.

So, he closed his eyes, leaned back into the welcoming embrace of his chair.

"Anything interesting in the post today?" Claude called out to him from the laboratory, behind the heavy leather curtain.

Zimenes shook himself, rubbed his palms over his high cheekbones, smoothed his beard. Straightened his spine and opened his eyes, turned his attention to the packet of letters. Time to end this silly, daily game. They were all addressed to him, of course. He searched, as he always did, for a familiar, elegant script, with rotund spines and thin, spidery swashes and tails.

As always, he did not find the script he sought. The envelopes, unopened, joined the others on the stand. He placed his head in his hands.

The burning wood cracked, and shifted in the hearth, sank into a puff of ash.

*Tesse*, he thought. *Oh, my dear, distant Tesse.*

# 2

Clarions shattered the morning stillness, reverberated through the courtyard. Zimenes, bleary-eyed, roused himself from bed and swung open the louvered window, peered into the yard below, squinting in the bright sunshine. Four fine chestnut stallions led the way through the large crowd that had gathered at the gate. Each steed carried a mailed man-at-arms, who each in turn bore an upraised spear, at the tip of which fluttered a yellow pennon, where the white unicorn rippled and snapped. The men's shields hung at their sides, each also depicting the white unicorn rampant on a flowery bed, surrounded by a field of gold.

Following after, two horses pulled an enclosed coach on four wooden wheels, escorted at the rear by another two men-at-arms on horseback. Curtains covered the coach's windows. The trumpets' echoes lingered after the final shrill tones had announced the royal arrival.

*The queen,* Zimenes thought. His heart began to beat again. *She has come after all.*

He turned away from the window, took stock of the room. His bedroom, lined with bookcases inset into the walls, doubled as his library. The air was close, stuffy, ripe. He left the window open to allow fresh air into the place.

*She won't be coming here, you nincompoop,* he admonished himself. *However—she may summon you.*

He lowered his face to the washbasin, splashed the chilly remnants over his cheeks and forehead, rubbed the sleep from his eyes as best he could. Reached for a hand towel.

"Clod!" He called for his apprentice. The lad's name was Claude, but Zimenes' foreign accent rendered it *clod* more often than not. As—it must be said—more often than not suited the young man. Claude was earnest, Zimenes would never deny that. Diligent. Punctual, at the very least.

Usually.

"Clod!"

Then he remembered. The day before he had dispatched his apprentice to Friedelheim, a two-day ride distant, to return a borrowed tome to Master Archytus. Zimenes hoped his assistant and his ornery nag were getting along.

He stripped out of his robe and nightshirt, inspected himself in the looking-glass. He ran his fingers through his thick black beard and his bushy black eyebrows, tried to pull these unruly tufts into shape. They proved defiant, and he reached for a boar's-bristle brush, worked in a smear of lampblack, to hide the few wiry gray hairs beginning to sprout, and then smoothed in a few drops of lamp oil, for sheen. He reached for a diffuser and sprayed a mixture of ambergris and musk into the air, lifted his arms and stepped into the cloud, eyes closed.

*The queen, here. In the castle. Today. Now.*

His heart beat double-time as he searched through his wardrobe for his best silk tunic and breeches, standard attire for formal gatherings in the Great Hall. When had he last worn them? In the autumn, Master Eirenaeus' funeral. That was when the wasting disease truly began to tighten its grip on King Adalmund. Zimenes shook his head as he pulled the clothes from their hooks: the white silk trimmed in gold thread appeared clean enough, but horribly wrinkled. He supposed he would find the clothes-iron downstairs in the laboratory, where Claude also kept his cot and few personal belongings.

In the sitting room he paused, draped the clothes over the tall back of his winged chair. He began to tidy up the sprawl of unanswered mail that festooned the desk and side table near the hearth. Envelopes slipped from his grasp, parchments scattered to the floor, and he cursed Claude for choosing to take off this day of all days. Not that either of them had any premonition of the queen's arrival. He'd never imagined that she might visit so soon. Had a hard time imagining that she would leave her cloister at all, even. It had been nearly ten years since she had sequestered herself.

*Ten years.*

*Silly fool,* he whispered. *She will not be coming to you, in your hovel.*

She would see the king, first, of course. Protocol would demand that.

Unless, perhaps, she wished to thank Zimenes for his letter, for alerting her to her husband's turn for the worse. She might consider that. She always was gracious. He shuffled the correspondence into several neat stacks on the table, then closed and gathered up the various books that lay scattered over the chair, the carpet, the table, and arranged them in a row on the mantle, in pyramids on the table, until the mantlepiece sagged and the boards groaned under their weight.

No, she would go directly to her husband. Not only would that be proper, but she had always loved him best. And why shouldn't she? He was much more of a man than Zimenes ever was. Perhaps not now, but in his day, when he was in full health. He'd been busy, that was all. Burdened by responsibilities. Traveling to the remote reaches of the kingdom, overseeing the implementation of his decrees, meeting his people and meting out justice on their behalf. Neglectful, perhaps. His worst offense. Never unloving, nor unkind. Never harsh, never cruel.

With an iron poker Zimenes rooted in the ashes for an ember to rekindle the blaze, but realized he would have to light a new one. Why, oh why hadn't Claude at least swept the hearth before departing? Hasty at the hour of lighting out for the countryside, of course, never when it came time for his duties!

He swept through the heavy leather curtain that separated the laboratory from the sitting room, lit the stove in the lab, fed it with firewood, finally found the clothes-iron and set it on top of the potbellied cast-iron container. He lit a stick of incense from the blaze, waved it to and fro as he moved back into the sitting room, spreading the sweet-smelling smoke as he went.

He was caressing the creases from his silks with the warm iron when a knock sounded at his door. His heart leapt into his mouth.

*The summons! So soon? It must be.*

"One moment!" he called out. He pulled his housecoat over his shoulders, hastily buttoned it, skipped to the door, hauled it open.

There she stood. Naught but a silhouette, framed in his doorway, deep blue sky beyond.

*Tesse.*

After all these years. Her regal bearing unmistakable. Her posture, her attitude. Her grace. Her benevolence. The light from beyond, from behind, fired her hair into a brilliant blond halo.

She stepped across his threshold, into his sitting room. She took another step forward, came within touching distance. He recoiled from this vision from his past. This green-eyed specter. Her milky-smooth cheeks, marred only by a small mole near the left corner of her mouth that, somehow, he had forgotten. The fullness of her unpainted lips bore a hint of chapping, perhaps from the long journey.

He stumbled backward, bumped into the winged chair.

*Tesse.*

Every bit as vibrant and beautiful as he remembered her, from all those years ago. As though for her, in her cloister, no time had passed, while beyond those walls the days had turned into weeks, had stretched into seasons, had blurred into years that wreaked their slow poison on Zimenes and the rest of the world.

No, it was more than that. This was Tesse as he remembered her from his first sight of her, even. As though time had somehow reversed its course. This was not a trick of the light. Nor of careful shading and painting, as some women were wont to resort to. Tesse had always abstained from such deceit. No, there was a strange magic afoot.

This was sorcery.

He reached for the chair back to steady himself. Clung to it as though this construction of wood and batting and leather would moor him to the earth, anchor him in reality.

"Tesse," he gasped.

The queen *tsked* and rolled her green eyes.

"I should hope not," she said. Then, as he still gaped, "It's me, you ninny." She slapped her palm over his left breast. "Vialle."

"Vialle?"

The princess Vialle. The king's daughter—the king's only daughter. Carlès older sister, by three years. She shook her head and swept past him into the room, surveying it all with those avid green eyes.

"My god," he breathed. "But you look—"

"Your tower is so much smaller than I remembered it," Vialle said, as she came to stand in front of his hearth. "Isn't it strange how diminished things seem when you return after a long absence?"

An older woman followed after Princess Vialle, tiptoed hesitantly onto the threshold. She wrapped her shawl more tightly about her, touched her dark hair tied into a bun, secured with long needles, decorated with a square of black lace.

"Vialle?" She peered into the gloom.

Embarrassed, Zimenes straightened himself. The older woman stepped across the threshold, but did not close the door behind her. He smoothed his housecoat, assured himself that it remained buttoned. Cleared his throat.

"You remember Magda," Vialle said. "My chaperone."

The woman extended her hand, and Zimenes took it into his.

"Of course," he lied.

The woman pressed her lips together into a smile, sketched a slight curtsy. He inclined his head.

"Doctor Zimenes," she said. He released her warm hand.

"She remembers *you*," Vialle said. Magda's head pivoted toward Vialle and her eyes narrowed.

Vialle picked up a book from the top of the nearest pyramid, opened it to the title page. Nearly twenty years ago, shortly after befriending the king, he'd taught her to read: him sitting in his winged chair, she on the ottoman. He smiled as he remembered her dangling legs, her chubby little feet that didn't quite reach the worn carpet. Her mother smiling at her clever daughter's rapid progress, at her ruddy-cheeked promise. The princess's inquisitive nature had quickly outstripped his library, comprised largely of dull medical texts and herbal compendiums loaned to him by Master Eirenaeus, who had, at the king's urging, taken Zimenes as his apprentice. So, he had purchased, borrowed, even pilfered books in a wide range of fields—history, natural philosophy, alchemy, astrology, even logic and mathematics—to keep his pupil returning to his chambers. His pupil, and her mother.

Vialle had eagerly devoured them all. In this way he had continued his education as well, as he struggled to stay a step or two ahead of his student, to maintain the air of teacher, to justify her continued presence in his sitting room. She read much more rapidly than he did, and demonstrated an uncanny ability to digest and retain the material more thoroughly. By the end of their time together, he was just as often picking through books his "pupil" had devoured and cast aside. He was often distracted, in those days. Distracted by the presence of her mother at these lessons. The occasional glance stolen over her daughter's lowered head, finger swiftly scanning over the pages...

Then, at twelve, Vialle had been sent away to Gothenburg, the Imperial Capital. To a finishing school, where she would receive instruction in etiquette, hygiene, household management, diplomatic protocol. The sorts of things that would prove useful in a princess when she married.

It wasn't long after Vialle's departure that her mother decided to cloister herself away, in a convent outside Rotterham, a tiny forest hamlet at the edge of the Mirrenwood. The diametric opposite of Gothenburg in size and importance.

And here she was again, in his sitting room. The Princess Vialle.

The silvered mirror of her mother.

"You...here," he stammered. "I.... Where—?"

The princess laughed, a ripple that filled the room.

"I've never seen you at such a loss for words, Master Zimenes," she said. "Even in my mother's presence, you were always so... volubulous. The effect you're having on him, Mags." She shook her head. "You've practically stricken the poor man dumb."

"Girl!" the older woman said. "Hush!"

Zimenes stepped to Vialle's side, took the book from her hands and closed it, set it back carefully on the table.

"Voluble," he said. "The word you seek is voluble."

"Ah—so it *is* you." Vialle turned toward him, a slight smile on her lips, the light from outside dancing emerald in her eyes. He caught a whiff of her soap, lavender and sage. "I was beginning to wonder."

"Please"—Zimenes closed the door, turned toward Magda— "come in, sit by the fire. You've had a long journey. My boy is off for the day, but—"

"We won't be staying long," Vialle said. "I would see my father, of course. But I wanted to hear the truth from you first. I need to brace myself. How is he?"

Zimenes shook his head. "Not well. Not well at all."

"You might have written to me," Vialle said, "rather than to my useless mother."

"Really, Vialle," Magda said. She had moved closer to the chair, but did not sit, despite Zimenes' offer.

"I suppose she's not entirely useless," Vialle said. "At least she passed along your message to me."

"She read my letter?"

"What else is there for her to do in that horrid nunnery, but kneel and pray and cavort with all the other fallen women?"

Magda placed her hand over her heart, and lowered herself to the very edge of the chair. Muttering, she bowed her face into her hands.

Vialle wrinkled her dainty nose, angled her head. "What's burning?"

Zimenes jumped. "My silks!"

He ran around the table, pushed through the heavy curtain. Smoke curled from the edges of the iron, where he had left it sitting on his tunic. He lifted it away, revealing a brown smudge painted squarely over the left breast. He plunged the iron into the wash bucket, releasing a hiss and a cloud of steam.

"Shit in milk," he breathed.

From the part in the curtain, he watched Vialle paging through another tome she had selected from the table. The uncanny resemblance to her mother fooled not only his eyes, but his humors as well: his blood ran quick, causing his heart to pulse in his chest and roar in his ears; acrid bile dampened his armpits and extruded from his palms; phlegm pooled and roiled in his belly, left his mouth dry as a southern desert.

But there were notable differences as well, and as he observed the princess more closely, he scolded himself for mistaking her for her mother. The dark mole on her left cheek, below the corner of her mouth. Her eyebrows a touch thinner, her lashes a hint longer, her irises a purer green than her mother's hazel. Her ivory-colored dress, trimmed with violet curlicues, fit her more snugly than any he recalled her mother wearing, while she evidently eschewed the underlayers within which her mother had typically encased herself.

Vialle leaned forward over the table to choose another book, and her breasts strained against the creamy fabric, straightened the purple curls stitched there, pulled the cloth away from her lithe figure, revealing several more moles in that inverted valley that deepened into shadow down by her navel.

She glanced up, and he stepped quickly back, touched his index finger and thumb to his lowered forehead, covering his eyes. What was he doing? The silence of the room pressed in on his ears. What was he thinking?

He cleared his mind, then his throat, and passed through the curtain into the sitting room. Vialle turned the book in her hands toward him, splayed open to a woodcut of a unicorn, *passant*.

"Glad to see you're on the right track," she said.

"You know something of your father's condition, then," Zimenes said.

She nodded, licked her finger and continued turning leaves.

"I've consulted regarding his case with the finest physicians in Gothenburg. Doctors of physic, Imperial University licentiates. Not glorified self-taught leeches." She glanced at him over the book's spine. "Without meaning to offend, of course."

He generally ignored such slights. Master Eirenaeus had both graduated from and taught at the Imperial University, and often enough had directed pointed asides at what he had described as "ossified indoctrination" inculcated in students by the traditionalists back in Gothenburg. Coming from his former pupil, however, the barb carried an extra sting.

Vialle closed the book with a thump, laid it back on top of a teetering stack. She said, "Unfortunately, all are in unanimous agreement. The remedy requires the horn of a creature that no one has seen in my lifetime."

"That is not the eternity that a woman your age might suppose," Zimenes said.

"Twenty-two years is long enough," Vialle said. "Who knows if the one my father saw is still alive?"

"They are said to live for a thousand years," Zimenes said.

"There are also those who claim they have very short life spans. A few days, at the most."

"No one really knows." He could not stop staring at Vialle—at Tesse—at Vialle again. "They are so elusive."

"What are you two on about?" Magda asked from the chair.

"Don't worry your fool head about it, Mags," Vialle said.

Magda *tsked*.

"It doesn't help," Zimenes said, "that your father refuses to open the Mirrenwood to hunters."

"We'll see about that," Vialle said. "I can be very persuasive when I want to be."

"Hah!" Magda chortled. "Petulant is the word I would use."

Vialle shrugged and thrust her tongue out at her chaperone. "I get what I want," she said.

"All too often," Magda said. "As my mother always said, 'spare the rod, spoil the child.'"

Vialle moved behind the chair where Magda sat, wrapped her hands around the wings, pressed her belly and hips into the tall back, and cooed, "Your sole sworn duty is to spare me from any and every rod."

"Ay!" Magda cried. She swung in her chair and swatted at Vialle, but she had already skipped back out of range. "The things you say, girl! You're a scandal!"

Vialle grinned at Zimenes, who felt the blood rush to his cheeks.

"Seriously, now, Mags, get your plump butt off the chair. The adults must speak frankly for a few moments. See to the food or clothing or whatever it is that the magician has scorched back behind the curtain."

Before he could stop her, Magda had vanished into the laboratory, as though relieved to have a duty other than monitoring the princess. Meanwhile Vialle flopped into the chair that her chaperone had left vacant, pushed the ottoman toward Zimenes with her foot. She shoved it again into his shins, forced him to climb over the cushioned footrest lest she topple him back into the fireplace.

"I hope we did not ruin a medical miracle that you were in the process of preparing."

Zimenes shook his head as he sat opposite her. "Only my best tunic," he said.

Vialle laughed at him.

"*You* were ironing a shirt?" She laid her hand over her heart and fluttered her green eyes. "For *me*?"

Zimenes found himself—not for the first time since this young woman had arrived—tongue-tied.

"Of course not"—Vialle waved her hand airily—"silly me, the effort was for my mother. You thought you might see her today. You were expecting a summons to the Great Hall, weren't you? Yes, look at you, you thought that the good Queen Tesse might actually descend from her lofty perch in the clouds. That she might grace us mortals with her sanctimonious presence."

Now that he knew that the queen had not arrived with her daughter, he had to admit his disappointment. Only to himself, of course—not to the princess. No need to give her the satisfaction. And a denial would be as damning as a confession.

Vialle inhaled and rocked back into the chair, swung her legs up over the armrest.

"You and my father both—such sad sacks. Holding out hope for this woman who has completely rejected the both of you. Who has rejected you so thoroughly that she has dismissed the very *idea* of men. The philosophic *ideal* of men, even."

"Your mother is a special woman," Zimenes said. "Very dear to both of us, each in our own way."

Vialle rolled her eyes.

Magda emerged from behind the curtain with his burnt shirt. She held it up and shrugged. "This is beyond even my magic, I'm afraid. Do you have another?"

"Upstairs," Vialle said. "In the wardrobe. Find something suitable for court. He may yet have need before the day is through."

Magda moved toward the steps, and Zimenes opened his mouth and lifted his hand, but Vialle grabbed his upraised finger and lowered his fist. She winked at him as he swallowed his protest.

"Tell me about my father," she said. She released his hand, rapidly cinched her hair back behind her head in a ponytail, brought her knees together, clasped her hands above them. The ever-attentive pupil, just as he remembered her. A fond memory.

Until today, that is. This woman sitting in front of him had somehow, in less time than it took silk to scorch, managed to shatter his memories not only of the young girl he thought he knew, but also of her mother, whom she so closely resembled in appearance if not in spirit, whom she rivaled in outward beauty if not in grace and quietude. No—in front of him perched an entirely new, entirely foreign creature.

"I need to know about this delusion of his," she said. "Can he truly believe his body is made of glass?"

"He won't even allow me to bleed him anymore."

"Probably just as well," she said.

Zimenes told her everything he knew about her father's condition. He barely even noticed Magda as she returned from his bedroom with another gaberdine—green this time—and passed through the sitting room into the laboratory. He found himself quite pleased to discover that the princess's mind was as sharp as her tongue, her intellect as vibrant as her eyes. She was familiar with most of the authorities he referenced, and in turn had read others mentioned in his books that he had as yet been unable to acquire for himself. The Imperial Archives in Gothenburg were an invaluable resource, and she had clearly spent many, many hours there reading and researching, poring over dusty grimoires and moldering tomes.

"Most days I find myself wishing that Master Eirenaeus were still alive," Zimenes said. "All I've managed to come up with are palliatives, sleeping draughts, lozenges to quiet the catarrh."

"That's something, at least," she said. "And, even if that old coot were still around, I doubt my father's situation would be any different. Every doctor I interviewed in Gothenburg declined to take him as a patient."

"You asked?"

Vialle leaned forward, laid her pale hand delicately over his. A friendly touch, but still it sent a jolt through his arm, sat him up straight. As though Queen Tesse herself had reached across the vast distance that separated them.

"Being my father's best friend doesn't necessarily make you the most qualified physician," she said.

He retrieved his hand from hers, picked up a book from the pile on the stand next to him. "Believe me—I, too, have sought help from outside. I summoned Master Archytus in from Friedelheim."

"Archytus?" She raised an eyebrow. "Here?"

"I also consulted with Aben Zakariyya, from my homeland, when he passed this way on pilgrimage. Both men, after a thorough examination and consultation, agreed that without the unicorn horn, there was little more to be done."

She pursed her lips and nodded slowly. "All the doctors at the Imperial University concur in that his situation is intractable, lest we obtain the horn. Of course, they also demur due to the distance between the capital and our little province. They make excuses of their rheumatism, or gout, or cataracts, or consumption. Physician, heal thyself, say I."

"Your father has told me that your suitors also complain of our remoteness. Tells me there have been those who have backed out of betrothals as a result."

"A contributing factor, perhaps," she said, then smirked, dimpling her left cheek, just above the tiny mole there. "But I'm pretty sure that wasn't the only reason they ceased their pursuits."

A knock at the door roused them from their conversation. Both leaned back, startled by the sudden noise. Before Zimenes could rise, Magda bustled to the door and opened it.

Prince Carlès stood outside. Next to him stood another man—slightly taller, slightly older, slightly more handsome—long dark hair pulled tight behind his head, dark beard combed to a fine point at his chin, huntsman's cap slashing a jaunty angle over his brow.

Carlès stepped onto the threshold, peered inside.

"Sister," he said.

"Brother," she said.

"We heard of your arrival," he said. Then, "Lord Guillem accompanies me."

The dark stranger stepped forward, swept the cap from his head and bowed low into the room.

"Princess Vialle," he said. His voice slightly deeper than Carlès'.

"Guillem," Vialle said. Magda nudged her, and she stood, curtsied. "How d'you do."

"Most excellently, your grace," he said as he deftly returned the cap to its precarious perch. "I trust thou art as hale as thou art lovely."

Vialle slouched into the chair, where the tall winged back hid her from the doorway. She rolled her eyes at Zimenes.

Magda coughed. Vialle sighed. "Quite well, thank you." Magda kicked the chair leg. "My lord," Vialle called over her shoulder.

"Your suitor and I were disappointed not to have seen you sooner, sister," Carlès said.

"I needed to speak with father's physician, brother."

Carlès chewed his lip and nodded.

"Common courtesy would suggest—" Carlès began.

"I'm not the courteous sort," she cut him off.

"Perhaps that is why at twenty-two," her brother said, "you remain unmarried."

Magda clapped her hands loudly. "Let's have some port, shall we, gentlemen? Doctor, do you have any—?"

"No," Vialle said. "My brother is right. Besides, the time has come to see my father."

The princess stood up.

"Come Mags," she said. Magda wrapped a shawl over the princess's shoulders.

"Don't look so distraught," Vialle said laughingly to Zimenes. He blinked and forced a smile, suddenly aware that the prospect of the princess's departure had left him crestfallen. She leaned toward him, touched his knee lightly.

"I have an idea that may solve all our problems," she said, voice lowered for his ears only. "Yours, mine, and—not incidentally—my father's."

The one called Lord Guillem stepped forward. Smiling blandly, he offered his elbow to Vialle. She did not loop her arm through his, but placed her hand on the inside of his forearm, near the crook of his elbow. The sleeve's fabric was black, sheer.

Zimenes stood up, and his knees crackled like logs settling in the fireplace. How long had they been conversing? It seemed to have passed in a moment, but his body told him otherwise. He bowed as far as his stiff back would permit.

"Prince Carlès," he said. "Always a pleasure."

The prince ignored him, strode from the threshold, making way for Guillem and the princess to squeeze together through the doorframe.

"Fare thee well, princess," Zimenes said.

Vialle turned over the shoulder furthest from her escort and winked at him.

"Till again we meet, my dear Master Zimenes."

# 3

Zimenes lifted his head from the book he was reading, or attempting to read: Archytus' *The Physitian's Compleat Herbarium, with Notes Astrological and Horticultural.* His eyes ached, bleary and weepy; his nasal passages were congested with an accumulation of dust and oil smoke inhaled during the hours that had marched steadily from the afternoon through the evening and now well into the night. Shoulders hunched, neck crimped, buttocks numb.

*I might as well be a miner,* he thought. A miner of words, digging through tomes rather than tombs, searching for the glint of ore—the hint of a cure—in the dim light of his lamp. Seeking a cure that did not call for an impossibly far-fetched ingredient.

He wondered about the princess's visit with her father. Wondered whether she had been able to change his mind regarding the Mirrenwood. Wondered—no, worried would be more accurate—what she would think of her father's decline. Worried whether she would blame him. As she should. As he blamed himself.

Master Eirenaeus had always complained that he was a dismal student, head drifting among the clouds, feet never firmly rooted on the earth. That he was too easily distracted, too prone to moping and sighing and giving himself over to prolonged bouts of lethargy. "Like a lovestruck young lass, you are," he would often chide. Zimenes had always chalked these reprimands off to the old man's cantankerous nature. To the fact that Eirenaeus resented the king foisting Zimenes upon him, arbitrarily replacing the man that he'd been grooming as his successor. To the old curmudgeon's natural distaste for foreigners—especially those, like Zimenes, who hailed from the "savage lands" beyond the southern mountains.

Now that he had come up against a malady that resisted his every effort—that confounded his skill, training, and intuition—he wished that he'd been a more adept pupil, and that Eirenaeus had been an even stricter instructor. Wished he had a genuine talent for physic and alchemy, instead of being the slavish reader of recipes he knew himself to be.

Wished he had a qualification for his title beyond merely being the king's friend, as the king's daughter had so aptly phrased it.

He turned down the wick and snuffed the lamp. The moon shone brilliantly through his solitary window, splashed a bright rhomboid onto the threadbare woolen rug. After the princess's visit, he'd worked through his correspondence while awaiting the summons to the Great Hall, but as the afternoon wore on, still no messenger had arrived. And so, his green gaberdine and white pantaloons also waited, neatly pressed by Magda, stretched flat over his bed. He gathered them up, hung them in his wardrobe. He needed to sleep.

He reached for the curtain to draw it tight, but instead threw the window open. The night air felt fresh, pleasant. The smell of cherry blossoms wafted into his room.

He turned to the washbasin, when a clattering against the window spun him round. Followed by a whisper, as faint as the scent of the flowers, but as distinct: "Zimenes!"

He stepped to the window, peered down into the courtyard.

A more urgent hiss—"Zim!"

Wrapped in a dark robe and hood, a figure crouched in the shadow of one of those cherry trees. A hand, pale in the moonlight, reached from the tree's shadow, beckoned him to come down from his tower. Then the figure moved, swift and silent and elastic, skipped lightly through the gate that led to the castle gardens.

Vialle. Perhaps with news about her father. But at this hour?

He splashed some water on his face to wake himself up, smoothed his eyebrows and his beard, buttoned up his housecoat, and headed downstairs.

He spent a great deal of time in the gardens supervising the planting of the herbs, flowers, and berries that he required for his medicines, salves, and unguents. He passed swiftly through the beds and planters, though—he had a feeling he knew where he would find the princess.

He stepped into the oval-shaped hedge labyrinth, turned

right, followed the outer path around a gentle bend to the left. Once among the tall, neatly trimmed hedges—each taller than the tallest man by an arm's length—there was no way to see to either side, only ahead, and behind. But he was familiar with the twists and turns, as he had helped the master gardener design the maze, many years ago. He turned left through an arched gap in the hedges, followed that bend to the right.

Soon he arrived at the center. He slowed, and cautiously peered through the rose-bedecked trellis toward the cherry tree, whose artfully pruned branches extended over a stone bench. He'd come across his share of young servants, pages—even nobles—dallying on the stone bench beneath the blossoms over the years.

The bench was empty. But a faint humming drew him further in, through the trellis, and there she sat, on the ground, the hood lowered, her hair a moon-silvered waterfall cascading down her back. She leaned forward, rocked gently back and forth as she hummed absent-mindedly, her attention fixed on a series of colorful playing cards spread out before her.

Zimenes cleared his throat as he stepped through the trellis.

"Master Zimenes." She glanced over her shoulder. "What has you awake at this hour?"

"I am nocturnal by nature," he said, as he stepped further into the maze's central patio. "And you, princess?"

"I am bored, by nurture."

She scooped up the cards, spread them out in her hands, faces up. "Recognize these?"

He did, from years and years ago. He moved toward her, barely aware of his legs or his feet, as though he drifted there, hovering above ground, pulled by some strange magnetism. As he reached for the cards, she retracted her hand, patted the gravel next to her.

This brought him to his senses. Finding himself alone with a woman in this secluded corner of the garden at any time of day would make him uncomfortable—being so with this particular woman, at this especially late hour, twisted his stomach into knots, turned his head on a swivel. But it was impossible to see beyond the dense hedges that formed the labyrinth.

His knees crackled as he folded his legs under him and sat facing her, rather than next to her.

"May I?"

She relinquished the cards into his hand. It was the deck he had painted for her, when she was his pupil. Not very long before she left for the Imperial capital.

"You must handle them, in fact," she said, "if we are to cast them."

He snorted. "We won't be doing that."

He turned the cards face up, began riffling through them. He smiled as he slowly passed the cards, one at a time, from left to right, studying each in the moonlight.

He'd spent weeks working on these. Months, all told. Several hours daily in his laboratory, beneath the solitary window, a giant magnifying glass suspended by a brass armature between his face and the cards, enlarging his fingertips, his horsehair brushes, his pigments.

He had based the deck on the twenty-three cards of the tarot's Major Arcana, and as he scanned through the cards he recognized the Magician, the Fool, the Hanged Man, the Moon, the Sun, the Tower, the Lovers, and more. However, he had substituted a few, mostly animals—here pranced the hart, with hounds nipping at his heels, and here perched the wise old owl on a leafy branch, crescent moon over her shoulder—because he knew that the animals would delight the princess.

"I'm surprised they survived," he said. He cleared his throat; his voice had emerged quieter than he'd intended.

"I always took these cards as proof that you were a magician," she said.

"I'm nothing of the sort," he said. "No matter how much people around here wish me to be."

He came to the Empress. She sat regally on a throne, gazing to the right, the scepter of the world in her left hand, cradling in her right a shield bearing the unicorn on a gold field. Her eyes were green; her dress red, fringed in blue. Though the painting was small, the shading delicate, he still recognized her clearly. He had painted her to be beautiful, and she was.

Vialle leaned forward to peer at the card that had given him pause. "You painted her in my mother's likeness," she said. "In my first years at Gothenburg, I looked at this card more often than I looked at the locket she had given me with her portrait on ivory."

"She was the first card I painted," he said. He'd labored for many hours over this card—not to mention many previous attempts that he felt didn't do the queen justice. They had all wound up in his fireplace.

*Tesse.* The Empress still looked like her, even though the coloring had faded somewhat, rubbed away in places, presumably from her daughter handling the card so often, to remind herself of her mother. After the Empress he had gone on to paint the Emperor, in King Adalmund's likeness.

He held the card out between him and the princess, shifted it to the side, comparing the two: one a pallid, flat, amateurish simulacrum; the other a very real being of flesh and blood and bile, her skin pale in the moonlight, but her emerald eyes bright, a few loose blond strands wafted by a sudden breeze.

"She looks like you, now," he said.

"You must've really liked me," Vialle said. "To lavish so much time on these cards."

"Naturally," he said. "You were my star pupil."

"Your only pupil." He looked around them as her laugh lifted toward the cypresses.

"Had I as many students as there are stars in the sky," he said, "you would've outshone them. Just as the full moon outshines the collected shimmer of all the stars combined."

"Too much poetry," she said. "Not enough natural philosophy. Each star is actually infinitely brighter than the moon, which does not generate its own light, but rather reflects light to us from our nearest star, which we call the sun."

"Is that so?" he asked. "Is that the sort of abstruse metaphysics they teach you at Gothenburg?"

"No," she said, with a pout. "My so-called instructors only attempt to fill my head with silliness and my heart with submissiveness. But if you know where to look—and if you know how to ditch your chaperone—you can discover all sorts of magic and miracles in the Imperial City. It's called modernity."

"Speaking of your chaperone—" Zimenes said. "Where is she?"

"Snoring away," Vialle said. "She can be a heavy sleeper. Especially when she lets me brew her evening tea."

Zimenes' eyebrows lifted. Vialle raised a hand to her mouth, perhaps to hide a smile.

He came to another card of his own devising: a gnarled old yew tree, dotted with that tree's poisonous red berries, that he had based on the tapestry that decorated the king's throne room.

The twenty-third and final card he had painted, and his personal favorite of the entire deck, even though the yew's branches drooped, rendering the card gloomy, foreboding. He felt he had captured some of the solidity of the tree that hung in the throne room.

"How did your father seem to you?" he asked.

"Pathetic. Hollow. Angry."

"Angry?" It had been weeks—months, even—since Zimenes had seen the king in any sort of distemper that he would describe as angry. Impatient, perhaps.

"That may have been partly my doing," Vialle said. "However, the Mirrenwood is officially open."

Zimenes gasped, leaned forward. "To hunt the unicorn?"

"Tomorrow my father will make the announcement," she said, "and issue a royal decree."

She did not fight to hide her smile now.

"Your father agreed to all of this?" he asked. "In one afternoon?"

"I told you—I can be very persuasive," she said. "I've brought a hunter, hounds, horses. All we need now is the unicorn. And I think I know how to find him."

"You do?"

"Have you read Garrimault?"

"Surely you don't mean the magician?"

"Why not?"

His shoulders slumped. She had given him hope, only to dash it, cruelly, with her naiveté.

"Oh, I see," she said. "Because she's a woman, she can't figure among your 'authorities.'"

"Hardly!" he said. "It's because she's a—a charlatan." The word that Carlès had hurled at him earlier in the day curdled on his tongue. "She preys on the credulous."

"Master Zimenes—the unicorn is, by his very nature, a magical creature."

"But at least he's been seen," he sputtered. "The ancients have described him in his natural habitat. They have used his horn to make medicaments. They have recorded recipes, and formulas."

"And yet we can see that your precious 'authorities' are not always correct, when it comes to the unicorn."

"How so?"

"Do they not insist that only a maiden of noble blood will draw the unicorn out into the open?"

"Actually," he said, "they are divided regarding whether she must be royalty."

"But they are unanimous regarding her gender," she said. "And her purity."

"Truly."

"Then how do you explain such a beast appearing to my father? Or rather, how would your authorities explain away this anomaly?"

It was a question he'd asked himself countless times before. Carlès' accusation from the previous day echoed in his mind: *In that feverish state, one can see all manner of things.*

"Perhaps they do not have all the answers they pretend to possess," Vialle stated, triumphant.

"Your father certainly *believed* he saw a unicorn." Zimenes chose his words carefully. "But that doesn't mean—"

"If you don't believe," she said, "then why plead with him to open the Mirrenwood? Why pin your hopes—and my father's—on finding a magical beast you don't believe he even saw?"

"At least then we have a hope!" he said. "A last, desperate hope, perhaps—but hope nonetheless."

"Doesn't it simply make sense to use magic to lure a magical beast?" she asked. "That's all that Garrimault—"

"What has this Garrimault ever accomplished?" Zimenes asked, attacking Vialle's "authority" in exchange for her assault on his. "What does she have to show for all her purported command of magic? I hear she is driven from town to town, can barely scrabble together the coins for crusts of bread, for the rags on her back."

"Have you ever read her?"

Zimenes waved his hand. "Master Eirenaeus described her views as heterodox. Verging on the heretical. And undoubtedly hysterical."

"Eirenaeus," Vialle sighed, gathered herself, then continued dispassionately, "was an old man with a broomstick shoved so far up his ass he no longer had need of an actual spine."

Zimenes guffawed, then looked about them, at the surrounding hedges, aware that their voices had begun to rise. She, too, glanced back over her shoulder at the rose trellis, as though expecting somebody to pass through.

"He was that," Zimenes conceded quietly. "But he was not

often wrong. He was fond of saying 'magic is just another word for wishing.'"

"Let's see what the cards have to tell us," she said. "Shall we?"

He'd given up on this parlor game as a means to reliably predict the future years ago. "The cards are too susceptible to manipulation," he said. "Too prone to the reader's desires and projections."

"That's not what you taught me about them," she said.

"They are a children's game," he said. "And you were a child."

"But I'm not anymore," she said. "So stop treating me like one. You know the power the cards have. The secrets they can reveal. That's why you taught me how to cast them. That's why you invested so much time in fashioning this deck for me."

Zimenes lifted his head, glanced through the towering cypresses at the full moon, smiling down at them.

"We don't even know if this is an auspicious night—"

"Master Zimenes," she said. "It's a full moon, on the eve of the vernal equinox. Mercury, Venus, Mars and Jupiter are all visible in the night sky. Or were, before Mercury and Venus set."

"You seem determined."

"And you seem frightened."

He smiled wanly. "They've certainly taught you the not-so-subtle art of manipulation at that finishing school of yours."

"How else is a princess to get her laggard husband to obey her?" She returned his smile, batted her lashes exaggeratedly. "Not that you're a laggard, of course."

"Well, I'm certainly not your husband."

"Shuffle the cards, Master Zimenes," she said. She held up her index finger. "One card. Humor me."

He shuffled the cards. The princess watched the cards intently as he passed them hand to hand. In the days before Vialle's birth he used to cast the cards for Tesse nearly every evening after supper, the dining hall empty except for a servant or two clearing dishes or polishing the service for the morrow—him sipping his postprandial brandy, she her glass of ruby port.

"I have no question to ask of them," he said.

"Of course you do," she said.

And she was right. The question came to him: *can the princess's plan, whatever it entails, possibly succeed? Will she—will we—finally produce the panacea we seek?*

He ceased shuffling, placed the cards in a neat stack on the ground in front of him. Cut the deck into three shorter stacks, recombined them.

He closed his eyes, thought back over the day—from the moment that Vialle had crossed his threshold, the moment that she had burst back into his life. The disturbance that she had brought with her. The emotions that she had resurfaced. Memories of the many hours spent with her—and with her mother.

Opened his eyes, to see her daughter leaning forward eagerly, looking uncannily like her mother all those years ago when he would read her cards in the banquet hall.

"Will we find the unicorn in the Mirrenwood?" she asked. "Will we find the cure for my father's malady?"

Her voice had taken on a remoteness, a trance-like distance that prickled the small hairs on his neck, behind his ears. That she had formulated virtually the same question as him caused him to gather his robe closer around his shoulders as he, too, leaned forward.

As he touched the uppermost card, he hesitated. Let his fingers rest on the deck.

He was afraid he would fail his friend. Afraid the king would die on his watch. He didn't care what might happen to himself after that. He could lose his standing at court. He could lose his tower. His apprentice. His salary, his gold and silver coins. He cared nothing for these things. He'd been a homeless, country-less vagabond before. The angered people might even capture him, sentence him to death. Stone him without so much as a trial. He wouldn't care. The worst would already have happened, if he were to lose his friend. If he were to fail in the one job he'd been charged with.

*Will we find the cure?*

He picked up the card, turned it over, laid it face up on the pebbles between them.

The Unicorn.

Vialle squealed and clapped her hands vigorously. But he felt a clammy palm constrict his throat, making it hard to swallow. Hard to breathe.

"An auspicious omen!" she said.

The unicorn was another of his additions, painted just as it appeared on shields and banners across the land, facing *dexter*, rearing up from a bed of brightly colored flowers, white against a background of gilt paint with a bright white star in the upper left corner.

"No," he managed, finally. He swallowed. Daubed sweat from his brow with his sleeve.

"What's wrong?"

"The Unicorn is the first card I painted that was not one of the tarot's Major Arcana."

"I remember you telling me that, long ago."

"But what I never told you is that I swapped out the Death card for this eminently more appealing image. Because I didn't want Death's skeletal appearance to disturb you. It was only after I made that substitution that I decided to add others, mostly animals, figuring it would please you to have a special deck that was all your own. So, in your deck, unbeknownst to you—this is the Death card."

She chewed at her lips as though she were digesting this new information.

"You taught me that the Unicorn stood for change," she said. "Revolution. Transformation. The unicorn seems to us a symbol of light and good, and Death stands for darkness and evil, but in this deck, they are one and the same. Change can mean so many things."

*Change can mean so many things.*

She was saying what he wanted to hear—which didn't mean that she wasn't correct. Already, in one short day, the princess's arrival had brought a great deal of change. Along with all the turmoil and tumult that typically rode alongside.

The card might be telling him that the king's condition would change. It might also be telling him that only death awaited him here. The death of the king. His own slow death, of stagnation.

"Think of it this way," she said. "Your younger self swapped out Death for the Unicorn. So that your older self, ten years later, could draw it instead of Death."

Now it was his turn to ponder the vagaries of fate.

"And you say you're not a magician," she said. She reached over the deck and patted his left knee. "You altered your own destiny!"

He shook his head, collected the Unicorn card and inserted it into the middle of the deck, held the twenty-three cards in his hand for a moment. Then he handed them back to her.

"It grows late," he said. Gingerly he unfolded his legs from beneath him, then stood up. "Dawn cannot be far off."

She lifted her hand for him to help her to her feet. He did so, but she did not release his hand. She dropped the cards into a pocket of her skirt, then took a small step closer. He stepped back, and she took another step in pursuit, still clasping his hand firmly in hers.

"Do I make you uncomfortable, Master Zimenes?" she whispered. The moonlight shone bright on her pale cheek, her emerald eyes.

"You look so much like your mother," he said. "It's... distracting."

He took another step back. His slippered feet crunched over the fine gravel underfoot. He tried to pull his hand free, but now she held it in both her hands, and she lifted the knot of their hands between them.

"Was she so beautiful?" she asked.

"Yes," he said. "She is."

Another step—his retreat, her answering advance. Above them, the cherry tree's limbs waved, bestirred by a soft midnight breeze.

"Am I, then?" Vialle asked. "So beautiful?"

"You are too forward," he said.

The flowers' cloying perfume swirled about them. Made it hard to breathe, even.

"I've learned it's the only way to get what you want, Master Zimenes," she said. She opened his fist, ran a finger lightly over the creases and callouses of his palm. "Nobody can read your mind, after all. Unless he truly be a magician."

She leaned forward, lips parted, as though to press those lips to his palm, or even to take his thumb into her mouth—another involuntary step backward brought his calves in stumbling contact with the unyielding stone bench. Surprised, his knees buckled, and he sat down.

She leaned toward him, and her hair spilled into the space between them, washed over their hands. He could taste the anise on her breath.

"Go and sleep now, Master Zimenes," she cooed. "Tomorrow will be an eventful day, I predict."

She released his hand, turned on her heels and strode through the trellis, into the labyrinth. Her dark robe snagged momentarily on the rose thorns, then swirled along in her wake.

He sat there, on the hard bench, its marble chill seeping through his robe, breathing in the cherry blossoms' fragrance. He considered his open palm in his lap, as though it were a thing foreign to him, a strange gift he'd been given. With his other hand, he curled those fingers closed, placed his elbows on his knees, and lowered his chin to his fists, one wrapped around the other.

*What on earth is she?* he wondered. *What is she doing here?*

*More importantly, what is she doing to me?*

The cherry branches sighed above him, and he stood. It was late. He wanted to retire to his tower. To his solitude. He picked his way by rote through the labyrinth, head lowered, hands clasped behind his back. Once free of the maze, the hedges no longer shielded him from the breeze, and the chilly night air caused him to wrap his housecoat more closely around him, and stuff his hands into his pockets. As he did, the fingers of his right hand closed around a slip of paper. He pulled it forth, into the moonlight beaming brilliantly over his shoulder.

The blank back of a playing card. A card from the deck he had painted as a present for the princess, all those years ago. He turned the stiff card over, though he already knew what he would see when he did.

The Unicorn.

# 4

The Great Hall hadn't been this full of people since the days when King Adalmund would hold public audiences with Queen Tesse at his side. The nobility and the heads of the craft and trade guilds had answered the summons, as well as the chiefs of the castle bureaus and administrative despatches—in all, thirty, maybe thirty-five men, as well as the Marchioness of Friedelheim, a glittering jewel in her spangled finery and painted fan, set against the dark costumes of the noblemen and the drab outfits of the bureaucrats. Wooden chairs had been provided, in three semi-circular ranks—nobles in the front row, guild heads and bureau chiefs in the second and third.

The attendees filed briskly into the hall. The chamberlain had informed them beforehand that there would be no time for formalities or politesses—frivolities that King Adalmund did without, for the most part, even when healthy. They would be seated, be silent, listen to the king's proclamation, and then leave, with instructions to pass along the king's decree to their sundry constituents.

The throne remained empty, but Adalmund had been propped upright on his couch in the center of the room. On his left sat his daughter, Vialle. Zimenes studiously avoided looking at her, though he felt her eyes seeking out his, sensed her pleased smirk at discomfiting him with her late-night revelations.

Instead, he peered toward his patient, vigilant for signs of fatigue. The king seemed alert, lifting his hand in acknowledgment and mouthing silent words to one attendee after another as they arrived. Encouraging them to take their seats, as some clearly felt compelled to remain standing, out of respect.

Magda sat to Vialle's left, and Zimenes had been given a chair on the far side of the chaperone. On the king's right sat his son,

Carlès. To Carlès' right sat Lord Guillem, the princess's suitor. Zimenes recognized the young man's father, the white-bearded Earl of Guillemôn, beaming proudly in the front row.

To the right of Guillem sat a large, broad-shouldered, bald man. The hunter, he presumed. He occupied the heavy, cushioned chair that Zimenes himself usually sat in when he attended the king. A long, mottled scar trailed from the crown of his shaven head down along his left eye and vanished into his bushy beard. A battered but well-oiled leather carapace clung snug to his body; the armor looked as though it had accompanied the man for many years on campaign, sleeping out of doors, under the heavens. He was the only guest who wore any sort of armor, though it seemed generous to call it that.

Behind this man knelt a much younger man, with dark eyes but smooth of chin and countenance, younger even than Carlès, Zimenes supposed. He absently petted and played with the king's favorite hunting greyhound, an aloof animal named Willit that Zimenes had never known to tolerate anyone's touch but the king's.

The chamberlain closed the doors, and after some rustling and coughing, a preternatural still fell over the assembly.

"Today you see me as I am," King Adalmund said. His voice was thin, and tremulous, but still it carried through the hall with authority. He lifted his left hand, straightened a finger toward the image of the unicorn hanging on the wall. "I am, once again, that boy you see in the tapestry. Lost, in the dark. Near death."

Murmurs of protest floated through the hall.

Zimenes turned to the image, to the boy in the lower left, the bright unicorn in the upper right. In between them swirled a dense tangle of trees and roots and rivulets, a convoluted labyrinth through which Zimenes—only sometimes—believed he could detect a faint hint of a continuous path connecting the boy, through many twists and turns, to the fabled horned horse.

He could not tell if this trail was an ingenious trick of the weavers, or his own mind playing tricks on himself, convincing himself of something that wasn't there during the long hours of vigil at the king's side, when he would stare at the tapestry with intense concentration, determined to remember every turn, so that upon encountering a dead end he could retrace his mental steps to that earlier point and try again in a new direction. Losing himself in this depiction of the event that caused the people to believe that their king had been chosen to lead them, not only by virtue of his birth, but by the favor bestowed upon him by the heavens, who had graced him and blessed him with a glimpse of the unicorn in the Mirrenwood. All those years ago.

He, too, felt as lost in that thicket, in that maze, as the boy.

He turned to the king, whose eyes were closed. Zimenes feared that he had fallen asleep, but he was only gathering his breath. He opened his eyes and swallowed.

"My physician," he lowered his hand slightly without turning his head from his audience, "in accord with Eirenaeus before him—bless his soul—tells me that the horn of the unicorn is required to cure me of this affliction. He has been urging me to open the Mirrenwood, where I saw the unicorn as a boy. He has been pleading with me to permit the hunting of this animal, so that he might produce the cure. Others have seconded his recommendation. I have been reluctant to do so, for—as you all know—this wondrous creature saved my life, all those years ago."

He paused, smiled. Cleared his throat.

"However, I do not wish to die. I will not allow this wasting illness to vanquish me. It seems that, once again, I must rely on the unicorn to find my way from this thicket. So, I have decided to open the Mirrenwood."

A cry of gratitude rose from the assembled nobles and tradespeople. Clasped hands lifted heavenward as though to give thanks for answered prayers. Some even looked toward Zimenes, and he could not help but return their smiles. The king lifted his hands, and the people became quiet, and still.

"But only to a select few, whose names I will recite today. I will not have the Mirrenwood overrun with well-meaning hunters, sportsmen and amateurs."

Murmurs and nods at the wisdom of their king's restraint.

"I have called to my side the renowned huntsman and lymerer, Borek of Slavikiya."

A ripple ran over the crowd, as people in the rear row leaned and craned their necks to see. The scarred man in the leather armor lifted himself partly from the chair and raised his right hand in acknowledgment.

"His fame precedes him," the king said. "He counts among his trophies the heads of a lion, a rhinoceronte, an oliphant, and the fearsome long-necked giraffa. He and his berner, Kurk, also of Slavikiya"—the kneeling boy ceased petting the king's hound for a moment, at the sound of his name, then resumed—"will guide the hunting party."

Borek scanned his eyes over the gathered crowd, nodded once, and sat back down. Though he did not know the man, had not heard of him, Zimenes found himself nodding. A professional hunter, an expert tracker, an experienced woodsman: to all appearances, at least, this seemed a good selection.

Before her father could say another word, the princess Vialle stood up, stepped to the end of her father's couch, laid her hand gently on the rise in the blankets created by her father's feet.

"I, too, shall go," she said. "As the lure to draw the unicorn into the open."

The crowd gasped. Magda, crouching as though this would keep the crowd from seeing her, inched forward until she could grab Vialle by the sleeve. She tried to pull her back to her chair, but Vialle snatched her arm away from her chaperone.

"My daughter," the king said. A faint smile played across his wan, bloodless lips. "I am pleased to accept your offer."

At this, Prince Carlès, Lord Guillem, and Borek of Slavikiya all stood and stepped forward, hands raised.

To his surprise, Zimenes found that he was also standing, even though he could guess from the previous night's conversation with the princess that this was her intent. Even though he supposed she must have already discussed this with her father. He raised his hand, leaned toward the king.

"Are you sure that's wise, sire?" he asked—but his words were drowned out by Carlès and Guillem, as they knelt at the foot of the king's couch and proffered their services, their swords, their shields, their lives on behalf of the king, as Carlès put it, and to protect the princess, in Guillem's words.

The king ignored Zimenes and looked past the two young men, toward Borek.

"You have an objection, master hunter?"

Borek thrust his chest forward and said, "Tis true we need a lure, sire. But, perhaps someone...younger would serve us in better stead."

As though pinched, Magda straightened and launched herself between Vialle and the hunter.

"Word of honor," she said, "I will strike down any who dare impugn the virtue of this girl!"

Vialle grabbed her chaperone's shoulder, looped her other arm around the woman's elbow, restraining her.

"The nerve!" Magda cried, her voice cracking. "The gall!"

"There is no better choice than my daughter," the king said. "Indeed, the authorities are unanimous in stating that the girl who will draw the unicorn from hiding must be a maiden of noble blood. Correct me if I am mistaken, physician?"

He turned his head to the left, toward Zimenes, who closed his gaping jaw, swallowed, and nodded.

"Still, sire, this seems needlessly risky," Zimenes managed. He ignored Vialle's steady glare, her eyes burning with green flame. "As your only daughter—"

"And I, as your only son, shall also go," Carlès said. He had thrown himself to his knees next to his father's couch. "I will slay the unicorn and provide the ingredient that your physician requires." He bowed his naked head to his hands.

The king lowered his hand to his son's head, gently ruffled his hair as he had when Carlès was a chubby-cheeked boy scampering about the castle grounds. He did not acknowledge his son's claim, however.

Lord Guillem, who knelt beside the prince, hands clasped together at the side of the king's couch, lifted his head and said, "I would safeguard the princess's life on this hunt, and would lay down my life to preserve her own without a moment's hesitation, should the need arise."

The king nodded. "I accept your brave offer, noble Guillem of the house of Guillemôn."

Guillem sighed, and his shoulders relaxed. "Thank you, my king," he breathed.

From the front row of nobles, Guillem's father, the Earl of Guillemôn, harrumphed and turned, smiling, to his right, and then to his left, as though accepting his fellow nobles' silent applause.

"And me, father," Carlès said.

"I'm going, too," Magda interrupted. She crowded toward the king on his couch. "You can't keep me from—"

The king raised his hands as though to ward away blows and buffets.

"Yes, dear Magda, yes, of course," he said.

The scowl that clouded Borek's face darkened even further. "Sire," he began.

But the king began to cough. A hush fell over the hall. The king's body shook, until the seizure slowly left him and his head and chest stilled. Borek sat, Guillem stood and returned to his chair, Vialle and Magda moved from the center of the room back to their seats. The prince continued to kneel at his father's side. Zimenes realized that he was the last one standing.

"The king tires," Zimenes said. No sooner had he said the word "tires" than he, too, felt a wave of exhaustion overtake him. It had not been a restful night. His knees protested loudly as he sat heavily in his chair, and energy drained from his body.

Carlès lifted his head. "Father? I would go, too—"

"There is one more who will join the hunt," the king said.

It was clear to Zimenes, from the way Adalmund turned a deaf ear to his son's pleas, that the king did not intend to send his heir along on the hunt. The pained contortions twisting the prince's face—as he, too, realized that he would be left behind—erased any gratification Zimenes might have felt at seeing callow Carlès brought low.

He turned from the writhing prince and scanned the faces of the noblemen in the front rank, quickly discarding each in his turn: *too lame...too near-sighted...too cowardly...too corpulent...too weak...too feckless...too much of a drunk....*

"This man will ride in my stead, since I cannot be present. He knows my thoughts nearly as well as I do, and his decisions will carry all of my authority."

"Me," the prince whispered, bowing his head a final time.

"Master Zimenes, my physician," the king said.

Zimenes' heart filled his throat, prevented him from swallowing, silenced his protests, blocked his breath. The eyes of the nobles all shifted toward him, judging his fitness for such an expedition as he had judged theirs only moments before, and finding him sorely wanting. As he found himself.

Prince Carlès leaped to his feet. "Him?"

Zimenes turned toward Vialle, and glared at her, but now she resolutely refused to acknowledge his existence. Just above that mole, at the corner of her mouth, her cheek dimpled.

"Master Zimenes has been studying these matters," the king said. "He is uniquely privileged to know how to find this creature, how to draw him out, and how to harvest what we need from his horn."

Prince Carlès stammered, speechless, his face flushed.

"I have need of you here, my son," his father said. "I cannot have my heir risking his life."

"Yet you send your daughter?" the prince cried, voice strangled. "And this—this charlatan? This impostor?"

The king glanced toward Zimenes.

"I must say," Zimenes began. Carlès' brow darkened, his eyes smoldered, twin blue embers. "The idea of sending either of your children on this quest seems...ill-advised."

The king frowned. "You tell me the horn of the unicorn is indispensable."

"Indeed, sire," Zimenes said.

"Father—" Carlès pleaded.

"You would not have us trifle with half-measures, would you?" The king spoke to Zimenes, ignoring his son.

"Of course not, sire," Zimenes said. "I only—"

"Very well then." King Adalmund turned back toward Carlès. Lifted his eyes to the gathered nobles beyond. "I have decided. I have spoken."

Red-faced, mouth pressed tight, Carlès extended his right arm and pointed his finger directly at Zimenes, though he refused to turn his head toward his father's physician. The gathered nobles— their faces placid, dumb, gaping—waited expectantly on the prince's pronouncement.

"Your illness has worsened under that fraud's care," the prince stated in measured tones. "He will lead these fools on a merry chase, I am certain."

Head held high, the prince turned stiffly, and strode directly through the center of the audience. The nobles and guild heads swiftly rose from their chairs and parted before him with a screeching of wooden chair legs over flagstones, providing the prince plenty of berth to pass. The heavy oaken door to the Great Hall slammed shut behind him with a violence that reverberated the length of the hall several times over.

"He shall come to see the wisdom of my decision," King Adalmund said.

The nobles regathered their ranks, though many remained standing. All faces returned toward Zimenes. He did not look away. He had to recognize the prince's declaration as a fact. A truth. He had to shoulder that responsibility. He had no defense.

"Let only the hunters remain," the king said. He then waved toward his chamberlain, who clapped and set in motion a troop of scullery boys and groundskeepers doubling as pages on this momentous morning.

The nobles and guild heads and courtly officials stood and bowed. The king closed his eyes while they filed from the hall, stumbling as though drugged, the muffled shuffling of their feet over the stones soon drowned by their steadily growing murmurs and grumbles of rumor and speculation, question and doubt.

Zimenes found that Borek, too, stared fixedly at him, face unreadable, scar livid and white against his weather-beaten hide. He traced that scar with the index and middle finger of his left hand, from his crown to his beard, which he gathered into his hand and pulled to a point, then released. The hunter turned his gaze toward the princess, and Zimenes did as well.

He stared at the woman who looked so much like Tesse before she became the queen. Somehow, he knew that she had arranged this all with her father. He did not appreciate being compelled to undertake this expedition. Shamed into it in front of the nobles and courtiers. Still, she refused to meet his gaze.

"Sire." He rose to his feet. "I beg you to reconsider. I am needed here, by your side. Who else will monitor your vital essences, administer your palliatives, formulate and apply your poultices—"

"Your expertise is needed to find the unicorn," the king said.

"I am too old," he said. "I would only hinder—"

"Nonsense," the king said. "If I had your health, I would—" His body suddenly spasmed in the throes of a coughing fit. Vialle handed him a glass of water, while Zimenes stepped toward him, ready with another lozenge to counter the catarrh.

"Had I your health," the king finally managed, "none of this would be necessary."

Vialle, Magda, Borek, and Guillem also stood and crowded into a small circle around the king's couch. Kurk continued wrestling with the king's greyhound, oblivious to the gravity of the situation, clearly accustomed to his master speaking for him and making all decisions on his behalf. Feeling it inappropriate to be looking down on their king, they all knelt by his side or at his feet, Borek on one knee, large hands clasped over his other. The hard stone floor dug sharply into Zimenes' kneecaps. The chamberlain, having closed the doors to the Great Hall, stood at the periphery awaiting further instructions, hands behind his back.

"Father," Vialle said. She did not look at Zimenes. "Know that we are here for you."

"I have one more charge for the hunting party," the king said. "And it is a weighty one."

"Name it, father," Vialle said.

"I would have you capture the unicorn, and shave from its horn only so much as is needed to fabricate the medicament," he said. "Rather than kill the beast entire."

"King Adalmund, with respect," Borek's voice boomed and rolled, his accent halting and harsh. "Hunting any creature is challenge enough. Already my companions are dictated to me rather than of my choosing. Now you suggest I hunt with one hand tied behind my back and my legs tied together!"

"I will double your initial fee," the king said. "And triple the bonus if successful."

Borek touched the scar with the fingers of his left hand, tugged at his beard.

"Quadruple the bonus," he said, "and I shall agree."

The king's brow creased as he glanced first toward Zimenes, then toward his daughter. He turned back toward Borek.

"Very well," the king declared. "You must consider the unicorn as though he were a friend of mine," he said. "A dear friend. You must promise me that you will not kill it."

"I have promised to bring his majesty the horn of a unicorn," Borek said. "That is the language in our contract. I will add a proviso in which I shall swear that I will do all in my power to do so without killing or mortally wounding the creature in question. But I must have your new offer in writing as well. With your majesty's signature."

"My chamberlain will make the arrangements," the king said.

Borek bowed deeply, straightened.

"Kurk!" he called. The young man pushed away the king's courser, tumbled into a somersault that projected him to his feet. "Tend to the horses, while I see to the paperwork."

The hunter, the chamberlain, and the hunter's apprentice strode from the hall. The king's greyhound trotted amiably after them, then whimpered for a moment at the closed door that separated him from his newfound friend, before galloping gracefully back to the king's side.

The king reached for his greyhound's head. "Yes, Willit," he cooed, "You want to go, too. And you shall, you shall."

"Sire." Zimenes cleared his throat. "I must beg you—"

"You will be my eyes, and my ears, Zim. You will act as my heart, and my head. I am entrusting you to guide these men and women in their quest, and relying on you to tell me of it in great detail when you return."

He still couldn't believe that he was really being asked to do this. To upend his life. He would do anything for his king—for his friend—but this seemed a colossal waste of his strengths, and certain to expose his weaknesses. He was not a hunter. He was not a woodsman. He was not a soldier. Yes, he'd been in the army. Yes, he'd slept in tents on the hard ground while on campaign—but that was nearly twenty years ago.

Still Vialle refused to lift her head toward him. As though she feared she might burst into laughter at this joke she had played on him if she were to see the stunned expression that he knew to be etched across his face.

"I would go, sire," he said, "in exchange for the princess remaining safe at your side."

Vialle began to shake her head, opened her mouth. Zimenes pressed on.

"The Mirrenwood is a dangerous place," he said. "It's a true labyrinth, not some neatly trimmed hedge maze. It's crawling with wolves, and bears, and...and lions."

"I will not remain behind," Vialle said.

"Unicorns are fickle beasts," Zimenes continued. "Their horns are long, and wickedly sharp. We ought not risk the princess's life to lure one."

Now she glanced at Zimenes, gave him a narrow smile, her green eyes flashing with anger. "Father," she began.

"Besides," Zimenes spoke over her. "I can think of no other whom I'd rather leave with instructions regarding your medicaments and schedules. If I am to leave your side, then I need someone here whom I can trust to read the stars and the cards as well as I."

King Adalmund spoke, in a voice reminiscent of his healthy, stentorian tones of yesteryear: "Everybody out."

They all rose to their feet, bowed to the king, turned to take their leave.

"Not you, Zim."

"Sire."

# 5

When only the two of them remained, King Adalmund motioned for Zimenes to sit at his right side, in the carved mahogany chair that Carlès had occupied.

"You're trying my patience, physician."

"Please, Adalmund," Zimenes said. He hadn't called the king by his name in, how long—maybe a decade? "I belong at your side."

"Zim, my friend," the king said, with a trace of a smile. "In devoting your life to my well-being, you are wasting away here right alongside me. This disease has thrown me in its dungeon, but I in turn have imprisoned you. Today I set you free, so that you may, in turn, liberate your king."

"I will only hinder the hunters," he said. "I am too old."

"Hogslop," the king said. "You are too comfortable."

Zimenes hung his head. The king spoke the truth, and he knew it.

"I have given you everything, Zim. Everything that you have—everything that you are—stems from me. I have asked for very little in return over the years."

Zimenes swallowed, and nodded. Of course the king was right. Still the word "but" leapt to his tongue. He kept his lips pressed firmly closed, however, did not allow the word to leave his mouth.

"I'm not a leader of men," Zimenes said. "I'm not like you."

"You must become one, then."

"Send your son in my place," Zimenes said. He recalled the boy's accusation: *never a kind word about me to my father.* "He would relish the challenge."

The king stared at the tapestry. "You know he's not ready."

"Vialle can lead them. She is headstrong."

"She is young," the king said. "She is a woman."

"What of this Borek?"

The king wrapped his hand around Zimenes', startling the physician.

"You're the only one I trust." The king's grip was surprisingly firm, insistent. "I trust you with this mission, just as I trusted you to keep my wife company, all those days and weeks and months when I was tending to my kingdom."

Zimenes lowered his head. "It was your wife who kept your trust, sire," he murmured.

King Adalmund smiled. "She's beautiful, is she not?"

"Sire."

"I would see her again."

Zimenes tried to remember what the queen looked like, but her daughter's face leapt to his mind in her mother's stead. He remembered the glimpse he had of her from behind the curtain. Shook his head as though to dislodge this image from his closed eyes.

"There are other reasons why I have kept the Mirrenwood sealed, and prohibited the hunting of the unicorn."

The king had turned away from Zimenes, toward the tapestry. High above them, in the dim recesses of the Great Hall's arched ceiling, the unicorn glowed with an unearthly light that seemed to emanate from within.

"I followed Master Eirenaeus' wise counsel on this matter," the king said. "There are those who would seek the horn not for its curative powers, but in search of other, more selfish aims." He turned back toward Zimenes. "My daughter tells me that you've assembled quite a collection of books about this wondrous beast."

Zimenes nodded. "Indeed, I have, but they've mostly proven to be alchemical texts, symbolical treatises, mystical sophistry—very little that could be described as practical. Almost nil drawn from firsthand experience."

"Your teacher warned that if the unicorn were to be slain by human hands," Adalmund said, his voice soft, "a curse would befall the land."

"I have read hints of this, in one or two older texts."

"Eirenaeus did not discount the idea," Adalmund said.

"Hence your request to preserve his life," Zimenes said.

"Not a request," Adalmund said. "A condition. Though it makes your quest more difficult. And decidedly more dangerous."

"If not outright impossible."

The king withdrew his hand. "Damn your eyes, Zim!"

He slapped the edge of his couch, then stared curiously at his hand, as though surprised that it had not shattered under the impact.

"I wish to see Tesse again," he said. "But not like this." His voice lowered to a whisper, as though the sudden outburst had exhausted him. "Not like this."

He squirmed on his couch, dug with his elbows among the cushions, fought to sit more upright. Zimenes stood up, moved to help him, but Adalmund winced and waved his help away.

"She left to preserve our friendship," the king said.

Zimenes gaped at him. "She told you that?"

"She didn't need to."

"What did she tell you?"

"This was something she believed she had to do. For herself. For us. Possibly even for the kingdom."

"How could you not demand that she stay?" This was a question he had wanted to ask ever since Queen Tesse had departed the castle. A question he had never dared ask.

The king sighed. "I will not command someone to do something they truly do not wish to do."

Zimenes opened his mouth to point out the obvious contradiction, but the king cut him off.

"Just as I did not command her to stay at my side when she made it clear that was no longer her place, so too I will not command you to go on the hunt. If it is a charge you truly cannot bear."

Zimenes lowered his head.

"You've saved my life before," the king said, his voice growing stronger with each word. "I'm asking you to save it again. Bring back this accursed horn. Make this cure work. Queen Tesse sacrificed herself for us, and now the time has come to repay her sacrifice. To earn it, you selfish bastard."

Chastened, Zimenes found himself marveling at the king's newfound stamina and strength. It actually gave him hope that the king might not have reached a point of no return. If the ingredient could be found in time, perhaps there was a chance to save him. This thought also made him realize that he had despaired of curing his friend, even if the hunters had been able to obtain the horn, so far gone had the king seemed. He felt ashamed of himself. Ashamed of his reluctance, ashamed of his pessimism. Ashamed of his fear.

"Sire—you seem stronger today."

Adalmund stroked his wispy white beard, smiled. "It's that girl."

"Vialle?"

"Indeed. She brings a vitality with her that is contagious. A vivacity that is infectious."

"I've noticed."

"She has reminded me of who I was—nay, of who I *am*. She has inspired me to fight."

"Perhaps she ought to remain at your side, then," Zimenes said.

"She does not belong—"

The king chuckled, which turned to a spate of coughing.

"You've seen how headstrong she is. No, she will go along. Eventually she will marry, and settle down, I hope in the Duchy of Guillemôn, bringing our neighbor together with us in close alliance and familial friendship. So let her have this adventure, Zim. Let her have a grand tale to tell her children, and her children's children. Let her set an example of what a woman is capable of in this day and age."

"She ought to be your heir," Zimenes muttered, though he regretted the words as soon as they had left his mouth. *Never a kind word about me to my father.*

King Adalmund frowned. "I wouldn't go that far."

"I merely meant that as a compliment to her," Zimenes muttered, "and to her parents who reared her."

The king's eyes drifted to the tapestry. Zimenes followed his friend's gaze as he traced a course from the boy to the unicorn across the tangled thicket of time, and memory.

What did Adalmund see in the Mirrenwood, all those years ago? Was it the unicorn? Or a forsaken boy's fever dream? And if it were indeed a unicorn that rescued him, was it possible that this same creature still roamed the forest? Or were Vialle, her tutor, her chaperone, her suitor, her hunter, and his boy about to embark on an epic folly? One destined not to be sung by troubadours for courtly audiences in years hence, but instead the subject of bawdy marionette shows to amuse children in the market?

"He was so beautiful that I could not look upon him for very long," the king said, startling Zimenes with how he seemed to divine his own doubts. "As though, in the darkest midnight, I suddenly stared directly at the noonday sun."

Zimenes lowered his gaze from the tapestry. When he was in

the presence of his friend, when he could see the sincerity engraved on the king's face, the belief in his clear, crystalline eyes, Zimenes believed.

"Sire," he breathed.

It was only afterward, alone in the quiet dark of night, when the doubts stole in on crepe soles.

"I'm counting on you, Zim," his friend said, with a wan smile. "These sore eyes would see the queen again. These aching bones would embrace her once again. Once more."

Zimenes swallowed. His king was asking him to swear a pledge that he could have no reasonable expectation of fulfilling. Despite the sunlight slanting into the hall, he could feel the vast, dark Mirrenwood out there, waiting for him. An interminable, forested labyrinth with no escape, eager to swallow him up.

"I will do everything in my power to make that happen," he said. "You have my word."

"Then fetch me my hunting horn," the king said.

The horn hung from a wooden plaque between two windows on the wall opposite the tapestry. Zimenes dragged a chair to stand on, and he lowered the ivory horn from its pegs. It was surprisingly heavy. As though it bore the weight of all the king's hopes and expectations.

He cradled the gracefully curved horn in both hands. Fashioned from a tusk of the fabled rhinoceronte, decorated with carvings of men on horseback, pursuing an antlered stag through tall trees, wrapped with copper bands at both the bell and the mouthpiece. The king had always sounded it to lead the charge and to rally his troops to his banner: to the unicorn.

"It's yours now," the king said.

"Adalmund." Zimenes fell to his knees, grimaced at the sharp pain from the impact. In many ways this was more significant than being granted the king's sword, even more a symbol of his authority and power.

"Rise, Master Zimenes."

"I don't even know how to sound one of these," he said.

"Put your mouth to it and blow," the king said. Zimenes tried, but nothing more than a spittle-inflected hiss emerged.

The king chuckled. "Doesn't exactly inspire."

"No," Zimenes said. "Hardly."

"Here," the king said, "hold it to my lips."

Zimenes did so, but the king did not have much more success.

Zimenes laughed. "Reminiscent of a fart passing through parchment."

The king glowered, pushed it back toward Zimenes. "Come on, put your lungs to a better use than flapping your lips."

Zimenes shook his head, inhaled deeply. Pressed his lips together at the bouche, as he had seen the trumpeters do. Nothing came out, no matter how hard he pushed. He felt his cheeks swell, his face grow red. Sweat stood out on his brow. He relaxed his lips slightly, pulled the mouthpiece from his teeth while keeping his lips pressed tightly, and suddenly the horn rang out clear and true, causing both men to wince their eyes closed, as though sound entered through their eyeballs.

"Cease!" the king called out.

Zimenes lowered the horn from his lips. "Sire!" he exclaimed.

The king palpated his body through the blankets, seemed relived. "You might have cracked me."

The door opened, and Vialle ran into the hall, Magda and Guillem and the chamberlain close behind.

"What on earth?" Vialle said.

Zimenes raised the horn in his right hand. "Your father's horn," he said. He turned to the king. "I want to blow it again."

"No!" the king said. "Save it for when you see the unicorn. Or for when your life is in peril. Save it for when it is truly needed."

Zimenes grinned. Vialle crossed the hall while Magda remained behind. Magda tugged on Guillem's cape, indicating that he ought to wait as well.

"I suppose this signals the commencement of the hunt," Vialle said when she reached her father's side, standing opposite Zimenes. He ignored her, though she seemed to seek out his eyes. He kept his focus on the king. On the weighty charge the king had laid upon his shoulders.

"Now you are truly committed to the quest," the king said to Zimenes, with a smile.

"I serve you as best I can, sire," he said. "In the capacity of your choosing."

He slung the horn's chain over his right shoulder, turned to take his leave.

Vialle touched his left elbow. He halted, but did not turn toward her.

"I'm glad you shall be accompanying us, Master Zimenes," she said.

He reached into the pocket of his vest, removed a slip of stiff paper.

"I would hate for your deck to be incomplete," he said.

She seemed surprised as she hesitantly took the card into her hand and turned it over, revealing the unicorn he had painted for her a decade before, the gilt background still gleaming, the blossoming flowers still vibrant. With that, he strode the length of the hall, to return to his chambers.

"We leave on the morrow, Master Zimenes," she called after him. "Soon as the sun has cleared the horizon."

He waved the horn over his shoulder in acknowledgement.

# 6

King Ethelred of Averonne stood at the parapet, gazed through the battlements toward the vast forest on the far shore of the Dulcamarra River, broad and sluggish here by the bustling town of Friedelheim.

He motioned for one of his men-at-arms, instructed him to get down on all fours so his son could stand on the man's back and peer through the crenellations as well, so he could see what his father saw. Ethelred's heir was growing taller with each month it seemed, but at twelve had not yet reached his full height.

"Addie," the king spoke into his son's ear, as he pointed out through the battlement, "do you see what I see?"

"The Mirrenwood, father."

Ethelred nodded. "Indeed, my boy. But what do you see there?"

"I see many trees," young Adalmund said. "And the Mjolnur Mountains, away to the west."

"Go on."

"The treetops ripple in the wind. Like waves in the Infinite Ocean."

"Bah." Ethelred partially straightened, looked down at his son. "You've never even seen the sea."

It was true—Averonne was, after all, a landlocked kingdom—but Adalmund had read about the Infinite Ocean, on the far side of the Mirrenwood. And he'd been many times on a boat in Lake Lauzas. Once during a sudden summer storm that had terrified him, but he hadn't let it show, and afterward his mother and her attendants praised him for his bravery.

"Ooh! I see boats on the river below us," Adalmund said, standing now on tiptoe. The "bench" he stood on shifted slightly beneath him.

"What kind of boats?"

"The ones with flat bottoms."

"Barges," Ethelred said. "Can you see what they're loading onto the barges?"

"Trees," Adalmund said. "Trees that have been chopped down."

"We don't call them that when they've been cut," the king said.

"Timber!" Adalmund quickly said. "They're loading timber."

"Good lad." Ethelred picked Adalmund up in his right arm, even though he was getting too big for this sort of treatment, clenched him to his waist with his forearm while he reached his left arm out over the battlement. Adalmund turned away initially, leaned back from the wall, leaned into his father's burly shoulder and bushy beard.

"Look, my boy," Ethelred urged.

Adalmund remembered to be brave, and lifted his chin, followed his father's hand as it swept out over the vista below them.

"This shall be the source of our nation's wealth," Ethelred said. "An infinite ocean of trees. We shall ship timber down the Dulcamarra to the bowyers and coopers in Wisselheim, to the carpenters in Donchester, and the largest, straightest, strongest pieces go on to the shipyards in Gothenburg. And you know what they'll ship back to us in exchange for all this wood?"

Adalmund, his voice still caught in his throat at the dizzying height, shook his head.

"Gold, my boy. Gold marks and silver shillings. Imperial drachmas."

Adalmund bit his lip, found his voice. Tentatively raised his own arm, though he feared to unbalance his father. He pointed at the immense Mirrenwood. "That's all ours?"

His father laughed. "All of it. Every single last tree."

"And the barbarians?"

Ethelred's face clouded. He set Adalmund down on the back of his man-at-arms, still kneeling patiently. The king laid his hands on his son's shoulders, stared directly into his eyes with a ferocity that made Adalmund desperate to turn away, yet rendered him powerless to do so.

"The barbarians have invaded from the broken lands, to the east. They are nomads, goatherders, scavengers. Their lands are very poor, so they have entered the Mirrenwood seeking to steal our treasure. That is why we are here, inspecting the town defenses, because they have grown very bold lately. On the morrow my men and I will ride out, and repel them, and drive them before us."

"Can't we just tell them that the forest is ours? That they must leave?"

King Ethelred shook his head slowly. His eyes still held Adalmund's.

"They are not people of learning, like you and I. They only understand fear, and the sword. So, we must make them fear the Mirrenwood, and fear the men of Averonne." The nearby knights murmured their approval.

"They shave their heads completely bald," Adalmund said. He had never seen a barbarian, but had heard them described many times. His father said he might get to see one on this trip— Adalmund's first to the north—though his father had then laughed cruelly after he said this. "And they tattoo their pale skin with blue ink."

"Ugly bastards," one of the king's men said, to laughter. The king nodded along. He clapped his hands down on his son's shoulders, and straightened, turned back to the view that surrounded them, briefly. It was time for the inspection to continue.

In the morning the king rode into the Mirrenwood with a hundred and fifty knights to seek out the barbarians that had been attacking foresters and loggers.

Adalmund, secretly, was among them. Reminding himself to be brave. Determined to prove himself to his father. His guardians were all occupied in cheering the king and his men as they thundered across the drawbridge that connected Friedelheim to the forest. The knights were a mix of the king's hand-picked companions and the town guard, so if any local man happened to notice the spindly lad that rode among them, he assumed him to be one of the king's fellows, and vice versa.

The helmet he had cadged made it difficult to see, difficult to breathe, and the pony that he had picked was nowhere near as swift as the chargers in the vanguard. The shield on his arm and the heavy broadsword at his waist made guiding the horse—a feat he had only recently learned—cumbersome. Once the men veered from the highway of packed earth and rode into the trees, he fell behind. No matter how much he urged his horse on, be it with spurs or whispered promises of sugar cubes, he could not keep up.

Soon the other men vanished into the forest ahead of him. He allowed the horse to slow to a trot, and then come to a complete halt. The sighing of the trees around him the only sound. He turned back the way he had come, ashamed.

A horn rang out in the distance, answered by others. *The enemy sighted! A rallying cry! Charge!*

Adalmund fought to turn his reluctant horse around, plunged once again through the trees, urged his mount to a canter whenever possible. Surely soon he would hear the sounds of battle, or come across the men's camp. But the sounds faded, and here the trees grew closer, the branches hung lower, the underbrush pressed in upon him. His horse, lathered, labored, no longer heeded his spurs. He diverted his course. Came to a halt in the deepening gloom. Night was coming on, and twelve-year-old Adalmund knew he was lost.

He was inexperienced, and unprepared, but he was not dim-witted. He would wait until dawn, and then give the horse rein, hoping the beast would carry him home, both with proverbial tails between their legs. He hung the shield and his sword from the pony's saddle, and looped the reins around a low branch. He sat with his back to a tree, the helmet in between his crossed legs, and waited, reminding himself that it was only the dark, that he had nothing to be afraid of. That he must be brave.

The light of morning woke him, and as he rubbed sleep from his eyes, he realized that the pony was gone. He hurled his helmet into the underbrush. He wanted to cry, but knew if he let that dam burst, it would not stop, and that crying would not solve his problem. So he began to walk, in the direction that seemed to be whence he'd come, changing course only when necessary due to the thickness of the underbrush. If only he'd kept his sword at his side, he could've used it as a machete, and hacked a swath through the vines and nettles, much as he supposed his father was carving a path through the barbarians that dared stand against him and his men. Every so often he would stop, and listen, for the sounds of men, or of flowing water. But only the birds, and the whispering of the boughs waving above him broke the silence.

His feet carried him deeper and deeper into the Mirrenwood. At first, he moved with trepidation, aware that barbarians might also be found in these woods, while scouting keenly for any sign of civilization, for men of Averonne. But after a few days, he just wanted to see people, of any band. He wanted food, and water. And company. He missed his mother. He missed his aunt, and his sisters. He missed his father, too, though he feared the man's wrath, feared the punishment he would incur upon their reunion. Before long he decided that no punishment would be too much to bear, if only he could see his father and his family again.

He ate pine nuts when he walked through a vast tract of such trees, where the going was easy, the soft ground carpeted with needles, and the scent that filled the air gave him hope. He came to a stand of berries and gorged himself, only to become very ill, reduced to writhing on the ground and retching for two whole days and nights. When he caught two crayfish in a brook and smashed them open with a rock, that seemed a feast. He drank water from that brook and laughed at his distended belly, and then followed the rivulet's meandering turns and twists, hoping that it would flow into the Dulcamarra, but instead it led him to a miasma choked with gray, leafless trees that rose from water coated with green algae, and teeming with biting flies and tiny gnats that swarmed into his eyes, and ears, and mouth.

For more than a week Adalmund wandered the woods. He lost track of the days. His head burned. His legs ached. Blisters made every step painful, but it was all he knew to do anymore: place one foot in front of the other, and then again, and then again. He was bereft of hope. Daylight seared his eyes, made his pulse throb in his head, so he slept during the heat of the day and walked among the trees in the moonlight. Perhaps this saved him from the nocturnal predators that stalked through the forest alongside him, that otherwise might have come upon him asleep, unawares, dead to the world.

One night, beneath a waning moon, as he picked his way among mighty, ancient yews, climbing over their gnarled roots, a brilliant blaze of blinding light caused him to shield his eyes, even as he quickened his pace, plunged forward, toward the light, heedless of scrapes and bumps and torn fingernails.

The unicorn. It waited for him. Did it allow the boy to clutch at its withers and climb onto its back, and then carry him swiftly through the forest? Or did its mere presence buoy him up, give him the necessary strength and hope to follow this bright beacon through the trees? Adalmund himself was unsure, in the immediate aftermath, and years later. All he knew was that he became suffused with energy, with a divine presence, that made it seem as though he were floating, as though the roots and brambles and nettles and branches and mud and rocks that had impeded him before no longer presented any obstacle to his way forward. He saw in his mind's eye where he needed to go, and so he moved in that direction, borne as though by the wind.

And thus, as dawn brightened the horizon on what would turn out to be the eleventh day since his disappearance, Prince Adalmund, his tattered clothes falling from his nearly skeletal frame, staggered into the outskirts of the quaint, even picturesque little mill town of Rotterham. He was saved.

The same mill town where the hunters arrived on this day, to make their final purchases and preparations, and to spend a last night in soft beds before entering the Mirrenwood, to hunt the same creature that had guided their king to safety, thirty-three years ago.

# 7

The travelers arrived in Rotterham before noon on a warm day after two full days' ride along the well-tended road of packed earth that connected the castle to the hamlet. Vialle the princess, Magda her chaperone, and Guillem her suitor rode in one royal coach, while Zimenes traveled in a second coach with Borek the lymerer, Kurk the berner, their three bloodhounds, Nigredo, Albedo, and Rubedo, and the king's greyhound, Willit. Zimenes elected to ride most of the way topside with the driver.

As Borek and Magda made arrangements at the town's sole inn, Zimenes sat on a bench on the inn's portico, looking out over the cobblestone road. A serving girl emerged from the tavern across the way, began unbarring and opening the shutters protecting the windows. Vialle sat next to him, and Guillem sat on her other side. The three of them watched—and were watched by—groups of people in twos, threes, fours, heading toward the market. Some stared, some pointed, some waved, some even paused and bowed in their direction.

"Long live the king!" called one. Vialle rose and waved, with a smile. That became the hailing shout, from all who passed after. "Long live the king!"

"Word has spread," Zimenes said, as the princess sat back down between him and Guillem. Before departing the castle, the king had dispatched a herald to alert the inn and the cloister of their impending arrival. It was only natural for news to make its way, from bird to bird, as it were, from tree to tree.

"They've come to see us off," Vialle said. "And wish us well."

"They love your father dearly," Guillem said.

"It would be best," Zimenes said, "if we don't return empty-handed."

Vialle turned to him, as though shocked to hear him suggest that was even a possibility.

"Faith, physician." She nudged his arm with her elbow. "Faith, and courage."

Borek set out to procure necessary victuals and other equipment that the party would need. Kurk escorted the hounds to the stables around back. Having observed the youth on the road, Zimenes supposed that Kurk would probably sleep in the stables with the dogs—he seemed infinitely more comfortable in the company of the animals than he did with the humans, and had barely exchanged more than a few words with any of them, even Borek, his master, so far as the physician could tell. He seemed adept at anticipating his master's needs, based on little more than a hand gesture, a frown, or a cluck of the tongue.

Vialle, meanwhile, would visit her mother in the nearby cloister whence she had ensconced herself all those years ago. Only Our Sacred Lady of the Mirren had received a royal dispensation to remain on the forested side of the Dulcamarra, just within the Mirrenwood, where it stood a couple of leagues downriver from the series of falls that powered the mills. Zimenes had heard King Adalmund describe the place, as he had gone to visit Tesse there once, not long after she had departed the castle. To plead with her to return? To see to her comfort? Simply to see her again? Zimenes did not remember. So long ago.

*Not that long ago, ten years,* he thought. *Long enough—look how much Vialle has changed in that time. Then again, look how little you've changed.*

*And Tesse? Had she changed?*

Magda, of course, would accompany Vialle. She had been one of Tesse's ladies-in-waiting before she became Queen. Guillem announced that he would accompany the women to the convent, to make sure that no ill befell them along the way. Vialle assured him that such precaution wouldn't be necessary, that the presence of the renowned Champions of the Mirren—the guardians of the forest—would surely dissuade any would-be highwaymen. But Guillem insisted. Determined at every opportunity to impress upon Vialle his valor, and his value.

"You're not joining us?" Guillem asked Zimenes. "I assumed we would all—"

"I imagine men are not even allowed to enter," Zimenes said.

"My mother is still the Queen," Vialle said. "Exceptions can be made. You ought to join us. It might do you good."

He frowned at her. Vialle wishing to see her mother seemed perfectly reasonable. But there was no reason for him to disturb the queen. No benefit that might be gained.

"Seeing her might prove...liberating," Vialle said.

"Am I imprisoned?" he asked.

"She could give you her blessing," Vialle said, "as we undertake this quest."

"I would not presume to see the Queen before her husband," he said. "Only after we have succeeded in this mission and I am satisfied that your father has been completely cured of his malady, only then will I have proven myself worthy of an audience. Should she be so inclined."

"Physician, suit thyself," Vialle said. She rose to acknowledge another party saluting her father, with a smile and a wave.

Magda emerged from the inn, looked down at the three on the bench.

"Shall we?" she asked.

Vialle and Guillem got to their feet. Magda looked inquiringly at Zimenes.

"He's not going, Mags," Vialle said.

"*Och*, of course he's coming," Magda said to Zimenes, rapping him on the shoulder. "What are you going to do, stay here drinking with this lot?" She gestured toward the people passing before them—some of whom Zimenes was sure had already passed them by. Around for a second look, he supposed. "We'll be lucky if these hooligans let us get any sleep tonight."

And with that, it was settled. Zimenes would join them on their little expedition downriver. Truth be told, he did not relish the thought of staying behind, on his own, among the growing tide of curious gawkers.

"You'd think it was Midsummer's Eve from the way folks are carousing!" Magda said, with a cluck of her tongue and a shake of her head.

They set off along the cobblestone road, walked past enormous mill wheels slowly turning, the churning water pushing their broad scoops.

Past the mills, the road reverted to packed earth. The path paralleled the river, sloping gently uphill all the while, until the

Dulcamarra was lost to view below them, hidden first by trees and then by a sheer drop as the river entered a gorge.

They reached the stone guardhouse at the head of the narrow wooden bridge that spanned the river, connecting the cloister to civilization. In front of the gate, two Champions of the Mirren stood at attention, the butts of their spears at their feet, the tips high in the air, graced with the white and yellow pennons Zimenes was accustomed to seeing at the castle.

The Champions were charged with guarding the few entrances to the forest and patrolling its borders. These honored knights were all veterans of the fierce wars against the barbarians. They were entitled to bear the unicorn on their pennons and their shields, to incorporate the unicorn's horn into their familial coats-of-arms, and to wear the white and gold ribbons of the brotherhood. They were known to tattoo an image of the unicorn over their left breasts, though tattooing was considered a savage custom, embraced only by the barbarians they had so recently vanquished.

The knights crossed their spears in front of the travelers to bring them to a halt, and two more guardsmen emerged from the guardhouse, hands resting easily on sword pommels. On recognizing the princess, the knights parted their spears. She stated her intention of visiting the cloister.

"May the unicorn guide your way, m'lady," the Captain said, with a deep bow, as they passed him by.

This was an old expression of good fortune that Zimenes recognized from his days in the army, though he hadn't heard it in years, as the expression had fallen from fashion, at least in the castle. Clearly here, so close to the Mirrenwood, and among the unicorn's champions, it still pertained.

On the far side of the narrow bridge—a quick glance down through the planking underfoot had sent Zimenes' mind reeling at the precipitous height—they passed through a stone arch.

Directly ahead of them a road of broad flagstones—the old highway—led straight into the Mirrenwood. The trees here stood tall and proud, separate from each other. The early spring undergrowth grew sparsely; the branches above had begun to bud and flower, but were not yet clothed in their full greenery.

A track wound away to the left, toward the cloister, through smaller scrub pines and cypresses that clawed an existence from the shallower, rocky soil near the gorge. The cloister perched at the very edge of the ravine, the building's southern wall even leaned out over the chasm, peered down at the Dulcamarra rushing along far below.

"Seems so precarious," Magda said. "I don't think I should like to live in such a place, at all."

"Better be a good girl, then, Mags," Vialle teased.

They passed through a gate, and were greeted by an elderly, hunched woman, wearing a dark tunic and a shallow, broad-rimmed hat. Behind her rose a graceful statue of the Lady of the Mirren, naked except for a girdle of flowers, her arms swept low, palms open in welcome, as though about to gather them all up into her sweet embrace. Locks of her hair swirled about her head, caught in a permanent gust. Though sculpted from marble, the pale white stone seemed translucent somehow—diaphanous, even. Perilously fragile.

The woman guided them, haltingly, not through the principal doors, but around to the side, away from the gorge, to a gate that led into a square courtyard. The woman motioned toward a small wooden door set into the far wall, but then reached with gnarled, knotted fingers for the sleeve of Zimenes, and then of Guillem, restraining them with the gentlest of tugs.

"Not you," she said. "The women only."

Vialle turned, shrugged her shoulders and flashed them a smile, then she and Magda ducked their heads, and continued into the chamber. The door closed behind them, and then the older woman departed back the way she had come, leaving Zimenes and Lord Guillem standing in somewhat awkward silence. A wooden bench waited next to the door, and they both sat down. Guillem splayed his legs out wide, pointed his toes upward, slowly rotated them around.

"So," he drawled. "A physician, eh? You like that sort of work?"

"There are days when I'd rather be anything else," Zimenes said.

"If I were to learn a trade," Guillem said, "don't think I'd be much for doctoring. Too much responsibility. Don't think I could take it if a patient of mine died."

Zimenes stared at him. Soon the young nobleman realized the implication of what he had said, and became quite flustered and apologetic.

"Don't worry about it," Zimenes said. After all, Guillem hadn't said anything he hadn't already considered, many times over. "What profession would you choose?" he asked, to change the subject. "If you were required to dirty your hands, so to speak."

"Horse trading, that would be more my speed," Guillem managed, after he had ceased his spluttering. "But what I really love to do? I know you can't really call this a trade, *per se*, but I do love to race them."

He began to harangue Zimenes about the glories of racing at the hippodrome that his father's father had built in Wisselheim.

As the young man spoke—animated, gesturing with his hands—Zimenes became aware of whispering and tittering. He glanced up, toward a window in the wall looking down over the courtyard, and three pale, oval faces quickly disappeared. He averted his gaze. When he glanced back, they were there again, hands over mouths, but they didn't notice him looking in their direction, as their eyes were fixed on handsome Guillem, now up on his feet and astride an imaginary horse, demonstrating as he narrated how he would lash his mount's flank with his crop, urging him on to the finish line, fending off a challenger making a desperate final assault.

Flushed and beaming, Guillem threw himself back down on the bench, stretched out his skinny legs, clopped the heels of his magnificent leather boots.

Zimenes nudged him and indicated with his chin the upper-story window.

Guillem shrugged. He was aware. Had been aware all along, Zimenes realized. He was handsome. He was rich. He was royalty. He'd come to expect that kind of attention from women.

"I do love her, you know," Guillem said.

"The princess?" Zimenes said. "That seems obvious."

"Is it?" Guillem asked. He leaned toward Zimenes, lowered his voice. "Is it *too* obvious?"

Zimenes chortled. "I'm not the one to ask about such subtleties," he said.

"I understand that you and she have a long history," Guillem said.

"I was her tutor, for a time," Zimenes said. "She was my pupil."

"I want you to know that I would always encourage you to maintain that special bond," Guillem said. "I know she has great respect for you."

"Fortunately for her," Zimenes said, "she has long since outgrown my tutelage."

The young man lowered his voice further, to a whisper: "Does she ever speak of me?"

Zimenes tried to recall something positive the princess had said to him of Guillem since her return to the castle. Tried to recall anything she had said to him regarding the young man.

"She does not complain of your presence," Zimenes said. "You might take that as a good sign."

Guillem sighed and slouched back into the unforgiving bench. "She despises me," he said.

*Does she?* Zimenes suddenly felt some sympathy for the princess's suitor—despite his youth, his dashing looks, his broad chest, his easy athleticism, his charming demeanor, his family fortune. He was pretty sure that the princess didn't *despise* Lord Guillem. Her attitude seemed more one of...*indifference*. Which, he supposed, might even be worse.

"I suppose her heart can be hard to read, at times," Zimenes finally said.

"At best," Guillem said, with a faint sigh. He crossed one ankle over the other, waggled his toes. "It would mean a great deal to me if you were to put in a word on my behalf," he said.

"I don't know that I—" Zimenes began.

"She looks up to you," Guillem said. He suddenly sat up straight, touched Zimenes' sleeve. "She always speaks so fondly of you. She admires you so."

At that moment, the door opened, and Magda filled its narrow frame. "Lord Guillem," she whispered, waving at the younger man. "Come meet the queen."

Zimenes gave the nobleman a valedictory pat on the knee. "I'll do what I can," he said. "But—trust me—a good impression on the mother-in-law will do more for you than I ever could."

Guillem exhaled heavily, clasped Zimenes' hand in his. "Thank you, physician," he said, somberly. As though the odds were good that he would not return from this encounter alive. "Wish me luck."

"Hop to it, lad," Zimenes said. "Give 'em hell."

Magda stepped back to allow Guillem to fold himself at the waist and duck in under the lintel. From the shadows that darkened the chaperone's face, Zimenes could not be sure whether she winked at him as she closed the door after them.

Disappointed, the three young women turned from the window, leaving Zimenes sitting alone in the courtyard, aside from the bees dancing from flower to flower.

*She admires you. She speaks so fondly of you.*

The bees, not unlike his thoughts, flitting from subject to subject.

*Will they tell her I've come? Will she want to see me?*

# 8

He stood in the corner of the courtyard, watching a spider knitting her web in the angle between a column and the colonnade's eave, when the little door opened and Magda, Vialle, and Guillem emerged and straightened. Vialle blinked and stretched in the waning afternoon sunlight. The door closed, and Zimenes crossed the small lawn to join them for the return to Rotterham. He was growing hungry, and the thought of a glass of brandy at the tavern facing the inn held a certain appeal.

"How seemed your mother?" he asked. Quietly, so that his voice would not carry through the door.

"Dried and shriveled," Vialle said. "Like a prune left in the summer sun."

Magda *tsked* and swatted at Vialle with her fan.

"Stuff and nonsense," the princess's chaperone said. "Her grace is every bit as beautiful as she's always been. The forest air favors her."

"Good," Zimenes said. "That gladdens my heart. Shall we return to town?"

Vialle shook her head. "Your turn," she said. She hooked her thumb toward the door.

Zimenes turned to Magda to see if Vialle was teasing him. The older woman simply shrugged, her thin lips pursed.

"I dare not—" he began. His breath came shallow, his mouth suddenly dry while sweat dampened the base of his spine. The sun warm, now, and close.

"Go on, silly," Vialle said. "She asked for you."

He threw back his shoulders. Ran a hand through his beard.

"Let me." Vialle removed a comb holding her own hair pinned behind her head and ran it several times through Zimenes' beard. She licked her thumb and pasted down first one eyebrow, then the other. She removed his robe, straightened the collar of his gaberdine. Finally, she pinched his cheeks between her thumbs and knuckles.

"To restore your color," she said, as he pulled away. "You look like you've seen a ghost. Or like you're about to."

He turned toward the door, bent forward to push it open. As he stepped through, head bowed to avoid the low lintel, a hard swat across his buttocks startled him, caused him to stumble forward into the dim room. He could hear Magda scolding Vialle as the door was pulled shut behind him.

He straightened, gingerly, waiting for his eyes to adjust to the low light. A curtain had been partially drawn over the room's single window, set into the wall next to the door, to screen out the afternoon sunlight. He found himself in a small chapel, the nave no more than two rows of five pews facing a humble altar. A large sculpture of a tree adorned the wall of the chancel, carved from wood, the leaves painted green, dotted with pale white flowers and red berries.

In the first pew sat a woman, her back to him. Zimenes moved down the aisle, came to stand next to her. He couldn't bring himself to look at her. He dropped to one knee. The side of the pew screened her from him.

"I apologize, my queen," he said, head bowed. "I am ashamed. My patient has fallen so far under my care. I had resolved that I would not seek an audience with your grace until our king had recovered to his full health and strength."

"What changed your mind?"

"You—you summoned me."

"My daughter said you sought my blessing."

He chuckled to himself, though the laugh echoed in the small nave. "She likes to stir up trouble," he said.

"She always has had a mischievous streak," her mother said. "But it's just as well. Rise, my friend. Sit with me a while. It has been so long."

He gripped the end of the pew and hauled himself to his feet. She turned her face up to him, but a black veil hid her features. She scooted herself down the bench, made room for him to sit alongside her.

Instead, he sat on the second step of the dais that supported the altar. Facing her.

"How are you, Zimenes?"

"Must you wear that veil?"

"You look well," she said.

"And I, in turn, should like to say the same of you, as I'm sure is the case," he said.

"But first you need proof?"

"I would like to see your face, my queen."

"It's better, perhaps, if you don't," she said.

"Oh." He leaned back. "You don't believe I could handle myself?"

"I am in mourning," she said. She sat with her knees together, her hands in her lap. Even her hands were hidden by gloves. Black gloves.

"He's not dead yet, my queen," he said.

"I've been in mourning since I arrived at the cloister," she said.

He stared at her, tried to see through the lace, tried to divine her expression. Was there the hint of a smile? The trace of a teasing tone in her voice? He had no idea. There was a time when he would've been able to picture her features simply from hearing her speak one word—but it had been too long.

"That's a long time," he said.

The veil bobbed, up and down.

"Perhaps it can end soon," she said. "My daughter tells me that this expedition is under your command."

He straightened his spine, filled his chest. Did his best to look the part.

"To seek the horn of the unicorn," she continued. "To cure my husband of this illness that afflicts him."

"That's right."

"I have a charge of my own to lay upon you then," she said.

"Name it, my queen."

"Keep watch over Vialle," she said. "She is young, naive, and willful. With a touch of arrogance."

"She has a chaperone to do just that," Zimenes said.

"Magda, much as I love her," Queen Tesse said, "is not the most astute. I fear that Vialle is beyond her control."

Zimenes laughed. "She's certainly beyond my ability to control."

"She will listen to you, Zim," Tesse said. "She respects you. You were her teacher. You're"—and now he could detect, in the pause, her nose wrinkling in distaste—"you're a man."

"I'd bet good money that, mere moments ago, Lord Guillem also pledged to you that he would safeguard your daughter's life with his own."

Tesse's shoulders shook, once. Her right hand lifted from her lap, as though to hide her smile, only to realize that it didn't need to make that journey, as the smile was already obscured by the veil. It returned to embrace its partner in her lap.

"As I said," Tesse said, "you're a man. The heir of Guillemôn is but a child. As is my daughter."

*I'm not so sure about that,* Zimenes thought. *Regarding either Vialle, or her suitor.*

He stood up. He had energy, suddenly. He clasped his hands together behind his back, to keep from reaching out and swiping that veil from her head, laying bare her face. He paced toward the window, considered throwing open the curtain, letting the afternoon sunlight flood the chapel, letting it chase away these shadows, these doubts. Instead, he pulled it to one side. Through the gap between the curtain and the casement, he spied Vialle and Guillem standing in the center of the courtyard, talking, Vialle smiling, her green eyes glittering. Guillem, evidently pleased with a witticism, leaned forward while digging one boot heel into the turf.

"I will, of course, do all in my power to keep her from harm," he said.

He turned away from the window. The shaft of light that stabbed toward the altar only plunged the rest of the room into a deeper shadow.

"And don't you worry about me, my queen," he said, trying to lighten the mood, if not the room. "I'll be fine."

"Adalmund chose well," she said. "As he ever did."

Zimenes climbed the three steps to the chancel, walked behind the altar to the tree. He traced his fingers over the intricately carved trunk.

"How do you spend your time in this place?" he asked. He turned back toward her. "Your days?"

"I'm quite a bit busier than I ever was at the castle," she said. "I garden. I weave. I sing in the choir. I cook—I bake bread, mostly. There is always something more to do. Our work is never done."

"Is that—do you find that satisfying?"

"My first two years here," she said. "I didn't speak to anyone. I mostly prayed, or meditated, or argued with myself, whatever you would call it. I muttered to myself like a crazy woman. But I have since made my peace. With myself, with how I behaved. With what I wanted but could not have."

"Have you?" he asked, looking down at her, his hands braced on the altar. "Because I haven't."

"We can't have everything in this life," she said. "Not even one so fortunate as the Queen of Averonne."

He came down the steps, and she stood up to meet him. He opened his arms to her, but she raised her hand, gloved palm out, and said, in a powerful, strident voice that echoed in that small space:

"Zim!"

He stopped. Her voice reverberated in his head.

In softer tones, then, she said, "I'm told you would have my blessing, Master Zimenes."

He swallowed. Nodded. "Yes," he said.

"Kneel," she commanded.

His knees crackled in the quiet as he bent them, lowered himself onto them. The hard stone floor dug into his kneecaps.

She towered over him. She lifted her veil, swept it back over her head.

*Tesse.* Her hazel eyes glinted in the gleam cast by the window. The streak of gray hair pulled back at her temples, the tightening of the corners of her mouth, gave her beauty a severe, almost fearsome aspect. Abashed, he dropped his head, clasped his hands together, clamped his eyes shut. Prepared to receive her blessing.

She took one step closer to him, inclined at the waist. Lowered her head to him, and placed her lips soft against his forehead, where his hair fell away to either side. Her kiss lingered there for a moment, and then another. Her warmth swirled around him, her scent of orange peel and cloves.

From his knees, he wrapped his arms around her legs, pulled her close to him, even though she had to remove her lips from his head and place her hands on his shoulders to keep from pitching forward over his back.

"Zimenes!" she cried.

He buried his face in her skirts, in her lap. She regained her balance. Her legs relaxed. She placed her hands on his head. Ran her fingers through his hair. Gloved fingers.

"Zimenes," she said, in a softer tone. She tapped his shoulder now. "That's enough. You have your blessing."

He released her. He remained kneeling, back to the altar, as her skirts swished and her shoes clipped over the stone. A door opened—not the door to the courtyard.

"When you catch the unicorn," her voice floated across the nave to him, over the empty pews, "I want to hear the news."

He swiped angrily at his eyes. She did not deserve one tear, this woman who did not love him. Certainly not in the same measure that he had loved her.

"I want to hear it directly from you, Master Zimenes," she said.

"You have my word," he said. "My queen."

The door closed, leaving him in the dim chamber. Motes floated in the thin golden shaft that passed between the curtain and the window sill. The chime of Vialle's laugh filtered in from the courtyard, danced in time with those ever-falling particles of light. He placed his palms on the bench before him—the wood still warm—and lifted himself to standing.

Time to see about that glass—no, that decanter—of brandy.

# 9

Vialle studied his face when he emerged from the chapel. "How was that?" she asked.

"Fine," Zimenes answered. "We've been blessed."

On the walk back, Zimenes and Magda led the way, while Vialle and Guillem dawdled behind. By the time they reached the rickety town gate, the sun had nearly finished its descent, and bathed the budding, blooming trees in golden light.

Magda stopped at the gate and sighed. "I suppose I must wait on my charge," she said.

"Right," Zimenes said, seizing the opportunity to spend some time unaccompanied. "I'll see you all back at the inn, then."

Townspeople and country folk alike thronged through the market, a collection of a dozen or so semi-permanent stalls and stands, built of wood with striped cloth coverings providing shade, or cover from the rain on a cloudy day. No sign of Borek, nor of Kurk. The brightly colored vegetables and fruits, the pungent breads, the gooey beeswax, all reminded Zimenes that he was hungry, and he bought an orange, paid a ha'penny extra for the lass to hand it to him peeled and sectioned. The fruit burst between his teeth, filled his mouth with flavor, quickened his step.

Tucked in a far corner of the market, he came to a stall that was smaller, less substantial than the others, and did not sell food. An older woman perched on a stool behind the counter. She wore a simple, dark tunic and a shallow, broad-rimmed hat. Her table contained a number of brightly colored trinkets, including prayer beads and glazed ceramic cups and mugs. In front of her sat a narrow loom, and she passed the shuttle back and forth, to and fro, weaving together varicolored threads into an intricate pattern that she packed down with the beveled edge of the shuttle with each pass through the weft. Several finished woven bands of various lengths and widths stretched out on display over the table alongside the loom.

"What do you call these?" Zimenes asked the woman, while holding up one of the colored bands.

"They be inkles," she said, without removing her attention from the braided pattern she was weaving.

She continued passing the shuttle back and forth, switching the warp and the weft before each pass with a deft flick of her hand, packing the threads down into the pattern with the edge of the shuttle after. He found the movements entrancing.

"Do these inkles serve a purpose?" he asked.

"They can be used as a bracelet, a belt, a strap, a tie, a bootlace," she said, a well-practiced patter. "Some folks take them as reminders, or for prayers. They can be sewn together into socks, or bags, or placemats, or pillowcases."

"Did you make all these?"

The woman left off her weaving and looked up at Zimenes, neither pleased nor annoyed by the interruption. He had to admire her complete and total indifference.

"No," she said. "They are made by women in the cloister. All proceeds benefit Our Sacred Lady of the Mirren."

"I see," he said. "Even the queen?"

The woman smiled.

"Why yes," she said, clearly accustomed to the question. "Even the queen."

She glanced toward her loom, the slowly growing band taking shape there. He was keeping her from her pastime. Meanwhile, several people had begun to mill around behind him. Children grabbed the edge of the table, stood on tip-toe to see the wares on offer.

"Would you be able to tell me if any of these were made by her?"

The woman did not lower her eyes to the inkles arrayed before her, but instead narrowed them as she studied the face of her questioner.

"We do not identify the pieces that we make," she said. "That would be a sign of worldliness."

"But she does make these charms? These—inkles?"

"We all do," she said. "It's a pleasant enough pastime. All proceeds go toward upkeep and maintenance."

Zimenes' heart quickened. "Could you point out one she had made?"

The woman smiled and shook her head. "I'm sure I couldn't, dearie."

"I see."

Zimenes set about inspecting the various inkles while the woman returned to her loom and took up the shuttle. Some inkles incorporated bits of colored glass, or beads, into the pattern. Others had been interwoven with silver and gilt threads, still others shot through with what appeared to be fine copper filament.

He picked up a broader band, one that might serve as a belt, a rainbow of colors intricately patterned, studded with pale beads. As he held it up, the sunlight gleamed on threads of spun gilt that he hadn't even noticed in the pattern before. This was the finest example on the table, the work of a skilled artist. Surely this was the one Tesse had made. He wrapped it around his waist. It would serve him as a belt.

"The prettiest of the lot," a man's voice spoke at his side. He turned to see a broad face, deeply tanned, cheeks lined with creases that disappeared into a bushy brown beard. Zimenes placed the intricate inkle back on the table, suddenly aware of its ostentatious beauty. "You seek a belt?" the man asked.

The stall minder answered for him. "He's looking for an inkle made by the queen. As a token, I suppose."

The people gathered around him nodded and murmured in approval.

"To take with you into the Mirrenwood?" a woman asked. Somewhat unnecessarily, it seemed to Zimenes. He smiled blandly at her, returned his gaze to the trinkets on display.

The people pressed in closer, now, to aid in his selection. Hands reached forward, selected various lengths and thicknesses of woven cloth, held them up for him to inspect.

"Surely this one, milord."

"This is the pattern she favors, I've been told."

A tug on his robe caused him to look down. A little girl, her face sweaty from chasing around the market with her friends, held one up in a grubby hand for his inspection, clearly grabbed at random from the table whose contents she could not see even when standing on tip-toe.

"What about this one?" she asked.

The old woman cast a sidelong glance while she resumed passing the shuttle and packing threads down into the weave.

He was about to depart without making a purchase, deterred by the swelling crowd, when one of the inkles drew his attention: off to the side, a much smaller, narrower band. An alternating diagonal pattern of white and yellow—the colors of Averonne—shot through with two waves of emerald green that seemed to chase each other the length of the band. The color of Vialle's eyes. He reached through the arms of the solicitous people trying to aid him, and picked up the smaller one. It was much plainer than most of the other bands, but the elegance of it appealed to him. The humility.

"Ah, surely not that one," one of the women said. A few others shook their heads and clucked their tongues.

"As good as any other," the tanned man at his side said. He clapped Zimenes heartily on the shoulder. "They're all the same, my friend."

He could smell the brandy on the man's breath. It made him less inclined to visit the tavern. As did the way that everybody in town seemed keenly aware of who he was, and why he was there.

"I'll take it," he said. Studied the attendant's face as she glanced at the inkle, but she merely nodded. She opened her mouth, but only to tell him the price.

He handed over the coins without haggling, took his prize in exchange.

"Would you like me to convey to the queen a message on your behalf, m'lord?"

He couldn't tell from her placid expression whether she was teasing him. Though he was pretty sure she was.

"That's not necessary," he said, with a polite smile. "She does not know who I am."

"Of course not, dearie," she said.

The old woman's eyes shifted to a point beyond Zimenes' shoulder, and grew wide. Her lower jaw fell open. "M'lady," she said, then cast her eyes down.

The folks gathered around him fell back murmuring, whispering. Zimenes turned to find the princess standing at his elbow. Beside her, Lord Guillem, a preening crow in his black finery. Magda stood behind them, flanked by two bearded knights in the white and gold of Averonne—Champions of the Mirren. The people gave them room, but stayed near, so they could continue watching, and listening.

"Ain't she a beauty?" he heard a woman whisper.

"Did you make a purchase?" Vialle asked. "Let me see."

Zimenes had yet to pocket the inkle. The narrow band of woven threads dangled limply from his hand.

"An interesting choice," Vialle said, as she plucked it from his palm. "Let me help you affix it."

"I don't need help," he said. "I haven't decided—"

"Don't be ornery." His hand still hung in the air between them, and she grabbed it, looped the inkle around his wrist. "Like so?" she asked.

He nodded. Felt his face flush warm under the gaze of the knights, the nobleman, and what now seemed to be the town's entire population. He hoped that his complexion would once again hide his embarrassment.

"Didn't even know what an inkle was." A woman's voice emerged from the crowd.

"Course not," a man answered. "What do you expect from a southerner?"

"That's too tight," Zimenes said, as the princess twisted the ends into a knot.

"It ought to be snug," she replied. She looked up into his face as she secured the knot with her thumb and forefingers. "You wouldn't want to lose it."

Zimenes nodded his thanks to the woman who had sold him the inkle, then turned to walk back to the inn. Lord Guillem thanked the knights for their service. The knights bowed and bid them a good evening; Magda and Vialle curtsied deeply and elaborately, in a show of their gratitude. The knights then commanded the crowd to see about their business, to leave the gentlefolk be. Muttering, the crowd dispersed, some melting away deeper into the market, some falling back a step or two while continuing to gawk at the princess, some heading toward the fiddling and dancing that had started up in the square as the sun began to set.

Vialle skipped to catch up to Zimenes and walked along beside him. He rubbed at the band around his wrist, a strange new presence for a man who wore no adornments, not so much as a single ring on his fingers, nor an amulet around his neck.

"It suits you," she said. She wrapped her left arm around his right, startling him, but he did not break stride. She leaned into him.

"It's nothing more than a trifle," he said. "The proceeds benefit the cloister."

"Does it ever get boring?" Vialle asked. "This unrequited devotion?"

"It's not something I control," he said.

She snorted, removed her arm from around his. "Then you are nothing more than a slave," she said. "And that inkle is not a trifle, but a shackle."

Vialle was right. He devoted entirely too much thought to this woman who had been absent from his life for so long. She was no longer a woman he knew, but the mere memory of a woman whom he once had known well. Or thought he did. How well could he claim to have known her, after all, if she could depart from his life forever without explaining her decision to him? Without even saying farewell? He had devoted himself not to a flesh-and-blood woman, but to a fantasy of a woman. A fantasy that he clung to, stubbornly, for a reason that eluded him. As though he were under a spell that she had cast—although even that conceit made it seem like she wanted him to be thinking about her, wanted him to miss her, when he knew that wasn't true, when he knew that she probably spent the vast majority of her days without his name, his face, his voice even coming to her mind.

Running footfalls caused them all to pause and turn. Lord Guillem came running up. He fell to a knee in front of Vialle. He lowered his head and raised his hands. Across his upturned palms stretched the splendid rainbow-colored, bead-studded belt, the one that had drawn Zimenes' eye from the first.

"Princess—a token of my esteem," he said, somewhat out of breath. "And sincere affection."

"Oh, my, that's lovely," Magda said. She nudged Vialle.

"What is it?" the princess asked.

Zimenes turned toward the princess. "Why, it's a belt," he said.

"Ah, yes. Of course," Vialle said. "A symbol of my chastity."

Magda grabbed a handful of the princess's hair and yanked, causing Vialle to cry out briefly and raise her hand. Magda glared at her defiantly. Guillem lifted his eyes, then quickly lowered them again. A few titters reached them from observant passersby. Vialle composed herself.

"Rise, my lord," she said, as she took the elaborate inkle from his hands. "You have my gratitude."

She wrapped the belt around her narrow waist and cinched it with a simple square knot.

"Delightful," Magda said.

Zimenes turned and continued on toward the inn. But not before the princess detected his smirk. She smacked him on his shoulder.

"At least my shackle is of my own choosing," he said.

# 10

Early the next morning, Zimenes and Guillem led the way from the inn carrying heavy packs on their shoulders, followed by Vialle and Magda—the princess now wearing breeches like a man, Magda in her skirts. Behind them followed Borek and Kurk, each guiding a laden packhorse; the horses pulled a two-wheeled cart behind them as well. Some of the curious villagers and farmers escorted them from town, followed them on the road to the bridge—though they also walked past not a few sleeping off the carousing of the night before right out in the square, wrapped in heavy blankets brought for that purpose, apparently. The accompanying well-wishers hailed them with rousing cheers of "long live the king!" and "may the Lady of the Mirren watch over you!" that Vialle gracefully accepted with a wave and a smile each and every time. Kurk let the four dogs run out alongside to wear themselves out, calling them to heel every so often.

As they reached the guardhouse, two knights on horseback rode out and turned the townspeople back toward Rotterham. A last round of "fare thee well!" and "good luck!" and the crowd reluctantly turned away, headed back down the slope.

Again, the captain greeted them at the gate. As he did, three other knights unsheathed their swords, laid the blades across their palms, knelt on both knees, and lofted the weapons above their bowed heads. Offering their swords—their lives—to the princess, to aid her in her mission to save her father, their king.

"If it pleaseth your ladyship," the captain said, "these men would accompany her worship into the woods, to aid in the hunt and safeguard her person."

"Rise, brave champions," she said.

They did, and though they lowered their swords they did not raise their heads. On the face of the knight nearest Zimenes, tears trailed down his cheeks and into his beard. The man trembled with anticipation, or perhaps simply from coming so close to the princess—a second time in two days. What more could a knight desire from his life, than to accompany the beautiful princess on her noble mission?

"Should we require succor," she said, "you have my word as my father's daughter that we shall surely send for you in all haste, and expect you to fulfill every pledge made to my father, and to me as his daughter. Your presence at the gates of the Mirrenwood fills my heart with courage, and conviction."

"You heard the lady," the captain said.

The men, heads still bowed, sheathed their swords and stepped back from the gate. Thick, seaworthy ropes and chains suspended the bridge's wooden planks over the narrow gorge. It swayed slightly, but was broad and sturdy enough for the party to cross two at a time. Kurk put blinders on the horses, and while they were initially skittish, he cooed at them and petted them until they settled down, and then he guided them across. Borek brought up the rear with the hounds, now on leads.

Once the party had assembled at the far side, the captain of the guard unsheathed his sword, thrust it into the sky, and cried out, "Long live the king!"

"Long live the king!" the remaining champions echoed, and their cheers redounded through the deep gorge. They kept this chant up until all of the travelers had turned and passed beneath the stone arch that marked the entrance to the Mirrenwood.

To their left lay the cloister, the steeple of which Zimenes could just make out through the trees. What was the queen doing, in that moment, as they passed her by? Was she sitting at a table, weaving an inkle from strands of colored thread? Was she kneeling before the altar in the chapel, head bowed and hands clasped, praying for the success of their expedition? Was she cleaning up dishes from breakfast, or perhaps still sleeping away the morning? He had no idea.

Ahead of them stretched the old stone highway that led straight into the Mirrenwood. They expected to be able to find a clean water source and forage for some food within the forest, but they carried enough of both to last them for several days at least. The plan, as outlined by Borek to Zimenes in the tavern the evening before, was to penetrate as deeply as possible into the Mirrenwood along this road, establish a base camp—downing a tree or two as needed for lumber and firewood—and then send Kurk and the horses back to Rotterham as needed for additional supplies.

Borek led the way, with Lord Guillem alongside. Zimenes followed after the men, Vialle and Magda fell in behind him. Kurk, the hounds, the packhorses and the cart trailed after.

The forest here consisted of a panoply of oaks and maples and chestnuts and black locusts in flower and beginning to show buds, but whose leaves had yet to fill in. The air was fresh, perfumed by the white flowers high above, and petals drifted down about them not unlike a light snow flurry, carpeting the mossy road that stretched ahead of them. The falling petals reminded Zimenes of another time, two decades before, another forest—a dead, wintry forest, where the white petals really were drifting flakes of snow. Where his breath steamed in the frigid air. Before he could drift too far back into that time—before he could get lost in the thicket of his memories—Magda came to walk alongside him.

Her head turned from side to side, her neck craned, as she peered into the trees.

"We needn't be on the lookout just yet," Vialle teased her from behind.

"Oh, but I so want to see one!" Magda said. She wrapped her arm around Zimenes'. "None of this felt real to me, until now!"

"Be careful what you wish for," Zimenes said.

She tightened her grip on his arm and pressed in closer. "Are they terribly dangerous?"

"No," Vialle said at the same time as he answered, "Yes."

"He's teasing you," the princess said.

Zimenes halted, lowered his pack from his back, rummaged around inside until he found the book he was looking for: *The Unicorn: An Alchemyst's Vade Mecum*, by "A Devotée of the Rosy Cross." He reshouldered his burden, and then paged through the slim quarto as they continued walking.

"Here we are," he said, and he read aloud: *The unicorn is by nature a fickle beast. The mature male's horn is known to measure up to two cubits in length*—"a cubit is the length of a man's elbow to his fingertips," Vialle interrupted—*a lady's wrist in diameter, and culminates in a fine point, hard as adamant. The unicorn is not known to be aggressive, but can move swiftly when startled or threatened. When one of these creatures has formed a firm bond with a maiden pure of heart, mind, and body, he will come to see her as a father would a favored child, and also as that same man would treasure that child's mother, and also as he would revere his own mother; and will thus go to great lengths to jealously protect the maiden, even if, in so doing, he must expose himself to danger and forsake his natural habitat. It is in this circumstance when the unicorn is both most vulnerable, but also most fearsome, as the horn is a deadly weapon, and the creature possesses a keen intelligence, at once superior to the memory of the oliphant, the wisdom of the owl, the speech of the parrot, or the cleverness of the fox, whilst combining elements of all of these."*

"Do the...lady unicorns also have horns?" Magda asked.

"The literature is unclear," Zimenes said. "In reindeer and elk, males and females both bear antlers. Among the rhinoceronte, both males and females grow horns—indeed the female's horn is often longer than the male's, though slimmer."

Magda touched her forehead. "I shouldn't like to have a horn," she said.

"That's not where they grow, Mags," Vialle said.

"You're terrible," her chaperone said, as Zimenes and Vialle laughed.

"Truth is, there is precious little to be found in the literature regarding the differences between males and females," Zimenes said.

"Even less on their reproductive cycles or gestation periods," Vialle said.

"They may be asexual," Zimenes said.

"Asexual?" Magda asked.

"They might not have sex organs," Zimenes said.

Vialle stepped between Zimenes and Magda, wrapped her arms around their waists, and whispered, "Or they might have them"—she stepped back, and thrust the physician and her chaperone closer together, until their shoulders and hips bumped into each other's—"and simply never use them."

Magda turned and swatted at her charge, who skipped further back out of reach.

"Pay her no mind, doctor," Magda said, her face flushed red. "She's incorrigible."

Guillem fell back from the side of Borek, who was leading the way. "What's so funny?" he asked, with a grin, eager to be in on the joke.

At that moment, a dark figure clad in a brown cloak swung out from behind a tree. Borek had passed him by unnoticed, and Guillem's back was turned to the man. The stranger stepped toward Vialle, his hand raised as though to strike.

Zimenes pushed past Magda, seeking to put himself in between the assailant and the princess, keenly aware that he was unarmed. As he ran, he swung his pack down from his back—he would use this as a shield to absorb any blows until Guillem and Borek could enter the fray. But the heaviness of the bag unbalanced him as he ran, his toe snagged on the upraised corner of an old flagstone, and he crashed into the man as he swung his pack forward with both hands, arms outstretched.

The heavy pack's impact knocked the man backward, expelled breath from his chest with an "oof!" He landed on his backside at the edge of the road, his heels flew over his head, and he tumbled into the stone-lined culvert choked with weeds that ran alongside to drain rainwater from the highway.

A cry of pain was followed by a stream of curses.

Guillem had his sword out with a flick of his wrist, stepped past Zimenes, into the ditch. Then the nobleman sheathed his blade, stooped and reached down to help the man to his feet.

"Brother!" Vialle cried.

As Guillem hauled the man from the ditch, the hood lowered, and Zimenes could see that it was, indeed, Prince Carlès. In his hand he held not a weapon, but the pennon of the Champions of the Mirren.

The curses, it seemed, were aimed at him.

"I believed you threatened the princess," Zimenes said, by way of apology.

"I'm her brother, idiot!" Carlès said.

Vialle was laughing. Even Magda seemed to be having a hard time keeping a straight face. Guillem brushed briars from Carlès' cape.

"I couldn't make out your face," Zimenes said.

"Are you blind, man?"

"Your hood—"

"Well met, brother," Lord Guillem said. "What brings you here?"

"I'm coming with you," Carlès said. He ignored Zimenes' apologies. Which were sincere.

Borek had turned back to join them. He waited with a look of disinterested disdain on his face.

Zimenes leaned forward to retrieve his book, which had flown from his hands in his panicked charge. Several items had spilled from his pack, as he had not secured the flap. Among them the king's hunting horn, wrapped in parchment. Zimenes peeled back the vellum to inspect the horn for damage.

"Your father relented?" Magda asked.

"Our father doesn't know his son is here," Vialle said. "One would assume."

"Correct, sister," Carlès said, with a smile. His first.

"I don't think that's a good idea," Zimenes said. "Your father was quite—"

"I don't care what you think, mountebank," Carlès said.

"As your father's representative," Zimenes began. The rest of the party turned toward him, as a silence suddenly fell on the group, and the hush seemed to spread to the birds of the forest even.

"What does father's factotum say?" Vialle said. She looked at him curiously.

His first decision as leader. Everything hinged on this, it seemed.

"Where did you get that?" Carlès demanded. He stepped forward and reached for the king's hunting horn that Zimenes still held in his hand.

The prince's hand closed around the mouthpiece. Zimenes released the pack and wrapped his other hand around the horn's copper-bound bell.

"Relent," the prince said, as he wrapped his second hand around the horn. "This is mine by right."

Zimenes would not release it. He tightened his grip. "Your father entrusted it to me—"

"You'll break it!" the prince shrieked.

"It is you trying to take it by force!" Zimenes replied through clenched teeth.

Carlès kicked the pack out from in between them, spilling more books out over the road. He pushed the horn into Zimenes' chest, seeking to unbalance him, but the physician clung to the horn and backpedaled. He wrenched it and his body to the side, forced Carlès to follow him. The prince's foot stubbed into Zimenes' pack and he tripped, released the horn to throw his hands out to catch himself as he fell, once again, to the flagstones. Once down, the hounds were upon him, barking and nipping and licking, thinking this was all some sort of sport, before Kurk could call them back to heel.

The prince scrambled to his feet, breathing in heavily and cursing with every exhale. Surprised with his swift victory, well aware of the prince's extensive training in the manly arts of grappling and wrestling, it was all Zimenes could do to suppress the grin that fought to show forth.

Carlès reached for the bejeweled hilt at his belt, but Borek grabbed his hand, removed the slim dagger and pocketed it. "If there's to be a fight," the hunter said, "it'll be a fair one."

Carlès raised his hands, empty palms. Borek released him, but remained close by. Lord Guillem also stood nearby.

"I'm in command," the prince growled. Clearly, he was directing these words at Zimenes, not the hunter. The prince kicked one of the books that had spilled from Zimenes' pack further down the road.

Zimenes took a deep breath. The prince outranked him. Who was he to countermand the order of a royal? If Vialle were to command him to do something, likewise, he would feel compelled to do it. He had just hoped it wouldn't come to that.

"Your father, the king, put me in command," Zimenes said.

"You think you know what it is to command?" the prince said. "I suppose you're an expert in that as well, right? Maybe you read about it in one of your books."

He kicked another book away over the flagstones, and a third. The covers of this last one sprawled open as it lifted into the air with a flutter of pages, like a wounded bird.

Relinquishing command had a certain appeal. He hadn't asked for this duty. He hadn't wanted the responsibility. The king had insisted, above his strenuous objections. Before they had even entered the Mirrenwood the burden had weighed on him. The thought of simply turning around, walking alone back toward Rotterham, then wending his way home, lifted a yoke from his shoulders. He could remove himself from this fiasco completely, and absolve himself of all responsibility. That was certainly what Carlès would have wanted.

"You're the king's heir," Zimenes said. "If your father were to learn that you were here, that both of his progeny were risking their lives for his sake, it might well be his undoing."

Carlès took another step closer. "And that's precisely why he must never find out."

"If something were to happen to you," Magda said, repeating Zimenes' sentiment, though more succinctly, "it would kill your father."

"If I don't go," Carlès said, "there is a very good chance you won't kill this unicorn, and then he will die anyway."

"We are not to kill the unicorn," Zimenes said.

"Father was explicit on that point," Vialle added.

Carlès guffawed. "What are we supposed to do, capture it?" He turned to Borek, who nodded.

"We are to catch him, retrieve what we need from his horn, and release him," Vialle said. "Unharmed."

"Where's the glory in that?" Carlès said.

Borek sidled closer to Zimenes, and in a low voice said, "We could use another pair of hands, Master Zimenes. Another strong back. A young man's eyes." Though he did not speak loudly, the rest of the hunters had fallen silent, eager to hear what the hunter had to say.

"Well, what are we waiting for?" the prince asked. "Onward!"

"No," Zimenes said. He held up the king's hunting horn. The symbol of his conferred authority. "As the king's representative—"

"Listen, physician," Carlès said. "I am my father's heir, and I am now in charge of this expedition, as is my right. As I ought to have been from the outset. Do I make myself clear?"

Zimenes looked at those gathered around him. Kurk tossed a stick for the hounds to fetch while he waited for the convoy to begin marching again. Borek shrugged, apathetic. Guillem murmured to the prince, and Zimenes knew that Carlès must have learned of their point of departure and the day thereof from his friend, somehow. Magda was fussing with her hair, tucking it into her hood. Carlès glared at him in defiance, the corners of his mouth beginning to curl into a smirk.

That left Vialle. Her green eyes did not look away when his gaze met hers. She was the one who made him want to continue this fight. Pointless as it may well prove.

"You may join the hunt, prince," he finally said. "But I remain in charge—"

Carlès forced a harsh, guttural snort that drowned out Zimenes' final words. "As though you could stop me," he said.

White petals continued to drift down about them from the canopy above. The horses' hooves resumed their clopping, the cart's wheels their creaking. Seven hunters now followed the road deeper into the Mirrenwood.

Prince Carlès turned toward his sister. "What sayest thou, sis? Did you really believe I was going to let you have all the fun?"

Zimenes retrieved his books from the mossy flagstones, returned them to the pack, along with Adalmund's horn. As he lifted the knapsack to his shoulders, he cast one last look back down the highway, toward the tiny pinpoint of light marking the arched entrance. He sought out the cloister's steeple, but it was lost among the trees.

# II

At the end of the flagstones—which had become so cracked and broken by roots, slippery with moss, and overgrown with briars and nettles as to be more of a hindrance than a help to travel—the road split into three tracks. Once broad avenues of packed earth, these trails were now hemmed in by saplings and tangled with vines and weeds. To the side opened a clearing. Evidence of a loggers' encampment, in regular use until the king's decree had closed the Mirrenwood to commerce, some twenty years ago. A fire pit in the center of the camp would still be serviceable, once cleared of the leaves and debris that filled it. Slightly elevated platforms of earth marked where they would pitch their tents. A stream ran crisp and clear not many paces away, with a well-worn track leading from the camp to its banks, as well as a narrow wooden footbridge that sturdily straddled the creek.

"Perfect," Borek had pronounced, and the others had readily agreed, as the afternoon sun was lowering, and they all wanted to set up the tents and eat.

Borek and Kurk began unloading the cart while Zimenes set about guiding Carlès, Guillem and Vialle in the fine art of building a tent frame. This was where Zimenes' experience in the Averonne army served them all in good stead, as this had been one of his many duties when he'd first joined as a young man, scarcely sixteen. He'd been a tent-maker, and a tent-breaker. A drover. A sharpener of swords, a darner of socks—and, as a southerner, it was almost inevitable that the men would seek him out as a reader of cards, the company soothsayer. And, yes—as Carlès so loved to point out—a cook. But that had been a promotion, after a couple years on campaign.

Out of the corner of his eye he saw Borek lugging Zimenes' specimen case—a flat rectangular wooden box that came up to his waist when stood on its end. The hunter swung it casually onto several leather packs and sacks of feed, where it tottered precariously.

"Hey!" Zimenes called, as he moved to rescue his case. "Be careful with that."

Borek stopped and turned to look at him, then again at the case.

"This is mine," the hunter said. He stepped back, pointed toward a wooden case still resting on the nearly empty cart. "That one's yours."

Zimenes noted the subtle differences between the similarly shaped wooden boxes.

"An honest mistake," he said.

"What's in yours?" Borek asked.

"Would you like to see?"

With both hands, Zimenes carefully shifted the case, undid the two leather straps wrapped around it, and then the brass latches. Produced a key from his pocket, and inserted it into the lock—the lid popped as the catch released. He opened the case to reveal one of his prized possessions: a glass alembic. The cucurbit, the anbik, the receiver—all of finely blown glass—and the copper armature were all cradled separately and snugly in crimson velvet-lined depressions that had been shaped to fit their gracefully curved forms; velvet straps secured them in place. The alembic took up one half of the case; the other half was given over to several tiers of similarly velvet-lined trays that contained empty glass vials and beakers, each with a cork stopper. Some as large as a wine cup, most no larger than a man's thumb. Below the trays, also secured with straps and flaps and snaps, a hunk of resin and another hunk of red wax for sealing the vials, a collection of charcoal pencils for labeling and calculating, a small book of handwritten recipes and formulas, a set of flints, a ball of mercury in a separate glass tube, a loop of horsehairs, a ball of twine, a magnifying glass and a set of jeweler's loupes.

"Mighty fine work," Borek said. He picked up one of the larger beakers, held it up to the light. The clear glass contained no impurities, no trapped bubbles or ash. "How's this going to help us catch a unicorn?"

*Good question*, Zimenes thought. "These are for transforming any herbs or roots or flowers that I may find in the forest into medicines, or unguents. I can extract their essences. Distill their spirits."

Borek stroked his beard. "Distilling spirits, eh? You know how to make alcohol?"

"A very basic formula," Zimenes said. "All we need is—"

"I know what's required." Borek clapped a hand on the physician's shoulder. "Your value to this expedition just increased severalfold."

Though Borek was smiling, Zimenes wasn't sure whether to take his last comment as a joke, or a statement of fact.

Borek lowered the lid on Zimenes' case. "Want to witness some truly fine craftsmanship?" he asked.

"Certainly."

Borek retrieved his case, set it down on top of Zimenes', waving away the physician's muted protests. A quick glance showed him that the trio of Guillem, Carlès and Vialle were making progress in their battle with the second tent, did not require his immediate assistance.

As the hunter unbuckled the leather straps, Zimenes noted the rounded corners of the well-worn, but also well-polished case. With his finger he traced a deep gouge that crossed the grain at a diagonal, spanning the entire width of the lid.

"This old crate saved my life," Borek said. "As have its contents. Several times over."

He opened it. Brass chains at the hinges kept the lid from falling backward and unbalancing the box.

Within, six narrow shafts stretched the full length of the case, which was lined in dark brown leather rather than plush velvet. Each glossy black shaft was supported by two pincer clasps. The fletched ends—the feathers also brilliant, glossy black—alternated, three to the left, three to the right, so the feathers would not press against each other. The arrows' heads seemed strangely blunt.

Borek pulled one of the shafts free, handed it to Zimenes.

"Look down the length of it," he said.

Zimenes turned and pointed the arrow toward Carlès, held the fletched end up to his eye. The narrow dowel ran straight and true, without the slightest hint of warp or deviation.

"Impressive," he said. He lowered it, touched the dull tip with his finger. The light shaft was clearly made of wood, but its metal head was grooved, threaded in a spiral.

"The heads," Borek said, drawing Zimenes' attention back to the case. Strapped to the underside of the lid were a number of different arrowheads.

Borek unsnapped one from its leather stay and held it up for Zimenes' inspection: a flat black triangle that tapered to a narrow point. He screwed it onto the tip, then sighted down the length. He handed it to Zimenes, who scarcely dared touch the immaculately sharp point.

He proceeded to remove and show Zimenes the rest of the heads. One was barbed, similar to the standard, but with a series of hooks pointing back toward the feathered end that would fight any attempt to pull the arrow free. One was conical, tapering to a sharp point, that Borek described as "armor piercing. Good for thick hides." Another he labeled as "expanding," with a lead weight behind the short steel tip, that he said would spread out upon penetration. A much larger head he described as "fragmenting," made of ceramic, with four ridges rather than the flat two of the more standard arrowhead. The final one he showed Zimenes contained a glass well behind the tip, that could be filled with poison, or a soporific, as needed.

As Zimenes examined the hunter's instruments, he said, "the workmanship is remarkable."

"Four different craftsmen, all from my hometown," Borek said. "Dudijek makes the heads, Jerszy the shafts, Birstinj the fletches and the bowstrings. Milanovik puts them all together, and he made the bow. Oh, and this case as well."

"Where is the bow?"

"That's in a separate case. Don't want to string it up just yet."

"Right," Zimenes said. "Of course not."

Borek returned the arrowheads to their straps. Zimenes knew he had to say something. He peeked round the corner of the cart, made sure the others were still busy with the tasks he'd assigned.

"The king has charged us with capturing the unicorn," he said, voice soft.

Borek glanced at him, snapped the shaft back in place. He tapped the ceramic arrowhead. "That's why I'll use this one to start," he said. "A shot to the haunch. It'll wound, but it won't kill. As he runs, the fragments will work their way deeper into the muscles. Slow it down. Allow us to catch it and net it."

"What about this one?" Zimenes tapped the head with the

glass well behind the tip. "You mentioned a soporific?"

Borek winked. "Maybe you can brew one with your still."

He closed the case, snugged up the straps and buckled them tight.

"We can't kill this creature," Zimenes said. He lowered his voice to a whisper and leaned toward Borek. "If we kill it, we risk a curse falling upon the land."

"Says who?" He turned to face Zimenes, folded his arms across his chest.

"The authorities," Zimenes said. He cringed inwardly at how effete that sounded. How distant from their camp in the forest, in both space and time. "The king himself."

"Bah," Borek shrugged. He waved his hand as though shooing one of the gnats that occasionally flitted about their heads. "They say that about all these monsters. I've killed my share—believe me—and I've yet to see crops wither or women's teats dry up after." He nudged Zimenes. "It's just an animal. Does killing a hog bring down a curse from the heavens? What about a chicken?"

"This is different," Zimenes said. "It's... it's a magical beast."

"We'll see if it bleeds red like any other," Borek said. "Like any of us."

"You swore an oath," Zimenes said. "You signed a contract."

"And I will do my utmost to honor it," the hunter said. "But the king's cure is paramount—right?"

"Of course," Zimenes said. "But—"

"And if the king dies, and that son of his becomes king—would that not be its own sort of curse?"

Zimenes guffawed, then restrained his outburst. His three royal workers—the prince, the princess, and the nobleman—lifted their heads in his direction, then they turned back to their work. The hunter had a point.

"What's worse?" Borek continued. "Your king dying? And you losing your job, I might add? Or some vague threat of a pox upon the land?"

Zimenes folded his arms, stroked his beard, stared at the hunter's battered, mud-stained boots.

"The king's cure is paramount," Borek repeated.

Zimenes nodded. Met the hunter's stare.

"The king's cure is paramount," he said.

After two full days of concentrated labor by Zimenes, Magda, Vialle, Carlès, and Guillem, the camp was fully functional. They had built four tents with wooden frames, one for Borek and Kurk, one for Carlès and Guillem, one for Magda and Vialle, and a smaller fourth that Zimenes occupied by himself.

The camp centered around the fire pit. Nearby Magda had established a cooking station, with an awning to shield the area from sun or the occasional rain shower. They'd dismantled the cart and used the planks to construct a broad countertop, with shelving below. A large tree trunk sawed cross-ways already stood in place as a cutting board.

They constructed a lean-to for the dogs and a roped-off paddock for the two horses. Not the sort of thing that would keep the horses penned if they were to panic, but they were docile beasts, accustomed to recognizing and respecting the limits imposed upon them by their masters. Beyond these, they dug separate latrines for the men and the women.

While the five of them worked, Borek and Kurk spent those first two days scouting along the nearby tracks and trails—some made by man decades before, others carved through the sprouting underbrush more recently by game. On the very first day they returned with a plump wood grouse, shot through by one of Borek's black arrows.

Late in the afternoon of the second full day—their third in the Mirrenwood—satisfied that their work was more or less complete, Zimenes had set off with some of his empty specimen vials in a pouch at his belt, and Archytus' translation of Socoridides' *Materia Medica*—a cumbersome folio—slung under his arm. He took the path to the stream, then crossed the bridge and followed the fading trail till it brought him to a forest of pine trees growing tall and straight and evenly spaced, the forest floor beneath them bare except for the carpet of pine needles and the occasional fallen seed cone.

He came to a stand of plants at the fringe of the pines, with glossy leaves, hairy stems, and large, pale pink flowers the likes of which he had never seen before. He knelt, paged through his reference book, comparing what he saw in front of him in vibrant color to the somewhat crude woodcut illustrations.

"Boo."

The sound startled him so that he slammed the book closed. He looked over his shoulder. Vialle stood behind him. She waved.

"Didn't mean to scare you."

"Where are the others?" he asked.

She shrugged. "Camp."

"Have Borek and Kurk returned?"

"With a brace of coneys," she said. "Kurk caught them in a snare he set this morning."

"We're going to eat well again tonight."

He straightened, handed his book to Vialle. Found her muttered "oof" at accepting the weight into her arms somewhat gratifying. He plucked one of the pink flowers, and dropped it into a glass vial, sealed it with a cork, and placed the vial into the hardened leather pouch at his belt.

He began to walk back toward camp, content to let her carry his book for him. She skipped until she was walking alongside him.

She breathed in deeply. Smiled at him when he glanced in her direction. "Can't you feel it?" she asked.

"I can smell it," he said.

"You can?"

"Pine trees."

She slugged him on the arm with the cover of his book, knocking him off his stride. A weighty tome.

"No, silly," she said. "Magic! It's everywhere here. It's like this whole forest is enchanted."

He laughed. "It certainly does seem to have certain... rejuvenatory properties."

"So, you *can* feel it?"

He shrugged. "Maybe it's just that you're...in love."

She glanced at him with a sharp frown. "What—with Guillem?" She scoffed. "Please."

"You could do worse," Zimenes said.

"He's no eyesore," she said. She looked at Zimenes as she said this, as though to gauge his reaction. "But I don't love him."

"Perhaps you could grow to do so," Zimenes said.

"I don't think it works that way," she said. "Besides, I don't want to love him. I don't want to love anybody. I've got more important things to think about. I don't want to get distracted right now."

"Right," Zimenes said. "The unicorn."

Vialle sighed. "Yes—and no. Magic, Master Zimenes. I'm talking about magic. I want you to teach me."

"I've told you, girl—I'm no magician."

"I don't believe you."

"Well, I don't believe such a thing exists. At least not in any way that we can control."

She stopped. "I saw how you entranced my mother."

He, too, came to a halt. "You think I did?" Immediately winced at his own foolishness. Her words reflected the impressions of a little girl—and still his heart leapt. Still, he found hope. Even though he had seen her mother with his own eyes. Had heard from her with his own ears: *I've made my peace.* She might as well have said, "You are part of my past. A distant memory."

"I suppose I can understand," Vialle said. "A man from the south—everybody knows how passionate men from the south are. Lovely dark skin. A mysterious past. I suppose I could see her attraction."

"Keep in mind I weighed a stone less back then," he said, with a chuckle.

"You're not the sweet-talking type," she said. "Not like Guillem—that boy loves nothing more than to hear himself prattle on. Maybe you were a great kisser. Is that what it was?"

Perhaps he and Tesse hadn't been as discreet as they had imagined.

Or...her daughter was bluffing. Attempting to draw a confession out of him.

"Who says I ever kissed your mother?"

"Don't be coy," she said. "I'm skeptical though—that beard. All of my suitors have been clean-shaven. Some barely even need to shave, they just need a good scrubbing with soap."

"Princess," he said. "I'll take my book now, if you'd like. I know it's heavy—"

She swung the large volume behind her, clasped it in both her hands. The leather at the joints was worn, exposing the cords that held it all together. If she were to drop it, the impact would almost certainly shear off one or both covers.

"I've never kissed a man with a beard before." She tilted her head to the side. "Doesn't it scratch and tickle?"

He cleared his throat. "My book, if you please."

She shook her head, a teasing smile lighting up her green eyes.

"First I want to know," she said, her voice surprisingly deep and raspy. "How you bewitched my mother so."

"Let me show you," he said.

He stepped forward, and she shrank back, but then stood straight. Lifted her chin. In defiance. In offering. A lock of her hair had fallen forward, caught at the corner of her mouth. He took the fine strands in his fingers, fingers that felt to him, compared to the smooth softness of her cheek, like rough unpeeled ginger roots as he tucked the hairs behind her ear.

He leaned toward her. Her eyelids drooped. Her lips gently parted.

He reached around behind her and caught the book, first with one hand, then the other. She struggled and squirmed against him, wriggled and tried to turn her back to him so she could improve her grip, grunting as she writhed, but he kept her pinned against his chest, kept her arms pinioned behind her in an awkward, even painful position, and soon he had pried the volume from her fingers.

"Ugh!" she cried. She shoved him away with both hands, then rubbed her right elbow. "Brute."

"Maybe here is where we should set you out, to await the unicorn," he said, teasingly. "If magic is in the very air around us. Ought we tell Borek?"

She clapped away the dried leather that had flaked onto her palms from the book's scaly spine.

"For such a smart guy," she said, as she wiped her hands on her breeches, "you can be pretty thick."

She turned away from him, and strode resolutely back toward camp, at a swift pace that he did not have the desire to match.

# 12

The great hart's magnificent antlers swept back from his head into two large hands, from which spread several sharp fingers. The rack lifted into the slanting early morning sunlight. His bearded chin swayed from side to side as the majestic stag surveyed his surroundings with his enormous black eyes, ears cocked, listening. Satisfied, he lowered his head again to the turf, continued pulling at the furze.

The stately creature stood on a low, rocky rise that lifted from the forest. Zimenes knelt behind a tree several paces back from the edge of the clearing, from where he watched his wary prey. He held the king's ivory hunting horn, ready to lift it and blow. His hands were steady, but the hard exposed roots he knelt on drove into his kneecaps, caused a tingling in his thighs, a numbness in his feet. He slowly lifted Adalmund's horn. Seemingly in time with his movement, the hart lifted his head and stared downhill, peered into the trees.

Zimenes froze. Those enormous black eyes stared straight at the physician. Seemed to peer directly into his soul. The stag's neck and back tensed.

Zimenes glanced toward the tree nearest him, behind which Vialle crouched, an arrow nocked to her bow, the string stretched, though not completely taut. Her eyes remained fixed on the hart.

The dogs had scented the great hart's spoor the day before—their third day in the forest—and led Kurk and Borek to this clearing, where they'd found further evidence: trees against which the hart had flayed his antlers, a matted area where he had slept. The conversation last night around the campfire had been excited, as they laid their plans for the hunt. Zimenes had initially opposed the idea, as it seemed a distraction. Borek argued that stalking the hart would give them good practice with their nets and nooses for when it came time to catch their true quarry, and Zimenes had to concede that the hunter made a valid point.

Now, though, a pang of regret overtook him. It seemed a shame to kill such a regal animal. He knew the others were spread throughout the fringe of the clearing, hidden, equally tensed. Awaiting a signal. What if he were to blow the horn, commencing the hunt? This would startle the hart, of course, alert him to their presence, cause him to flee, probably far from their reach.

If he felt such pity for the hart, such remorse at the mere thought of slaying him, how would he feel if he were ever to see their true target? Surely the unicorn's fabled beauty would cause him to quail; might even cause all of them to lose their nerve.

He lifted the horn to his lips. He could say he thought he'd heard the signal. An honest mistake. Vialle's eyes shifted in his direction, briefly, then returned to the hart, as she lifted the bow and sighted along the arrow.

Suddenly an arrow shaft, black, stood from the hart's haunch, and the beast bounded into the air. Vialle sent her arrow after it, but the hart leapt from the outcropping, and her arrow clattered over the boulders in the animal's wake.

"Might as well blow the commence," she said as she slung the bow over her shoulder.

*The horn.* Zimenes stood up, lifted Adalmund's hunting horn to his lips, inhaled as deeply as he could, and blew.

A mournful wail emerged, sounding the beginning of the hunt. Off to his left, lost to sight among the trees, the hounds, overcome by the excitement of the signal that they'd been trained to listen for, began to bark. In moments they shot through the trees in mad pursuit of the hart, following his scent.

The prince ran into the clearing from the south, arrow nocked to his bow. He halted briefly at the base of the outcropping, allowed Kurk to catch up. Zimenes and Vialle moved into the clearing and hailed them, and the two young men glanced down in their direction. Carlès shook his head. Then they took off running after the dogs.

Rather than follow them directly, Zimenes climbed the slope toward the center of the clearing, then clambered up the mossy boulders of the outcropping, until he reached the exact place on the bald hill where the hart had stood. Blood darkened the furze that peeked out from between boulders, a few drops dotted the exposed rock. From the trees a horn sounded a cadence that indicated that the blower had sighted the hart, and another horn sounded in reply. The sounds of barking and the belling of the horns receded through the trees.

Zimenes kept climbing until he reached the summit, a single broad stone that seemed to have been sheared flat, forming a platform from which he could survey the forest around him. A solitary linden tree had taken root near the top; its graceful branches arched overhead.

He stood at the center of an enormous hedge maze, a labyrinth that spread out to all sides. The outcropping—an island, a lighthouse in a sea of trees rather than of water—allowed him to see the contours of the many paths available, without attaining such a height as would allow him to pick a path to the exit.

After retrieving her arrow and returning it to her quiver, Vialle followed him up the rocky promontory. She leaned her bow against the trunk of the linden and came to stand next to him, breathed in deeply as she took in the view, exhaled with a sigh.

At his feet several strange markings caused him to stoop, then kneel, and brush away the moss. His hands revealed crudely engraved runes. Vialle crouched with him, and as they investigated, they found more such indecipherable markings, at four points of the flat surface.

"The compass's four quarters," she said. "Can you read them?"

He shook his head. He hadn't thought to bring any of his lexicons, or compendiums of antiquities along on the hunt—they were all too bulky, anyway.

He traced the strange, angular letters with his finger, and then stood up. In the center of the platform lay a circular mound, a low stone that had been eroded by centuries of wind and rain, edges rounded by the mosses and lichens that clung to it. They stood in a sacred place, a place whose purpose he did not understand.

"This is no natural outcropping," he said. "It's a cairn. Erected by people, years ago. Perhaps centuries."

If ever there was a place that held magical energy, this was that place. If ever there was a time when he actually could sense magic in the ether surrounding them, as Vialle had suggested, this was that time.

A touch at his hand passed a jolt from his arm through his entire body. He recoiled, withdrew his hand from hers. Swiveled to survey the clearing below them. Only trees and their gloomy shadows watched them, in silence and stillness.

"What are you doing?" he asked.

She shrugged. Reached her hand out again, though this time she did not take his into hers, only allowed her knuckles to brush his, the back of her hand to touch the back of his. A gentle pressure, easily broken. He found himself reluctant, however, to surrender the contact. He looked into her eyes.

"Holding hands isn't so bad, is it?" she asked, with a hint of a smile.

"We're not holding hands," he said, his mouth suddenly dry, his tongue clacking against the roof of his mouth.

"Precisely," she said. She shifted herself ever so slightly closer to him. "What were you about to say?"

He cleared his throat, swallowed. "This is an auspicious locale," he finally said. "The hart—the runes—the—" He glanced over her shoulder, toward the endless trees. "The view.... This is where we ought to await the unicorn."

She laughed, and moved apart. His hand, as though on its own volition, drifted after her, but the contact was broken. He swayed unsteadily for a moment, a limp flag in a gentle breeze.

She turned toward the southeast, and shaded her eyes. He followed her gaze, toward the horizon where the sun was lifting into a bank of fluffy white clouds. Far away, at the limits of his sight, an object rose from the monotony of the trees, even taller than their vantage: a steeple. The same one he had seen on entering the Mirrenwood, the same one beneath which he imagined Queen Tesse might even on that morn be praying.

The horns sounded again—Borek in the lead, he imagined. The baying of the hounds grew fainter as the hunt moved down the hill and away through the trees below them. Vialle turned toward the sound. Time to rejoin the hunt, lest the hunters leave them too far behind.

"No, I'll not be set out here, exposed on this little mountaintop," she said with an exaggerated shudder, "feeling as though my mother is watching over me the entire time."

She grabbed her bow from where she'd propped it against the tree and slung it over her shoulder. She leaped down to a lower boulder and began her bounding descent toward the woods, graceful and sure-footed. He moved toward the edge of the platform closest to where the hunters had disappeared into the trees.

He raised the horn to his lips, and blew with all his breath, with all his might. As he blew an image came to mind of the wounded hart, dripping his life's essence over the earth as he ran, and the slavering, ravenous dogs chasing after in a desperate race to be the first to leap onto their prey's back, to rend his flesh, and the men following close behind, arrows and spears and swords at the ready.

He lowered the horn, let the copper chain take up its weight around his neck and over his shoulder, let it sway against his side as he clambered back down the boulders. Past the hart's blood, already dark and dried.

Away in the valley, horns answered his peal. Their distance, their remoteness, lent an air of melancholy to the sound.

# 13

He chased after Vialle as she plunged downhill through the trees. He followed, as best he could, the belling of the horns, the baying of the hounds. The dogs were trained to bark only when the trail changed direction, where they would wait for the berner to catch up before dashing off again after their prey.

The clouds gathered and hovered just above the trees, it seemed, and humidity warmed the forest. The chase led downhill, however, and while he wasn't tiring, he did not look forward to the eventual, inevitable, uphill return.

Vialle left him behind. He had his horn, and whenever he sounded it, an answering blast would orient him. But he no longer had need, as the barking of the dogs had steadily grown louder ahead of him. He reached a steeper slope that led to a clearing, and began to work his way carefully down the hill, when a waving arm caught his eye.

Borek stood near a tree at the bottom of the slope, a hundred paces away, off to the right. He held a bow in his left, an arrow crossing it, the string slack. He waved at Zimenes with his right, motioned for him to stop. A hiss from behind him then drew his attention, and he turned to see Vialle ensconced behind another tree at the top of the slope, her bow also at the ready. He flashed her a smile, when the damp ground he stood on gave way.

His feet slid out from under him, depositing him on his backside. He spread his hands out to the sides in an effort to slow his descent, but the loose stones and the steepness carried him the rest of the way down, until he skidded to a halt at the bottom of the scree. Rocks and pebbles bounced and clattered down around him; leaves swirled after.

Embarrassed more than hurt, Zimenes groaned and lifted to his knees, rubbing his sore buttocks, when a shout came from in front, through the thick underbrush—a hoarse cry and an oath. Suddenly the hart broke through a screen of leaves and vines, and charged.

The stag's immense rack of antlers—easily as broad across as Zimenes' arms when flung out to both sides—was covered in a strange webwork of vines, but the tines still protruded, sharp and spiky. The rack plowed toward him, low to the ground, gathering speed.

Willit raced in from the side and leaped at the hart, only to get thrust aside by those antlers. With a pitiful whimper the king's greyhound fell broken among the tree roots. Still the hart swept on, angry black eyes focused on Zimenes, who barred his way toward escape, toward freedom.

A blur flew from the trees, and a black arrow pierced the hart's neck. The hart belled, a throaty roar of pain, but still it came on, undeterred. Then another arrow appeared in his breast, and the stag's foreknees buckled, its heavy antlers crashed into a sapling, wrenching his neck, then dug into the earth. Dirt and leaves showered Zimenes as the great beast skidded to a halt barely a pace away from the cringing physician.

An arrow shaft stood from the hart's haunch and pointed toward the sky, another grew from his flank, and a third—the killing blow, that had flown from behind him—stuck from the deer's breast. Dark blood coursed from the wounds, stained the hart's rust-red pelt. What he had taken to be a web of vines and creepers entangled among the antlers was actually one of the nets they had brought with them.

Carlès crashed through the underbrush in the deer's wake.

"He's down!" Carlès cried.

Zimenes exhaled and sank back to earth, suddenly spent.

Nigredo, Albedo, and Rubedo quickly converged on the downed animal. They swarmed over Zimenes as well, licking and yipping, eager for him to give them their share of the game.

Borek shoved the barking dogs away and hauled Zimenes to his feet. Vialle came slipping and sliding down the slope, her bow in hand. Hers had been the final arrow. She had saved his life.

"Sound the mort!" Carlès held his hand out for the horn. "Or let me!"

Borek nodded to Zimenes. "Go ahead."

Zimenes raised the horn to his lips. The mournful cadence

resounded through the trees. The hart was down. The hunt was over.

Kurk arrived, and fell by Willit's side. The poor animal's breath came shallow. He whimpered weakly.

"Guillem!" Borek called into the trees. "What say you?"

"I'll live," came the reply through the underbrush, though the nobleman's voice sounded strained.

Carlès vanished in the underbrush, then reappeared supporting Lord Guillem, who limped along, cradling his left arm in his right.

"Doctor," he gasped. His breathing was labored, and seemed to cause him more pain.

"Some leader," Carlès said to Borek, with a glance at Zimenes and a shake of his head. "He brings up the rear, startles our quarry, and gets our best man injured."

Zimenes had become accustomed to ignoring the prince back at the castle, and knew he needed to continue to do so, for the moment. He asked Guillem what had happened. The nobleman's pain made it hard for him to speak; between Borek and Carlès, they told him that Guillem had cast the weighted net successfully, but when the wounded hart had suddenly bolted, the cord attached to the net had wrapped around his wrist, and the fleeing stag hurled the nobleman to the ground and dragged him along behind for a few paces before the cord loosened.

He gingerly examined Guillem's arm. Rope burns had left his wrist raw and bloodied. The dragging had torn his sleeve and scraped his forearm and elbow. However, the worst of it quickly became apparent: the sudden pull on the cord had dislocated the nobleman's shoulder.

He'd witnessed Eirenaeus deal with such shoulders in the early days of his apprenticeship, in the army. He knew he had to pull it out of its skewed alignment to position the head of the humerus properly in the socket. The pain was impairing the unfortunate nobleman's ability to breathe. It would have to get worse before it got better.

He instructed Guillem to lie on the ground. Borek ordered Kurk to leave Willit and leash up the other dogs so they wouldn't bother the nobleman with their attentions. "Give them their share," the hunter said.

Zimenes showed Borek and Carlès how to hold Guillem in

place, while he reached for the young man's forearm. He wrapped it in a handkerchief so the blood seeping from his scrapes there would not cause his grip to slip.

"Look away, and relax," Zimenes said to Guillem. "Don't fight me. Don't pull against me. If you do, it will take longer, and hurt more."

Vialle crouched at Guillem's head, whispered, "It'll be over soon."

With that, he tightened both hands around Guillem's forearm and elbow, braced his feet on the man's ribs, and pulled. Leaned away from Guillem, with all his strength. With a great shout, the man writhed, attempted to wriggle free—"He's going to kill him!" Carlès yelled—but still Zimenes leaned back, ignoring the man's cries, until he felt the pop. With his feet, he guided the upper arm back into its proper place.

Guillem moaned and rolled away from him, into Vialle's gentle ministrations. He took his arm back into his belly and held it there as though to keep it from moving again, ever.

For the second time, Zimenes fell back into the earth, exhausted, sweating, breathing heavily.

But his work was not done. He sat up, then knee-walked to Guillem's side. Gently he palpated the man's shoulder. Vialle watched him avidly, asked him what he was feeling for. He touched her fingers to the joint, showed her how to verify that the humerus was in proper alignment.

"You've been fortunate," Zimenes said as he got to his feet. Thankful that it only took him one try, as he had only ever witnessed Eirenaeus performing that maneuver, nearly two decades ago, and had never actually been called upon to do it himself.

"Doesn't feel like it," Guillem said. He moaned.

"Will he have to retire from the field?" Borek asked.

Zimenes guided the hunter a few paces from the nobleman. "That would probably be for the best," he said. "Back at camp I'll give him a poultice for the swelling and a palliative for the pain. But he'll need some time to heal."

"Forsooth," Guillem managed, complexion pallid, sweating profusely, "I feel much better already."

Kurk tugged at Borek's sleeve, and the two moved away, conversed briefly in hushed tones, with occasional glances at poor Willit. The king's greyhound tried to roll up to his feet, relented, and flopped back down onto his side, tongue lolling, flanks heaving rapidly, shallowly. Blood leaked from several punctures in the thin flesh that covered the dog's ribs. Willit wheezed with each inhalation, and the sound seemed to be growing louder, as the dog fought to pull air into his lungs.

Borek called Zimenes over. Carlès came with him; Vialle remained crouched at Guillem's side, drying his brow with her kerchief.

"The king's hound is dying," the hunter said. "Kurk says he's beyond hope."

Carlès glanced briefly at his father's dog. "A shame," he said. "Put it out of its misery."

Zimenes knelt at the dog's side—cautiously, as Willit had nipped at his hands more than once back at the castle. The hound lifted his head from the ground at the physician's approach, but let it fall back when he saw Kurk alongside him. Zimenes inspected the small holes where the stag's antlers had punctured the dog's flank. Bubbles formed in the blood there, never a good sign.

"He is beyond my power, I'm afraid," Zimenes said. Kurk nodded. They turned to Borek.

"See to the others," the hunter said to Kurk. He motioned with his head toward the other hounds, where they were worrying at the hart and snapping and growling at each other.

Once Kurk moved away and turned his back to them, Borek unsheathed the long knife at his belt. Satisfied that the lad and the other dogs were not paying attention, the hunter leaned over the wounded greyhound, stroked his head, scratched behind his ears, and dispassionately slit his throat. Willit's labored breathing stilled. The hunter shook his head, wiped the blade clean on the dog's pelt.

"Our first casualties," he said, with a glance back over his shoulder at Guillem, still lying on his side, knees curled, shoulders hunched, head bowed.

Vialle knelt near the nobleman, but he no longer held her attention. She was digging in the turf near his head, brushing aside the sedge, peering into the clover and other wildflowers.

"Zimenes," she called. "Come look."

He walked to her side, followed by Borek. She scraped some of the grasses away, revealing a broad, flat stone, dark slate, shot through with striations of a paler gray. Deep angular grooves had been carved into the lighter strips.

Zimenes traced them with his fingertips, dislodging the dirt that had gathered there. Ancient letters.

"More runes," she said.

Zimenes straightened, brushed the dirt from his hands, breathed in the air perfumed by the wildflowers that filled the glade.

They stood in a small canyon near a winding stream. Zimenes had skidded down a lower portion of the encircling wall, which swept away from them, rising as it went, then wrapped around the glade in a concave curve, rising further into a formidable slate cliff that dominated their view. A stream of water fountained down a narrow channel, disappeared from view into the tree tops on the far side of the glade. They could faintly detect the fall's distant roar; a burbling stream emerged from a cluster of broad-leafed spatterdock and curled its way through the flower-bedecked glade.

Just the sort of picturesque setting described at length in two of the books Zimenes had brought with him: *The Unicorn: An Alchemyst's Vade Mecum*, and the *Enchiridion Monstrorum et Prodigiorum*, the book that Carlès had briefly sent flying with a kick.

"Does this place feel magical to you?" he asked Vialle. "Because it does to me—even more so than the cairn."

Before she could answer, Borek approached, Kurk at his elbow. "The boy tells me the creature is nearby," he said.

Zimenes' eyebrows lifted. He leaned toward Kurk. "Did you see signs?"

The lad's eyes were red, and his nose running. He did not meet Zimenes' gaze, or answer his question. Willit lay heavily on his heart, Zimenes supposed.

Instead, Borek shook his head, "He just—" He lowered his voice, stepped a little closer to Zimenes. "He just has a way with these things."

The hunter stepped back, cleared his throat, pointed behind them. "We set our blinds here"—he shifted his arm—"and there. It's a half-moon canyon. Any animals approaching the water will have to pass within range."

"I believe," Zimenes turned toward Vialle, "we have arrived."

She nodded her agreement. "It suits," she said.

Borek motioned for them all to join him back at Guillem's side. They propped the injured noble into a sitting position, leaning against a tree trunk.

Borek squatted, dangled the knife loosely between his knees. Following his lead, the others squatted as well. Zimenes leaned forward, braced his hands on his thighs.

"We need to get him back to camp," Borek said. "And I need at least one to help me undo the carcass here."

Zimenes said, "Why don't Vialle and I accompany Guillem back to camp?"

"You know the way?" Borek asked.

Vialle glanced at Zimenes. They both nodded tentatively.

"Better take the lad with you," Borek said. Then he looked toward Kurk, pointed at him with the knife. "In the morning, you return with the horses to help us move the carcass. The prince and I will stay here and finish the work."

"Oh, no, no, no." The prince stood up. "That won't do at all. I shall escort my sister and my friend back to camp. Kurk can stay behind with his master. I know the way."

Borek glanced up at Zimenes. Much as he wanted to discuss the glade with Vialle—this feeling he had, this intuition, that this was where they would see the unicorn—he knew what needed to happen.

"Kurk should guide them," Zimenes said, as he straightened his back. "Carlès, Vialle, and Guillem, go with Kurk."

He glanced toward the dead deer. At some point, presumably while he was resetting Guillem's shoulder, Kurk had cut the genitals away and given them to the hounds—their share of the spoils.

"I'll stay behind," Zimenes said.

"Take Nigredo with you," Borek said. He stood, and the rest of the party rose to their feet as well. Guillem leaned forward, and Vialle and Carlès helped him to his feet. "Alby and Ruby stay with us to ward away scavengers, or warn us of predators."

Zimenes knew enough of the woods to know that a bloody carcass would soon draw attention. But he also knew that Borek would keep them safe.

Zimenes reached his hand toward Borek, toward the knife he still clutched in his hand. The hunter deftly flipped it and caught the blade, handed him the pommel. Zimenes took it and cut a broad strip from the hem of his robes. He returned the blade, then fashioned a sling to cradle Guillem's injured arm and hold it in place while he walked, knotted it behind the young man's neck.

"You're in charge," Borek said to Carlès, "but remember, Kurk knows the way, and you must get back to camp by nightfall. You should get going."

Carlès nodded somberly.

"Lead on," the prince said to Kurk.

The boy leashed Nigredo, and with a last glance at his master, began to climb the slope that Zimenes had slid down. Prince Carlès stooped at Lord Guillem's right side, lifted his friend's healthy arm over his own shoulders, thus supporting his weight and keeping him steady while they scrambled up after Kurk and the dog. Vialle followed after. The bow slung over her shoulder alongside her leather quiver reminded him of her feat.

"Vialle!" Zimenes called, once she safely reached the summit. She turned to face him, her hand at her ear.

He cupped his hands around his mouth. "Thank you!" he said. "You saved my life!"

She waved her hand and smiled broadly. "You're in my debt now!" she called down the slope.

Her voice echoed from the cliff face behind him, faintly: "debt now!"

"Help me with this." Borek turned back to the carcass.

He cut free the net that had tangled in the antlers, tossed the limp ropes away into the trees.

The antlers were impressive, larger than any Zimenes had ever seen. As a younger man he had occasionally accompanied King Adalmund on hunts, and he had seen his share of trophies returning to the castle in later years, but he had never seen a hart so stately. So regal. Zimenes placed his hand against the hard bone, felt the scratchy fuzz that grew there. He traced the graceful sweep of horn out from the head, where it grew thick as his wrist, to the broad palm that branched out, then branched again, finally trailing off into sharp, even delicate points. Had Vialle missed, several of these wicked tines might easily have plunged through Zimenes' own hide. Might've crushed him, flung him aside, broken. Like Willit.

Even so, he felt more sympathy toward the great beast than anything.

They rolled the hart onto his back, dug the antlers into the ground to hold him in place. Then Borek cut the skin from throat to vent, and scooped out some of the guts and tossed the steaming, reeking mess to Nigredo. He did this work quickly, with no pity, no remorse.

*I should have warned you when I had the chance,* he thought. Glanced over his shoulder at Borek to see if he had spoken this thought aloud. The hunter remained bent over the carcass.

How would he ever bring himself to kill a unicorn, if it came to that? How could he countenance such a thing? Staring into the hart's unseeing black eyes, he understood—for the first time, truly understood—Adalmund's reluctance.

"A hand, if you will, doctor," Borek said.

Zimenes turned to the hunter, and the hart. Borek had peeled the deer's hide down to the spine and spread the large flaps of skin out to either side of the ribs to provide a bed for the flayed carcass. Borek extended a second knife in his direction. Field dressing such a creature was hard, bloody work, but Zimenes knew how to butcher fresh game from his days in the army. This was no different.

He plunged the knife into the haunch, to disarticulate the joint there.

As his knife slid through flesh, a memory came to him, unbidden.

# 14

Eighteen-year-old Zimenes stole through the forest, fighting to catch his breath, to slow his pulse, to move as quietly as possible over fallen, dead, brittle leaves that hid roots and rocks that seemed determined to catch his toes and roll his ankles.

He was alone. He'd become separated from his fellows in the chase. They'd been hunting barbarians fleeing in a rout through the trees.

He was no soldier. He'd joined the army not long after crossing the southern mountains into Averonne, but not as a warrior. He was a drover, a cook, an entertainer, a blade-sharpener, a darner of ragged socks and undergarments. But when Prince Adalmund— no, King Adalmund, now—sounded the horn to throw in the rearguard, to commit the reserves, to turn the battle definitively, Zimenes had thrown on his leather apron and grabbed his heaviest carving knife and rushed forward when the rest of the men did, eager to see some excitement, hoping for a glimpse of combat, emboldened by his fellow auxiliaries surging toward the front. Inspired by the example of his new king, Adalmund, crowned on the battlefield only the day before, on the same spot where the prince had defended his father King Ethelred's fallen corpse for hours, rallying his troops again and again against the tattooed horde, battling the barbarians to a stalemate in the open field, where they were once presumed invincible due to their ferocity and their fearlessness.

The invaders threw wave after wave against Adalmund and his vanguard, only to see each wave break on that rock, and roll back into the churning, pale sea. Bewildered by this staunch defense, the attackers' resolve wavered. Their leaders began to doubt. Another day of pitched battle and the berserkers recognized the fear in their chieftains' eyes, smelled its stink permeating the camp at night. A fear that—until now—they had only known in their enemies, who had all melted away before them in panicked retreat. Until now. Until Adalmund, fighting beneath the golden banner of the Unicorn.

The tide that had swept forward brought Zimenes, puffingly bringing up the tail end of the rearguard, across the blood-matted, corpse-tangled battlefield, into the forest. A few flakes of snow drifted down like ash, and his breath steamed in the air before him, though he did not feel the cold. As he passed among the trees, he had stepped around a few dead bodies, mostly fur-clad, head-shaven, pale-skinned, blue-daubed. Occasionally, from far ahead, whoops and cries reached back to him, shouts and echoed calls, but even those receded, diminished, as the violent, bloody tide rolled away before him, carrying all with it but the trees, and the leaves underfoot, and the dead.

Then a nearby horn blasted away his solitude, and he quick-stepped to the largest tree in his vicinity. He embraced its trunk, pressed himself into it, did his best to put its thickness between himself and the source of the sound that reverberated through the woods.

A rallying call.

He peered around the trunk, glimpsed a man, pulled his head back. He looked again. The man had not seen him. He was too absorbed in his own struggles, as he staggered along, dragging one leg stiffly behind him. The man disappeared for a moment or two, blocked from view by close-grown tree trunks. When he again emerged into Zimenes' line of sight, he paused, raised the large ivory horn to his lips. His cheeks swelled, and the bellow shattered the stillness. The sound quickly faded, became choked, garbled.

The man's hair was long and blond, dirty, braided with blood. He bore the golden shield of the unicorn at his side, though his was battered and chipped.

*One of ours,* Zimenes thought, relieved. He emerged from behind the tree, raised his hand, moved forward. Though he stopped on seeing the long black arrow that stuck through the man's thigh, the feathers facing front, the dark arrowhead pointing backward. The man released the horn, let it bounce against his chest as he staggered forward, stumbled.

The man did not pay any mind to the painted barbarian lying

at his feet. Another corpse, among many.

Horrified, Zimenes watched the corpse move, watched it rise to hands and knees, watched it reach to the ground and retrieve its spiked club. Zimenes began to move, tried to call a warning but found he had no breath, no wind, needed it all because he was running, running through the leaves, dodging tree trunks, running as the barbarian stood to his feet, running even faster as the blue-painted visage turned into a snarl of rage and hate.

Terrified by what he knew he had to do—by what he was, stars help him, in the process of doing—Zimenes charged forward. He flung himself at the man, who had been focused solely on his own prey, and knocked him to the ground, jarring the club from his grasp. He landed on the man and drove his carving knife under the man's ribcage and into his lungs.

It was a mortal blow, but not immediately so, and the man beat at Zimenes' head, clawed at his eyes, then reached out for his club. Zimenes rolled from the man's chest and continued rolling, scrambling, diving out of the barbarian's reach, his knife still buried in the man's side. The barbarian's club dug into the earth behind him as he rolled, pinned and ripped a gash in his tunic but did not mar his skin. The painted man struggled to his feet, leaning heavily on his club, and took one step. Not toward Zimenes, no—he ignored Zimenes and staggered toward the other man, the blond man, who leaned against a tree, and seemed to be slowly sliding down its trunk, right leg stiffly outstretched, face tightened in a grimace of pain.

A face that Zimenes recognized, though he'd only had glimpses from afar—pre-battle speeches he witnessed from the fringe of the gathered troops, or a sighting as he strode through the camp, inspecting and cheering his men. Prince Adalmund. No, *King* Adalmund, he reminded himself. King Adalmund. The new king struggled to hold himself steady against the tree, tried to heft his own sword in defense.

Zimenes put himself between the wounded barbarian and the wounded king. He raised his bare hands, ready to defend the king from his attacker as best he could—he did not even carry a paring knife at his side.

The barbarian took a step toward them, then another. He would have to get through Zimenes before he reached his true target. He raised his war club, studded with glittering shards of obsidian, but in removing his walking support he tottered and collapsed to the ground, where he bled out the last of his blood, and wheezed the last of his breath.

Zimenes turned to the king. He was sure it was him; he did not need to ask.

"Sire," he said. "What can I do?"

The king grimaced in pain, slid the rest of the way down the tree trunk, sat heavily on the gnarled roots, cried out. Fresh spittle flecked his filthy blond beard.

Zimenes cupped his hands around his mouth and yelled as loud as he could: "Doctor!" He turned to shout in the other direction: "Physician!" His voice fell away among the impassive trees.

He fell to his knees in the leaves at the king's side. "What can I do?" he asked again.

King Adalmund touched the horn at his chest. It was fashioned from an ivory tusk, banded at both ends in copper, and the ivory bore intricate carvings of men hunting on horseback, pursuing an antlered stag through tall trees.

"Wind this," he said. "And don't stop."

He lifted the horn over the downed king's head, extracted the brass chain from between his back and the tree trunk. He raised it to his lips, and blew, but no sound came forth. He tried again. Nothing but a hiss of air.

The king made a gargling sound, his body began to quiver. In a panic Zimenes rushed to him, but realized that he was laughing. Laughing at him.

"Some huntsman you'd make," the king said. "What's your name, lad?"

"Zimenes, my lord."

Adalmund winced, held out his hand for the horn. "From beyond the southern mountains?"

Zimenes nodded, placed the large horn in the king's hand, which fell under the weight into his lap.

"Sit with me a while, Zim," he said. "We have to remove the arrow, but I must gather my strength first."

He closed his eyes. Zimenes sat on the ground next to him. Stared at the open, unblinking eyes of the barbarian he'd slain. The man he had killed. The bile welled within him, and he rolled away from the king and let it spill up from within, out into the leaves.

The fetid mess steamed in the cold air. He sank back against the tree, next to the king.

Adalmund's eyes were open again. The king appraised Zimenes' leather apron, glanced at the wooden handle of the carving knife that protruded from the barbarian's rib.

"Your first?" he asked.

Zimenes nodded. Leaned to the side and spat the bilious phlegm from his mouth. Swiped at his lips with his sleeve.

"Before, I was a cook," he said. "Now, a killer."

Adalmund placed his blood-stained hand on Zimenes' elbow, not far from the smear of vomit that he'd wiped from his beard.

"No, my friend," he said. "Now you're a soldier. A warrior."

The knife had slid into the man as easily as though he were slicing into a side of beef, or a pork haunch. This surprised him, though of course a man is even less meaty than those animals. The sharp instantaneity of it, the irrevocability of it, chilled him.

"I don't want to be that," Zimenes said.

Adalmund grinned, his teeth white against his dirty blond beard.

"We don't always want to be what we must become," he said. He coughed, and his grip tightened on Zimenes' arm. "My father told me that. Four days ago."

Zimenes felt foolish. How was the badly wounded king—his father recently deceased—attempting to console *him*?

"I was sorry, sire, to hear of King Ethelred—"

"He always said he wanted to die swinging his sword in battle, not wasting away in old age," Adalmund said. "He got his wish."

The young king winced with pain, shifted his weight away from the arrow. Leaned into Zimenes. Adalmund's body shook with a cough that would not stop. Not knowing what to do, Zimenes placed his hands on the other man's shoulders, tried to steady him, as though holding him still would quell the cough.

"Who knew," the king finally managed, "that an arrow could hurt so much?"

Zimenes stood up again, cupped his hands and called for aid to the four corners of the forest.

"Doctor! Help!" He knew better than to cry out the king's name, and he searched the trees suspiciously for any signs of other blue-painted survivors. "Physician!"

The few drifting snowflakes seemed to make the silence even more complete.

"We must pull it out," the king said, "from the arrow side. Can you see it?"

He rolled onto his left side, suppressing a groan of pain. The arrowhead stuck redly from his right hamstring.

"Yes," Zimenes said.

"First we must break the shaft where it protrudes from the skin," he said.

"Shit in milk," Zimenes said.

"And we must do it cleanly and quickly." Zimenes knelt at the king's right side, near the leg that bore the arrow. The head had entered squarely in the front of the thigh, and the shaft seemed as though it must be on the hip side of the thigh bone, rather than the groin side. Both men breathed heavily now, sweated profusely despite the cold. "Decisively, understood?"

Zimenes swallowed and nodded. "Shit in milk," he said again, as he reached for the slick wooden shaft. "Mother of mercy."

"Listen, Zim," the king said. "If I should—you know—"

"I'm not going to let that happen," Zimenes said.

"Just listen," the king silenced him. "There is a woman. Among the healers. Her name is Tristesse. You must tell her—" He winced with pain. "Tell her I love her. Tell her I would make her my queen."

"You'll tell her yourself," Zimenes said. "When you walk into their tent."

The King smiled and nodded. He removed Zimenes' hands, grabbed the shaft in both of his instead, lifted his leg and then drove it and the arrowhead down into an exposed root to anchor it.

"Here's how we do it," Adalmund said. He grabbed the arrow where it rose from the skin. "I'm going to pull this way. You put your hands here"—he indicated the fletched portion of the arrow—"and pull in the other direction. Toward the earth. When I say 'now.'"

"Shit in—"

"Now."

Zimenes pulled down with all his weight, as though he were slashing a cleaver through a slab of ribs. The shaft snapped with a crack and a hoarse cry from the king. Zimenes held the feathers in his hand—they were slick with his own sweat, and with the king's blood.

Footsteps rustling through the leaves caused Zimenes to reach for the king's sword and scramble to his feet, but it was several of the king's guard. An older man among them. The king's physician, Eirenaeus, as Zimenes would later learn.

"We'll take it from here," the physician said, brushing Zimenes brusquely aside.

"Easy," the king said. "Zim here saved my life."

The physician decanted an indigo syrup onto the place where the arrow stuck from the king's thigh.

"A cook saved your life?" one of the guardsmen said. "My humblest apologies, sire. I don't know how we could've let you—"

"Nonsense," the king said. "We had them on the run. You'll have to tell me all about the hunt."

"First we move him back to the tent," the physician said. "Then we remove the arrow."

Adalmund reached out his hand to Zimenes, who dropped the broken arrow to take it.

"Think of it this way," the king said. "With your first kill, you saved the life of your king."

"Yes," Zimenes said, suddenly proud. "That is precisely what happened."

"I want a man with that kind of luck at my side," Adalmund said to the gathered men. They returned his smile, but their faces were grim, their jaws set.

Six men bore him up in a bier made by their interlocked arms. Zimenes stood with them. As the king's men stepped away, the king's bloody fingers slipped from his grasp. Zimenes strode after them, but Master Eirenaeus—who would go on to become Zimenes' instructor—placed his hand on Zimenes' chest.

"He's in good hands," he said. "You'll only get in the way."

The king winced as the men stepped rapidly through the trees. He called out to Zimenes, "You'll cook for me and my men sometime."

"Yes!" Zimenes cupped his hands to his mouth, "I will!"

The six knights carried his newfound friend, his king, through the trees. Snowflakes drifted aimlessly about them. The king raised his hand in farewell, but then it fell back, and hung limply as the men bounced along.

# 15

The next day they feasted.
Kurk and Carlès returned to Borek and Zimenes with the two pack horses and helped them load the venison. Borek hiked back to camp carrying the hart's head and antlers, determined to keep it intact for mounting as a trophy; Kurk helped him bear the gruesome load.

Borek insisted that Zimenes ride one of the horses, and he did not protest. The sun soared high in the sky, and his horse was beginning to labor and lather, when he and Carlès rode into camp. Borek and Kurk and the dogs had fallen well behind, out of sight.

Magda was rolling out noodles and stretching them to dry. Freshly washed mushrooms waited in a bowl; several bunches of wild spring onions had already been chopped, to add to whatever stew Magda might have up her sleeve. As his stomach turned over, he realized he was hungry. There would be no hunting today.

Lord Guillem sat shirtless with his back against the enormous log that the men had dragged into the camp to use as a bench, his left arm cradled in his lap. Vialle crouched at his side, tenderly ministering to his damaged shoulder, applying a fresh poultice. Zimenes dismounted and knelt at Guillem's other side. The young man looked as immaculate as he ever did, his hair combed back and knotted, his face washed, his beard freshly oiled. He did not seem uncomfortable in the least.

"How are you feeling?" Zimenes asked.

Guillem lifted his injured arm slightly from his lap. "Better," he said. "Thanks to the princess. And to you, of course."

His professional jealousy excited, he questioned Vialle about her poultice.

"Cool mud from the stream bed," she said. "Mixed with crushed juniper, angelica, and valerian."

He lowered his nose to the burlap. "And mint?"

"So it smells tolerable."

An expert application. The swelling around the joint had subsided, somewhat. With Zimenes' help Guillem could lift his arm above his head, but his casual smile reverted to a set grimace, and sweat began to form on his unlined forehead.

"You need to rest the arm," Zimenes said. "Continue with the poultice, for now."

"Those antlers," Guillem said, with a shake of his head. "I thought they were going to run right through me."

"Good thing they didn't," Zimenes said. "Or we might not be having this conversation."

In his tent he found fresh clothes—laundered and folded by Magda—and headed for the stream with the cake of lye. He drank his fill, and then washed the grime from his hands, his forearms, his feet, his face, his hair. When he returned, Borek and Kurk were in the process of building a bonfire in the circular pit. At the far end of the camp the hart's antlered head hung between the lower branches of two trees.

The venison roasted on spits they all agreed was a bit on the gamey side, the old hart certainly more of a trophy than a target for tender meat. But Magda's bouillabaisse—in which she slowly simmered chunks of shoulder and haunch that had been only briefly seared in the hottest part of the fire, alongside potatoes, parsnips, onions, mushrooms, ramps, and various herbs, thickened with her fresh noodles, spiced with salt, black pepper, sweet paprika, coriander and fennel—was enthusiastically devoured by all.

Borek praised the hunters for their steadfastness, and Carlès declaimed that bringing down this hart proved that they were up to the larger challenge, just as soon as they found the unicorn that they sought. They extolled Guillem's bravery, and as he told of his encounter with the hart, Vialle rose from where she had been sitting, next to Magda, and sat at Guillem's healthy side, rested her hand on his. The young man smiled, and color returned to his cheeks, warmed by the fire, and Borek's brandy, and almost certainly by the nearness of his beloved.

As the afternoon wore into evening, smaller groups formed, split up, recombined with others. Borek and Carlès and Guillem broke down the events of the hunt, strategized and theorized over how they would do things differently the next time. Zimenes sat for a time with Magda and Vialle, and they discussed the alchemical precepts of transmutation, and how distilling the essences of herbs and flowers and roots to make medicines always struck him as more valuable than the pursuit of transforming lead and other base metals into gold. Kurk tussled with the dogs, though he still seemed dispirited by the death of Willit.

Their chatter echoed through the trees, faded into the forest surrounding them. The circle of warm red firelight shielded them from anything that might lurk out there, in the darkness beyond. Sparks lifted from the fire up toward the heavens, toward the stars that stood out in the sky above, visible through the broad opening in the canopy.

Borek came to sit on the log next to Zimenes. He unstoppered a leathern wineskin, took a deep draught, handed it to Zimenes. He lifted the bladder and the acrid vapors stung his nose; a tentative sip curled his tongue, and as he swallowed, the liquor scorched his throat, then his belly, all the way down to his bowels.

"Go on," Borek said, tipping the skin back up to Zimenes' mouth. "A proper swig."

He raised the bladder, leaned back and opened his mouth, gave the skin a squeeze, fountained the brandy into his mouth until it was full. He swallowed the stuff all at once, handed the skin back to the hunter with his eyes watering.

"Your health," he gasped. The alcohol burned deep within his chest, flushed his face with warmth, sent a tingle down through his toes and into the earth. Not for the first time, an image of the onrushing hart, his antlers lowered, the deadly tines sweeping toward him, filled Zimenes' mind.

"You also saved my life yesterday," he said. "I didn't properly thank you. I'm in your debt."

"Two arrows gone," Borek said. The shafts had snapped when the great beast had crashed to earth. "Hoped not to have to use that many."

Borek took another pull and then stoppered the skin. He grabbed a long branch, prodded at the blaze. The logs settled, crackled, ejected a plume of sparks up into the gathering gloom.

"Do you ever have any regrets?" Zimenes asked. "About the creatures you've killed?"

The hunter's shoulders shook, gently, twice. Zimenes had come to learn that this meant he was laughing. While he could tell when the man was laughing, he only rarely understood the cause behind the laughter, and this was no exception.

"That would be like me asking you if you regretted fixing the fop's shoulder. A neat trick, that."

Zimenes lifted his hand both to acknowledge the compliment, and wave it away.

"No—my only regrets these days," the hunter said, "are the ones that got away."

He tapped the branch he'd been using to rake the embers against Zimenes' knee. "Bound to be some of those, at our age. Eh, doctor?"

*The ones that got away.*

"And I don't even mind the ones where I missed the shot," Borek continued. "It's the ones where I had the shot, but didn't take it. That moment of hesitation—and then it's gone."

He remembered the night—cold, wintry, fresh snow covering the gardens. He'd been lying in his bed, awake, puzzling over comments the queen had made during dinner, when the faintest rap at his door roused him. So faint that he wondered if it wasn't the wind, or a trick of his mind.

But no, it was her. Bundled in her furs, shivering, her breath steaming. He invited her in, closed the door behind her. Busied himself lighting a fire—this was before he had an apprentice living with him. When he turned from the licking flames, she had removed her fur, beneath which she wore only her shift.

"Zim," she said. "I want to apologize—"

He took her into his arms. "Shh," he said. "There is no need."

He kissed her. At first carefully, delicately. As though those lips were made of porcelain that might break if pressed too forcefully against the teeth. He reached his fingers to the smooth skin of her cheeks, as though to assure himself that she was, truly, standing in front of him. To assure himself that this was no dream.

He opened his eyes. Hers were closed. The growing light of the fire glowed on her cheeks. He moved his fingers into her hair, soft and lush, and the firelight danced there as well. Pried open her lips with his. Within, the tip of his tongue found hers, warm and yielding. He'd never imagined a touch so tender, so intimate. His entire self stiffened as she leaned her yielding body into his.

His hands moved from her hair down her back, along her body, and he knew that under the shift she wore nothing, she was naked. Her hands roved over his body as well, seeking, exploring. Her mouth opened further to his, their faces fused together. Her tongue widened, pushed against his, overwhelmed his. She sucked his tongue and bit his lower lip, an alloy of pain and play.

She placed her hands on his chest and pushed back, separating their faces. His hands on her buttocks held her against him from their waists down.

"Zim," she breathed.

He was kissing the queen. His best friend's wife.

But also, the woman he loved. More than anyone he'd ever loved before.

"Please, Zim," she said. "Please."

He heard this as a plea for him to stop them from doing what they both knew to be wrong.

He released her. She gathered up her fur coat, wrapped it around her shoulders. She stood in front of him, stood on tip toes to kiss him again, this time with her hazel eyes open, staring into his. Her eyes glistened. Trembled pleadingly. He reached into her coat and pulled her close to him, squeezed her tightly to him. She moaned, and pushed away.

"I didn't mean to disturb you," she said, and then she was gone, out into the night. Winter midnight air swirled around him, and he sagged back into his winged chair, staring at the fire in his hearth that had just begun to take, and grow.

The next morning, she was gone. To the cloister. No farewell. No explanation. No further correspondence. Leaving only an absence that weighed heavier and heavier on him with each passing day.

Countless days, endless nights he had pondered over her visit. Stared into those hazel eyes again and again, shining brightly, tremulous—searching. Surely, she'd known that on the morrow she would be gone, forever. She'd come to him in the night, like a thief, or a spy. Kissed him like never before. Surrendered herself to him. She wanted him to take her. To ravish her.

*Please, Zim.*

And he hesitated. Demurred.

It hadn't been fear of discovery so much as a desire to be respectful. He respected her, respected their friendship, respected her husband. He wanted her to respect him.

Bah—*respect*—what did this word even mean? When she stood before him, nearly naked, practically begging him to have his way with her? Did she show any regard for respect, in that moment? If it wasn't fear that held him back then it was something perhaps even worse: timidity.

He let her go. Let her walk out his door. Watched her disappear from his life.

He reached for the wineskin. Borek unstoppered it and handed it to him.

"To the one that got away," he said, and squeezed a stream of brandy into his mouth, swallowed it down. Passed it back to Borek as he wiped the excess from his beard on his sleeve. He'd hoped the vapors would blast that image from his eyes, erase that memory from his mind. Of course, they did no such thing, only made him gag instead.

Borek raised the skin in his turn. "And to this one that *won't* get away," he said, then drank.

The two men stared in silence at the flames for a while, each lost in his own memories, his own regrets. Zimenes remembered claiming, as a young man about to cross the mountainous border into Averonne to seek a new life, that he would live that new life with no regrets. A rueful smile spread over his face. The tapestry in the king's throne room came to mind, the twists and turns of its mazy, woodsy tangle—who doesn't ever wish to return to a decision made years before, and decide differently? Take a different turn? See where that path might've led?

What if he had taken Tesse that night? Perhaps they would have departed the kingdom together, hand in hand, arm in arm. Headed back across the mountains, to his homeland. Started a new life. A new family. Might've even started a war. Burned a love story across the heavens that the historians would be writing about centuries from now. Rather than living the muted, flat simulacrum of a life he'd been living in the castle these past ten years, turning away from his inmost desires in exchange for avoiding the inevitable pain.

He stood, unsteadily at first. The fire swam in front of him, the smoke seemed to blow right into his face. He coughed, then moved away, seeking fresh air, needing to relieve himself. As he headed toward the latrine, he felt as though somebody was watching him from the darkness. He turned, only to see the hart's head, strung up by its antlers. Its dead, black eyes gleamed faintly in the distant firelight. Suddenly sober, he made his water quickly, and returned.

He stopped at the bowl of wine that they had poured over slices of oranges and lemons they had brought with them. The wine was nearly gone, but he didn't want to drink any more. He scooped out a slice of lemon, and put it in his mouth.

Vialle sat next to Guillem—she rested her hand lightly on his injured arm and he winced, she apologized and retracted, laughing. Borek was regaling Magda and Carlès with a story about some creature he had hunted in the past, making a face to imitate it. Zimenes tried to guess—a lion? A manticore? Magda placed her hand over her heart and leaned back, then forward again, eager for more, while Carlès affected an aloof disposition, but also studied the hunter intently, mildly annoyed by Magda's interjections.

He bit down on the lemon, let the sour juice, infused with the wine, flow over his tongue. He walked back toward the fire.

Adalmund had been right. He'd been a prisoner in the castle, lashed to the king and his duties as he had been, for years. He had needed this. More desperately than he could possibly have realized without undertaking it, without experiencing it firsthand. *Adalmund was right.*

"Why so dour?" Vialle asked him, as he rejoined the group.

He smiled down at her, revealing the lemon's bright yellow rind instead of his teeth, an old trick that he used to play with her at the dinner table when she was a child.

She squealed and clapped her hands. Every bit as she used to, all those years ago.

"Let me try," Guillem said. Vialle scooped an orange from her own cup of wine, and placed it between the nobleman's teeth. He bit down, worked his lips around the rind, and then revealed an orange smile. Juice dribbled from his lips into his beard, and Vialle dabbed at the slobber with a handkerchief.

"Look at you," Zimenes said. "Like an old married couple."

"Yes," Vialle said, getting in on the joke, "meet my invalid husband who can no longer keep from drooling."

They all laughed.

He missed Adalmund, he realized. If only he'd been able to persuade the king to join them on this trip, surely he, too, would've experienced the rejuvenating effects of the Mirrenwood. Surely he, too, would be right alongside them, telling stories, cracking jokes, and laughing, laughing. He remembered the deep boom of his friend's hearty guffaws.

A hand patted his thigh. Magda. The hand remained there. "Why so quiet?" she asked.

"I'm going to turn in," he announced, silencing the merriment. "Tomorrow the hunt begins in earnest."

# 16

Zimenes crouched and plucked a flower of the hellebore plant, held it in his palm, brought it close to his eyes. He examined the dark purple, nearly black petals, a stark contrast with the bright yellow anthers radiating out from the center. Sticky sap leaked from the place where he had pinched the stem free from the stalk. Poisonous.

For four days now, Vialle had gone to the glade where they had finally brought down the hart. Three of those days, Zimenes had gone with the hunters, sharing a blind with Kurk, while Borek and Carlès surveyed the entrance to the canyon from the other blind. Vialle sat in the clearing and waited while the men hid, watching. Every evening she would return to camp with a freshly braided crown of flowers.

And every evening, Magda would ask, "Any sign?"

"No sign," would come the reply, as the hunters lowered their gear to the ground.

"Supper's ready," Magda would reply, relentlessly cheery. "Wash up, then come get your fill!"

Today, however, Guillem had insisted on going with the hunters, claiming he felt much improved, determined that his injured arm—still in a sling—would not impair him. Someone needed to stay behind with Magda, so Zimenes had volunteered. Huddling in a cramped blind for three days with the taciturn Kurk had almost brought him to the point of requesting that Carlès partner with him instead. Almost.

Magda had taken charge of the camp, and proven herself remarkably competent and efficient. Zimenes assisted as needed with chores: fetching water, splitting firewood, chopping vegetables, repairing equipment—all things that he used to do on campaign with the king's troops.

One of the hounds always remained at her side, to alert her to the presence of any wild creatures that might come to investigate the smells of food, but in the days they had been there, none had shown themselves—perhaps driven away by the smells of men and dogs.

Zimenes collected a few of the hellebore's furry seed pods, dropped them into a glass vial. He added the vial to the hard-cured leather pouch that dangled from his knapsack. In a few spare hours, he'd already found so many wonderful plants—herbs and fungi, flowers and worts, roots and barks—that he could use in his practice back at the castle. The tools of his peculiar trade.

It was good that he was finding these specimens. They would serve him, and the king, and by extension the people of Averonne. Perhaps he might even write his own book. But he could not help feeling the pressure of onrushing time. The king could easily have taken a turn for the worse, and they would have no way of knowing until Kurk made another trip back to Rotterham to purchase supplies. Which the lad wouldn't need to do for another few days. The hart they'd killed was enormous, and even though the seven of them and the hounds had been eating their fill of it, and even though he and Borek had not been extraordinarily scrupulous in conserving every last edible part of the deer, they still had plenty of smoked and dried venison.

He straightened and inhaled, through his nose, the sweet, loamy scent of the forest. Two short weeks ago he could not have imagined a life other than the routine of the castle, the routine that he had followed for more than a decade—and yet here he was, in the Mirrenwood, surrounded by trees and a stillness so profound he could feel his heart beating in his chest, the pulse in his neck, the air fresh in his lungs.

He could breathe more deeply, more clearly than he had in years. He slept more soundly, too, though he was sleeping on the ground, nothing but a thin mat of reeds for a bed, rather than the plush mattress he'd been accustomed to. He felt rejuvenated. As though each day spent hiking through the forest, chopping firewood, hauling pails of water from the stream, had subtracted a full year from his age. His knees didn't complain as strenuously when he straightened them. His back no longer stiffened.

The belling of a horn echoed through the trees. So faint, so distant that had a breeze stirred the leaves above him he likely wouldn't have heard it. He began to move in the direction whence the sound emanated.

There, again. Off to the right. An answering call? Or the same horn? Too remote to tell. He changed course, moved through the sparse underbrush, past the tall and straight beeches that thrived in these low rambling hills and shallow creek beds.

He quickened his pace. What if the hunters had found their quarry? What if the final, true hunt was on?

He paused, then, and waited for another sounding of the horn. His heart beat loudly in his chest now, in his ears, as his breathing began to labor somewhat.

Nothing. He continued in the direction he'd been following. This part of the forest was unfamiliar, but the going was easy. The sun shone brightly far above, but the partial shade kept the air cool, dappled the forest floor. Occasionally a spider web caught at his beard or his hair, or glistened in the sunlight and he would part it with his arm. The few birds scolded him as he crept along beneath them in their high perches.

There it was again. Fainter, even, than before, if that were possible. Receding. Off to the left this time. He corrected his course again, moved further into the forest. The tall, nearly branchless beeches gave way to massive, sprawling maples, the shade here darker, a more solid presence, the sweat from his exertions stood out on his brow and dampened his collar and trickled down his flanks. He picked his way around the broad trunks, as his robes swept through the low, thick underbrush.

He took a step forward—out into empty space.

A yawning chasm opened up beneath his outstretched leg— the Fool in the tarot cards. Nowhere for his foot to land. The earth beneath him had vanished.

He flung his arms out to the side. His right hand contacted a pillar of stone, strangely; his left, thorny brambles. He grabbed at both as firmly as he could, hauled himself backward, away from the cliff's edge, as vertigo clutched him and whirled him about dizzily, threw him down to his knees.

Once assured of solid ground beneath him, he sprawled out onto his belly, splayed his arms and legs out wide, as though to hold onto the earth, as though to seep down into it, as though to burrow in like the measly, fragile, perishable worm he was. As though to never move, ever again.

He squeezed his eyelids tightly shut and lay there, panting, gasping, on a mound of broken stones that stabbed and dug into his thigh, his hip, his ribs. Reluctant to open his eyes until the world ceased its spinning, until the bile in his belly and the dull roar between his ears quieted.

He finally opened them, and an eye stared unblinkingly into his, a hand's breadth away.

Startled, he lifted his head, refocused his vision: it was not an eye, after all, but a circular rune, carved into the stone, with a dot at the center. Runes ran away to either side of the "eye," their angular march stretched over the stones that had fallen into this pile. The remains of the column he'd clung to, that had saved him from plunging over the sheer cliff that divided the forest.

He inched closer to the edge, gazed down a drop at least as tall and as sheer as the walls of the keep in Averonne. Mighty oaks grew below, oaks whose crowns rose above the cliff, giving the illusion of a continual forest floor to any who might be ambling along unawares, hiding the sudden drop.

The broken column, he realized, once formed part of an arch that had long since fallen. The runes resembled those he had seen at the cairn where they had spotted the great hart, and in the glade, where the hunters now kept watch over Vialle.

He picked his way over the rubble, still on hands and knees, not trusting his queasy balance or the broken, uneven footing. He followed the trail of runes. They led him to stone steps that descended the cliff-face, narrow and steep, hewn from the rock itself. They switched back and forth, connecting one landing to another.

His panicked breathing had slowed, his stomach ceased its churning. The roar never did quite leave him, however, and he realized it was the sound of rushing water.

He stood up, breathed in deeply, cinched his knapsack straps and snugged his belt, and began the descent, leaning into the cliff face as he went, cautiously testing each step, aware that if one were to give way, or if he were to lose his footing on the worn-smooth steps, the fall would likely be fatal. He guessed that the steps had been carved from a natural seam in the cliff face, a jagged chain of diagonal slopes.

The sounding of the distant horns had been replaced in his mind with a fascination, a desire to explore. To see where these steps would lead him—slowly, painstakingly, one after the other. The drone of rushing water grew steadily louder as he descended. A waterfall, perhaps. He continued carefully from one landing to the next, until he reached the final step, and came to stand on a natural ledge that projected out from the cliff face. He moved more confidently here, as the ledge was broad and flat enough for him to stand comfortably and the drop to his left was only the height of a tall man, while the cliff stretched away above him and became lost among the upper branches of the oaks. The steady drumming of the waterfall close at hand now.

The ledge sloped gently down as it followed the cliff's curve. The waterfall came into view, a white sheet of water that plunged from above, the source hidden by leafy branches. The ledge narrowed through brambles, the stone became wet and slippery, and then it led him behind the roaring plume. Here the rock opened into a cave, the height of a man and maybe equally broad, the floor a bowl of stone smoothed by ages of rushing water that was wet near the waterfall but dry further back. He wondered if this cave was natural or manmade. The afternoon sunlight reflected off the churning pool outside, refracted through the waterfall, and shimmeringly lit up the rock ceiling within.

Toward the rear, on the dry floor, a small pile of folded white fabric. Strange. He crept toward what he could see were clothes, as though they were a creature he might startle. A shift, a tunic, a skirt, a robe, all of a thin white linen. When had these been left here? It was hard to say. It could have been a few moments; it could have been years.

He might not be alone.

Slowly he crept toward the front of the cave. Through the thin sheet of water, in the pool beyond, something moved. He brought himself closer to that curtain. Parted it with his hand, splashing his sleeve, his robe. A human head bobbed there, wet hair plastered to the scalp.

He jerked his hand back, as though stung, and the curtain quickly closed. His pulse quickened. His heart pounded loud in his ears.

The head, blurred through the falling water, lifted, supported by a pale white body. Again, he parted the curtain, this time with a finger. Then two. A third.

A woman's body. Breasts swelled as she leaned forward, placed her hands on the grassy bank. She lifted a knee from the water, revealing a graceful calf, a slender thigh. As she placed her arched foot on the grass, her buttocks hove into view, and then she lifted herself clear of the water, dripping, in profile to him, but her head turned away, scanning the screen of underbrush that provided her with privacy. Unaware, it would seem, of Zimenes watching from behind her. She wrung out her long hair, squeezed it between her hands, causing a smaller waterfall to cascade down over her back, and then she flung her water-darkened tresses over her shoulders, several times, sending droplets flying in all directions.

She turned, naked, revealing her full splendor, her broad hips, the dark thatch of her pubic hair, her breasts still dripping. Her green eyes flashed in a sudden reflected splash of sunlight.

Vialle.

# 17

He retracted his fingers, and the curtain descended again. Hand dripping, he searched frantically for an exit, but he could not flee without being seen. He backed further into the cave, past the clothes that he now realized must be the princess's.

She stepped up surefooted onto the slippery ledge, strode around behind the waterfall.

"Master Zimenes," she said. She stood before him, naked, unabashed.

He looked away, blinded by that beauty, that pale skin, gleaming in the light pouring in through the sheet of water, light that played ripplingly over the curves of her body, the image of which stayed in his mind, though he clamped his eyes shut tight. The roar of the water filled his ears, filled the hollowed-out space between them. He fell to his knees. They thudded painfully on the stone floor.

"I beg forgiveness for this intrusion, princess," he said. "I know not how I came to be here."

She laughed. "I summoned you, silly," she said.

He opened his eyes, but still did not look toward her.

"You...you what?"

"Hand me my clothes, would you?"

He let his gaze come forward enough to find her clothes on the floor. Her bare feet—revealing surprisingly pudgy toes— came within his view, and he looked away, reached down in the direction where he knew the clothes to be. Felt for the flimsy fabric, grabbed a bunch of it in his hand. He held out his arm, extending the clothing toward her.

"My goodness, Zimenes," she said. "You behave as though you've never seen a woman naked before."

"I should not see you naked," he said. With his other hand he shielded his eyes.

"Why not?"

"I am your father's friend. I am your mother's loyal servant. I am your former teacher."

"So? So? And so?"

"So, take your clothes."

"I will not," she said. "Until you stand up and look at me as an adult. As an equal. As a human being."

He continued holding his arm out. His shoulder began to tire. He stood up, bent his elbow, relieved some of the strain. He turned to face her, eyes closed. Still, she would not take the clothes from him.

He opened his eyes.

She stood before him, hands on her hips, head cocked to one side, lips pursed, one eyebrow lifted over her upcast green eyes. The only item she wore was an amulet—a single red stone as big as a partridge egg—that hung between her breasts from a leather thong. She shook her head slowly.

"'Tis really so overwhelming?" she asked.

*Yes,* he thought. Then, "Yes, it is. You are."

She took the clothes from him, pulled a sheer white tunic over her head, then wrapped a similarly diaphanous skirt around her legs. She lowered the robe to the ground.

"Sufferest thine eyes from a surfeit of beauty?" she asked, with a smirk.

The outline of her figure was still quite visible through the fabric, and as the water transferred from her body to the cloth, it clung to her flesh, and her moles and even her dark arm hairs pressed visibly against the white. She pulled the amulet from beneath the shift, let it drop against her breastbone. It glowed in the reflected light. To either side, her nipples stood proud, strained against the fabric, pushed it into two pyramids.

This was no better than her being naked.

"You said you summoned—" he began.

She stepped closer to him. Close enough to reach out and touch, if he chose. He did not know where to rest his eyes. The glare of the sunlight reflecting into the waterfall was blindingly bright.

"Why have you been avoiding me?" she asked, as she gazed up into his face. Close enough now that the water dripped from her skirts onto his leather boots.

"I haven't—" he began.

"Oh, come on, Zim," she said. "You've spoken maybe twenty words to me since we slew the hart."

"You seemed intent on ministering to young Guillem," he said. "I did not wish to interfere."

Close enough now to feel the warmth of her breath against his face.

"Why are you scared of me?"

He pulled back from her, but her hands held his wrists, would not release them.

He breathed in. "I am not scared of you," he said. "I'm frightened of myself. Of my...feelings. Nothing can come of them."

"Everything could come of them," she said, her voice hushed. She pulled his wrists behind her back, where his hands naturally came to rest on the damp globes of her buttocks.

He lurched away from her.

"I don't know what this is," he said, wiping his hands dry on his robe. "I don't know what you want from me."

"This? This is but a dream," she said. "You can have whatever you want from me."

Was he dreaming? Touching her felt real. The brush of her breath on his face with every word felt real. But there was something about this place—the runes, the steps in the cliff, the waterfall, the shimmering cave—that felt dream-like. This wasn't the way things happened, in real life.

"You said you summoned me here—"

"How did you find this place?" she asked.

"I was walking in the woods, and I heard a hunter's horn," he said. "I thought the unicorn had been sighted. I followed the sound. I came across a series of stone steps, and they led me here."

"That was my call," she said. "Across time and space."

She stepped toward him, pressed her hips into his, and placed her hand over his breast, lightly. The touch sent another jolt through him, but he held himself still.

"That seems"—his dry mouth made speech difficult—"remarkably sophisticated."

"Garrimault describes this as a first step," she said, "on a long path."

He placed his hand over hers, but did not remove her palm from his chest.

"Are you saying that this is...magic?"

She glanced down, then back up into his eyes.

"If you want it to be."

"You're teasing me," he said. *But why?* "You enjoy tormenting me."

"You can kiss me," she said. She pressed her lithe, wet body into his. Pushed her soft breast against his hand, covering hers. "You can do with me as you please. You will wake in your tent, and it will be as though nothing had happened."

His entire body stiffened—his neck, his shoulders, his back, his buttocks, his thighs—followed by a surge growing from his groin. A driving force that returned her pressure, that pressed his body into hers.

"Vialle," he whispered.

"Would I behave this way if we were awake?" she asked him.

"No," he said, voice husky. "I don't believe you would."

"Then this must be a dream," she said. "Right?"

*Yes,* he wished, fervently. *Yes, a dream. If it's a dream, I can do as I please. I can do what I want.*

*Is that what I want to do with her?*

*Yes,* a part of him answered. A voice deep within, a voice he scarcely recognized. *Yes of course that's what you want to do with her. Do to her.*

She lifted herself up on tiptoes, pressed her body into his, pushed her pelvis against his prick, standing proud, straining forward and upward. She leaned her shoulders back, her wet hair fell away behind her, her lips parted, her green eyes closed.

"This cannot possibly end well," he murmured.

"Why are you so worried about how things will end?" she whispered. "Why can't you be present—right now, here, with me?"

He leaned forward. His lips met hers, plump, warm, wet. Her fingers entwined themselves in his hair, pulled his head even lower. Her lips parted, opened to his.

He opened his eyes. Hers stared back at him. Deep green pools. He lost himself in those eyes, lost himself in that kiss. He didn't know who he was anymore. A bewildering sensation—but also freeing.

Her tongue sought out his, her teeth bit down playfully on his lower lip, then harder.

Enough to wake him. Though still he stood in the cave, still he held this woman—this girl, his student, his friend's daughter—in his arms.

He gripped her shoulders in his hands and separated their mouths, their bodies. Her cheeks were flushed; his searingly warm. The room spun as the drone of the waterfall suddenly filled his consciousness. He maintained his grip on her shoulders to keep from spinning dizzyingly with the room, but also to hold their bodies apart, as she sought to close that distance again.

"I want you, Master," she said.

"No," he breathed. Then, more firmly, "No. This is lunacy."

"This is natural," she said. "You desire me, and I desire you."

"No," he said. "I do not."

She reached into his robe, grabbed his swollen prick through his trousers.

"Your body belies your words."

He pulled away, though he had to recognize that a part of him did not want to.

"Stop, Vialle," he said. "This is not a dream. This is me–this is you–this is reality. We cannot—we must not. If we are to find a cure for your father."

"Fine."

She pulled free of his grasp, bent over for her robe, wrapped that around her like a shawl.

"Now I'm chilly," she said. "Let us sit in the sun and dry ourselves, at least."

His hands, suddenly empty, hovered in midair. She turned and strode on the balls of her feet, hips swaying, through the narrow gap between the sheeting water and the glimmering, glistening stone wall.

He lowered his hands, balled futilely into fists, to his sides. He panted. His prick strained dumbly against the fabric of his leggings.

*How can she just leave?* he wondered. *Is her heart made of stone?*

He turned his back to the water, to Vialle. To the world. In that moment he felt a certain empathy toward her mother. Toward Tesse. He understood how the queen might have—once, long ago—felt a similar desire for him, while simultaneously bearing the suffocating weight of competing loyalties, duties, obligations, reputations. The burden of the kingdom.

He ought to avoid this situation altogether, following the queen's example.

*That's what a stronger person would do,* he thought.

His shoulders relaxed. The twisting, tightening knot in his gut loosened. His erection subsided. He gathered the last of her clothes, a camisole and slippers. He bunched the sheer camisole in his hand, buried his face in the fabric, inhaled deeply. Lavender and sage, and a hint of something else, a smoky incense. It smelled of her.

He followed her pudgy footprints from the cave, followed their trail along the ledge. Through the bushes and brambles, to a place where the stone was not damp from the splashing of the waterfall, and where the sun found its way through the leaves high above.

Her bare legs dangled over the edge, her back leaned against the cliff face. He would have to step over her to continue on his way back to the steps.

It would almost certainly be better if he departed the Mirrenwood entirely. Returned to the castle, retired from the field.

*That's what a better person would do.*

"Don't run away," Vialle said. "Sit with me for another moment or two, at least."

He sat cross-legged, his back pressed into the sun-warmed stone. He began to tell her that kissing her was a mistake, that watching her swim was a mistake, that coming here was a mistake.

She waved him silent. She leaned her head back against the cliff, tilted her face up to the afternoon sunlight, closed her eyes.

"Do you know why we haven't encountered the unicorn?" she asked.

"Because it doesn't exist," he said. "It never has."

He immediately regretted saying this, but he did not chastise himself, did not apologize, did not try to make amends. It was what he believed.

"No, silly," she said. She smiled a placid, radiant smile that he had never seen on her face before. It reminded him intensely of her mother—but from years ago. Not the Tesse he had glimpsed back at the cloister. "It's because we're looking for it. The unicorn will reveal itself only when least sought."

"Then what's the point of even entering the Mirrenwood?" Zimenes asked. "If the entire reason for doing so is to hunt this creature?"

"The act of seeking the unicorn proves you are not worthy of it," she said. She opened her eyes and turned toward him. "It's a lot like love in that way."

"What would you know of love?" His nerves were, finally, beginning to settle. Her radiant beauty, her brilliant green eyes, her low, throaty voice, all of which had so unnerved him in the cave, seemed to have a calming influence now.

"Enough to know it makes fools of men," she said.

"It makes fools of all of us."

"Perhaps," she said. "Have you ever, truly, found love?"

"I like to think so."

"But—has your love ever been requited?"

"When it comes to true love," he said, "that is not a necessary component."

"Wouldn't love be so much sweeter if it were returned in the same measure?"

"There is a certain sweetness in not expecting any return, in any measure."

"That must be what they call bittersweet," she said.

She tilted her face back toward the sun, closed her eyes. He imitated her posture, closed his eyes as well. Felt her hand cover his, her fingertips wrap down into his palm. He did not pull his hand away. Perhaps there was something to what she said. He'd grown so accustomed to unrequited love that it had come to seem normal, expected—simply the way love worked. This...*answer*, this response, was something entirely new to him.

But this couldn't possibly be love. While he had known the girl Vialle well, he had to acknowledge that he barely knew the woman she had become.

And yet...and yet...

They sat still like this, holding hands, until the sun drifted further to the west, lowered closer to the horizon. Treetops came between its warmth and their upturned cheeks, cast a pall over them, chilled their damp clothes. She retracted her hand.

"You said you summoned me," he said. "Were you speaking truth? Or teasing me?"

"You're here, aren't you?"

"Then, perhaps you can summon the unicorn in a similar way?" he asked, now teasing her.

"I hope to," she said. "I thought I would try with someone closer at hand, first."

"Why me?"

"You're the one who heard my call," she said.

"Why don't you try it now?" he asked. "With the unicorn?" Again, teasing her. Challenging her to demonstrate her purported command of magic.

"It certainly won't come with you here," she said.

He supposed she was right.

"Tomorrow then?"

"I was thinking," she said. "My father always said that the unicorn appeared to him 'in his darkest hour.' I wonder if we ought to take this literally. Perhaps the unicorn only appears at night."

"As in your father's tapestry," Zimenes said. "The one in the throne room."

"I love that tapestry," she said. "There is a maze, you know—"

"Hidden in the roots and rivulets!" he said.

"Yes! Have you ever solved it?"

"Several times," he said. "Though it always took so long as to—"

"Feel like a dream?"

"Yes!" He was not surprised to find that they had shared this pastime.

"I love it, too," she said. "It's the very first thing that proved to me that magic exists. The tapestry, and then your cards."

"Your father was very particular about that design," Zimenes said. "And about that tree. He spent many days at the Royal Fábrica, making sure they got it right. This was before you were born, of course. Maybe we ought to seek out that ancient yew. If we can find it, and wait in its shadow under the moonlight...."

"I believe you may be onto something, Master Zimenes—"

"Fortune might smile upon us."

"I wish you could accompany me every day," she said. She patted his hand briefly, and then stood up. "I get so bored, sitting around and waiting. It doesn't suit me."

She scooted forward and hopped from the ledge down to the forest floor, a man's height below.

"I should return the way I came, perhaps," he said.

"Nonsense," she said. "Come with me."

He, too, made the leap. He crouched on landing, and was pleasantly surprised at how easily his legs cushioned his fall.

She helped him stand with an amused grin, then led him through a narrow path in the trees that bent away from the waterfall and pool to the glade that Zimenes and Borek had discovered six days ago. A carpet of wildflowers of all colors filled the clearing. She picked up a silver bell and gave it a ring, three times. The agreed-upon signal to the hunters in their blinds.

She led him from the glade, down a continuation of that narrow path through the trees.

With a shout a man sprang from the underbrush, lunging with his spear directly at Zimenes. He stumbled back, fell and landed heavily on his backside in a patch of stinging nettles on the other side of the trail.

Prince Carlès. He seemed as genuinely surprised to see Zimenes as the physician was to see the prince.

"You!" Carlès cried. He turned to his sister. "What is *he* doing here?"

"He found me," she said.

Borek loomed over Zimenes, nose wrinkled in disgust. He reached down to help Zimenes to his feet. The nettles' sting had begun to set in, burning his neck, his ears, and his exposed forearms.

Carlès spear remained pointed at him, even as he rose. As though he were under suspicion of something. He pushed the tip away.

"Why is he here, though?" Carlès demanded, swinging the spear point free of Zimenes' hand and pointing it again toward the physician's chest, though more comfortably distant.

"I was walking in the woods—" Zimenes began.

"What were you doing with my sister?" Carlès asked.

"We were talking," Vialle said.

"Let's hear the charlatan's answer," Carlès said.

"Stop calling him that," Vialle said.

Kurk and Guillem came running up, panting, to join the other men. Guillem had his sword drawn—his other arm held against his ribs in a sling—but he sheathed it on recognizing Zimenes.

"Seems the physician was dallying with your betrothed," Carlès said to Guillem.

"We are not betrothed," Vialle said.

"And we were not dallying," Zimenes said.

"For all intents and purposes," Carlès said to his sister, ignoring Zimenes' protest.

"I'd like to hear what he was doing with you as well," Borek said.

"You are all being absurd," Vialle said. She gave Zimenes a haughty, dismissive look, then turned back to the other men. The younger men. "If you imagine that anything might have transpired between two old friends, then you are more childish than even I suspected."

"I'd like to hear the physician explain," Borek said, slowly, "how he found you without alerting us."

"I found a flight of steps in the cliff," Zimenes said. He pointed through the trees to the gray stone wall that rose in the distance. "As I was trying to tell you, I was walking in the forest, and heard your hunting horns—"

"We never sounded our horns," Borek said.

Zimenes frowned, looked toward Carlès and Guillem. "None of you?"

"Didn't sound my horn," the prince said with a shake of his head. Guillem similarly shook his head.

"Not once?"

The nettles' venom had taken hold, and Zimenes found himself scratching where the flesh burned and stung, as though attacked by a score of bees.

"Water," he said. Kurk handed him a leather canteen, and Zimenes splashed the water over his head, scrubbed at his neck and ears while he ran water over the exposed skin. Carlès snickered while he worked. Then Carlès and Guillem and Kurk moved off, to head home. Borek waited for Zimenes to finish scrubbing, but the burning sensation would not leave him.

"I can make you a more appropriate remedy back at camp," Vialle said.

"Yes," Zimenes said, aggrieved. "I can, too."

Borek led them along the narrow trail, followed by Vialle and then the physician. They made their way through the trees, traveling roughly parallel to the cliff face until it was well behind them, walking a gentle uphill slope most of the way.

As he walked, he kept replaying in his mind every word, every movement, every touch exchanged with Vialle in that cave behind the waterfall.

In that place set apart from time. Like a dream.

He nearly bumped into her. She had slowed her pace, thereby slowing his. Allowing Borek's broad back to move on ahead of them.

She glanced back over her shoulder at him. She smiled, her emerald eyes glittered in the slanting late afternoon sun, then she turned forward, continued walking. She'd caught him with the fingertips of his right index and middle fingers touching his lips, which seemed to burn even more than the places on his neck and ears where the nettles had pricked and stung.

"Was it a dream?" she called over her shoulder.

"No," he said, lowering his hand.

"You nearly believed," she said. She glanced back over her shoulder at him, smiled again. "Perhaps my magic simply isn't powerful enough."

She'd caught him remembering their kiss. Caught him wanting nothing more than to kiss her again, just like that.

# 18

The next day, late afternoon, Zimenes returned through the woods to camp. The familiar, broadly spaced maples told him he had nearly arrived; the canopy of their leaves high above screened out, for the most part, the gentle rain that had begun to fall. He absently hummed a tune, pleased to have found a mature patch of lichwort, whose leaves he would be able to mash back at camp and use as a soothing unguent for his neck and ears, where the skin was still inflamed from his fall in the nettles.

Pleased? He knew he shouldn't be. Knew he ought to be horrified by what had happened the day before. In the cave. With Vialle. The kiss. A kiss he had shared with the daughter of his best friend. The daughter of his true love.

*What a kiss, though.*

Feeling pleased—feeling good—was completely inappropriate. Of course it was. He knew that, he was not the village idiot. Or perhaps he was, for he cared not one whit. In fact, he ceased humming, and began singing. He sang "A-Wooing in the Wood," a bawdy ballad they had all sung round the campfire on their first night, led by Guillem strumming on his lute.

As he recalled the young earl-to-be, the physician had to smile. Lord Guillem had everything: a title, wealth, youth, good looks, confidence, charm.

*And yet—somehow—she desires me.*

He sang with a lilt to his voice, strode with a bounce in his step. He was tired of hewing to the appropriate feelings. Tired of abiding by decorum, and restraint. How had that served him in the past? Out of respect, he'd watched the one woman who'd meant something to him walk out of his life. Out of decorum he hadn't said a word in objection. Out of restraint he hadn't lifted a finger to stop her. Consigning himself—resigning himself—to spending the better part of a decade pining over her absence. To a life of numb, dumb routine.

Perhaps it was his "southern blood" finally boiling over, his "southern passion" finally freed from its northern shackles. He glanced at his left wrist, and there it was, the gold, white and green inkle. Considerably muddied from his rummaging and foraging. She had been right to call it a shackle. Funny how he now thought of Vialle as "she" rather than her mother—whom he now thought of as "her mother."

A welcome change. "Her mother" had made her decision ten years ago. Now it was time—*finally time, yes*—for him to make his own decision to accept hers, and move forward with his life. He grabbed at the loop of woven cloth, to rip it from his wrist. She had tied it tightly, however, and he could only get one finger in between the band and his flesh. The sturdy weave would not tear, and the knot refused to budge. He tried to slip it up over the heel of his palm, but the inkle stuck just above his wrist and would not move further, even when he folded his thumb across his palm to touch his pinky.

Not a problem. He slung his knapsack down from his shoulders, searched for his pruning shears.

Then he heard a shout. From ahead, at the camp. Followed by a scream. The agitated whinnying of horses.

*Magda.*

He ran along the narrow trail through the dense undergrowth, swatting aside the grasping brambles with his knapsack.

As he neared the camp, he slowed, horrified by what he saw: two of the tents were knocked over, flattened—Carlès and Guillem's tent, and Magda and Vialle's tent opposite—their heavy canvas coverings dragged away from wooden frames that now leaned at odd angles to the muddy ground. In the center of camp, Magda's large cooking pot lolled to and fro on its side beneath the dripping, sagging awning. The fire that he'd started that morning had been reduced to a smoky mound by the rain.

A colorful trail led from the wreckage of Vialle's tent. Her cards. The cards he'd painted for her lay strewn across the muddied turf, a haphazard trail that led to his tent. He bent to collect one: the Tower. A lighting bolt crashed into the top of the cylindrical tower, sending a man and a woman flying from the ramparts. They fell headlong against a spangled background—a shower of sparks, or flames, or falling stars. The colors had not run, but the sodden card was crumpled and stained, as though a heavy boot had trampled it into the mud.

Something moved in his tent. Something large shook the frame, stretched one canvas side, then the other. He wiped the card against his robe and put it in his pocket.

From within, a sharp snort, like that of an angry horse. Then the tramp of a heavy boot—or a heavy hoof. He crouched and backed away.

He called out, "Magda!"

A weak moan from the cooking area drew his attention away from his tent—it sounded like the chaperone—but he could not see her.

"Be careful," she answered, weakly, from the far side of camp.

He carried no weapons. He lowered his knapsack to the ground, pulled it open while keeping one eye on his tent flaps. He tossed aside the pruning shears. He removed the largest, heaviest item: the *Materia Medica*. He took the stout folio in both of his hands, one at the base of the spine, one at the lower corner of the fore-edge. The covers were panels of oak wrapped in goatskin, bound together with heavy cords across the spine. He extended the book in front of him and stalked slowly forward. Step by step, toward his tent, toward the rustling and snorting and shaking of the frame caused by whatever lurked inside.

"What is it?" he called over his shoulder in Magda's direction.

"A horrid beast!" she said. "A—"

She spoke further, but the splintering of wood and the crashing of glass, from within his tent, drowned out her words. Filled him with rage. His vials. His meticulously collected, identified, labeled, hermetically sealed samples were being broken open and destroyed. One by one, from the sounds of it.

He lifted the book, held it over his right shoulder, poised to swing down and crush the head of whatever beast was pillaging his tent. His home.

He kicked at the flap and a low squeal of rage and a thick blur of movement caused him to leap back. A massive bundle of bristled fur and bared teeth rushed at him. He swung the book down and made solid contact with a thud, followed by an angry grunt. But the monster ripped the book from his hands as it pulled the tent canvas free from the toppling frame. The thing's bowed flank brushed into Zimenes and bowled him over backward. He lost his footing in the rain-slicked turf and fell onto his backside, jarring his teeth in his head.

The beast ran low to the ground, on four legs, its bulk hidden by the straining tent canvas. The *Materia Medica* stuck on an upturned ivory spike as big as a dagger. The monster reared up and shook its head, trying to rid itself of the book. The front cover flew open, the pages riffled, and all the various leaves and flowers and stems and roots that he had pressed within the book's pages flew into the air, rained down over the wet ground, landed limply in shallow puddles.

The thing reared up and tossed its head again, snorting and growling, then again, until finally the book flew from its tusk, baring its snout, and the canvas fell away from its bristly black hide, revealing it for what it was: a massive boar with enormous tusks. Free of hindrances, the beast settled on all fours and trotted in a small circle, until its beady, bloodshot, close-set eyes settled on Zimenes: seated, solitary, unarmed. He got to his knees and tried to stand, feet slipping over the rain-soaked turf.

The boar charged. Before he knew it, the thing was upon him. He leaped to the side and rolled, ran for the nearest tree. No sooner had he wrapped his arm around the bole and swung himself behind it than one of those dagger-like tusks smashed into the trunk. Chunks of bark flew into his face, pattered off his robe. The tusk had missed his knee by a hair. The enraged beast bellowed.

As the boar fought to free its tusk from the tree, Zimenes took advantage of the delay to sprint toward the center of the camp. He needed a weapon. He needed fire to strike fear into the boar.

He leapt onto the low retaining wall of stones, reached into the blaze for the unlit end of a longer log. He pulled it free, but this unbalanced both him and the burning, smoking logs; he stepped forward into the pit even as the mound of logs crashed and tumbled down into his shins and over his feet. Smoke billowed into his face, blinded him, choked his nose, throat and lungs.

Suddenly he was lifted and hurled through the air, projected forward into the fire by a solid thump on his backside. He did his best to leap over the collapsing logs, even as the flames soared into the air. He passed through a wave of heat, crashed into the low wall of rounded stones marking the far edge of the fire pit. The acrid tang of his own singed hair gagged him as he fought to stamp and beat the flames from his robe, from his sleeves. The snuffling at his head told him that the boar had come around the wall to his side of the pit, and he instinctively rolled away from the huge beast, back into the fire.

He hauled himself to his feet, danced on tiptoes over the grasping, hissing flames. Grabbed another partially burning log, by the unlit end, and swung this in the direction of the boar. He stepped up onto the retaining wall, flames still clinging to his clothes. The fire was proving more foe than ally.

"Arrgh!" he shouted at the beast, and he swung the firebrand down in a blazing orange arc to land squarely on the boar's thick knob of a head, above its eyes. The thing squealed and lunged at Zimenes, its tusks and snout exploded stones into the air as though they were weightless. Zimenes leaped onto the creature's broad back and jumped toward the muddy turf, where he landed, lost his footing, rolled, and came up swinging his flaming club from side to side with his right, swiping the rain and soot from his eyes with his left, only to realize that flames still clung to the sleeve. He cursed and slammed his arm into his side repeatedly.

"Shit in milk!"

The beast growled and trotted around to face him. Seemed to consider another charge, but also seemed dazed from its impact with the stones and possibly wary of the flames that his prey seemed to control. But still he moved closer. With his left, Zimenes swatted at the flames rising from his robe, even as the fire at the end of his log sputtered, and vanished.

"Hey!"

Vialle stood at the highway. She had returned, and grasped the dire situation. She sent an arrow whistling into the boar's shoulder, but this only seemed to further enrage him.

"Over here!" she called.

The boar swung his low, large head in Vialle's direction. Angled those deadly tusks toward the princess. She pulled another arrow from her quiver.

"Careful!" Zimenes called.

"Quite a brute you chose to fight!" she returned, with a smile and a gleam in her green eyes. She nocked the arrow and drew back the bowstring. The boar charged her, and she loosed the arrow, which flew just overhead, dug into the turf behind. The beast moved too quickly.

She stood still as a post, an inviting target for the thundering, snorting boar. At the last possible moment, she side-stepped the beast, and drove a dagger that he hadn't seen her draw straight down, toward the place where the neck met the spine. But the point stuck in the shoulder, and the beast snarled and wrenched away.

The dagger's pommel waved to and fro over the slim blade, like the metronome Zimenes would use in his laboratory to mark time on an experiment.

"This way!" He waved, urging Vialle to join him at the fire pit. Their best bet was to keep the smoldering, smoking fire between them and that creature.

That was when they both saw Magda's crumpled body, curled in a ball. The boar saw her, too, and turned from them to investigate.

"No!" Vialle cried. She waved at the boar to distract it from her chaperone.

The boar snuffled at the woman's frozen body, at her back. It shoved its snout into her, those razor-sharp tusks perilously close. Magda whimpered helplessly.

Grimly, silently, Vialle raced toward the boar, as though she were going to leap onto its back, unarmed.

The thing swung round to meet her. Its beady, red-rimmed eyes fixated on her, and he lowered his head, until the tusks pointed directly at her. She skidded to a halt, feet slipping in the muddy, mangled turf.

Zimenes ran after her, to pull her back, but then moved instead to the side, and yelled, waving his arms, hoping to distract the monster toward him instead. "Remember me? Over here!"

The wild boar wheeled toward Zimenes, pawed the ground with his cloven hoof and snorted, ready to charge.

A black arrow appeared at the boar's throat, triangular head emerging from one side, fletches from the other. Stunned, the beast staggered a step, swung its head. The monster emitted a bellow that turned to a gurgle, a strangled cry.

Borek stood on the flagstones. He nocked another arrow to his longbow and let fly. This arrow struck the creature directly behind its foreleg, and buried itself deep in the boar's flank. Kurk came running up behind, frantically calling to the hounds, trying to restrain them, but they were off leash, and had the boar's scent. Ignoring the hapless berner, they raced toward the boar, swarmed over him, biting and barking.

"Magda!" Vialle cried as she fell to her knees beside her life-long companion. Her friend. Guillem entered the camp, sword drawn. He ran toward the women.

The boar bellowed and swung his tusks at the dogs, scattering them. The darkest one fell limp to the turf. The boar lowered his hideous head and drove his tusks into poor Nigredo, flung him into the air. Kurk cried out, and raced toward the bramble bush where the dog had vanished.

Another arrow pierced the boar's flank, this one not as deeply as the other two. The beast gave a groan, and sank to his knees. Albedo and Rubedo leapt onto his back, snarling and biting.

The beast rose up again, shook the dogs free like they were nothing more than rainwater, and charged at Kurk as he crossed the clearing. Borek shouted at his apprentice, and the boy turned in time to dive out of the onrushing boar's path. He ran for his tent, ducked through the flaps. The enraged boar pursued the boy, blood streaming from his flanks. He crashed into the side of the tent and knocked it over. The boar bulled into Kurk's huddled outline, but the wet, waxed canvas prevented the tusks from piercing or puncturing. Still the beast trampled over the collapsed structure, snuffling and snorting, blood dripping from his snout, from his foaming mouth. Again, the hounds hurled themselves at him, forcing Borek to lower his bow and draw his long, curved hunting knife. He ran at the boar.

Zimenes grabbed a heavy stone from the retaining wall in both hands and ran as well.

Carlès beat them both there. He stabbed his spear into the flank that had not been pierced by arrows. The boar squealed at this new insult, reared back, and then as he came forward lifted his back end into the air and kicked out, scattering the dogs once again. His rear hooves slammed into the prince's gut, sent him reeling backward into Guillem, as the nobleman attempted to enter the melee.

Borek flung himself onto the boar's back, drove his knife into the boar's neck and attempted to draw it across, as though to sever head from body. But the brute lifted his heels into the air once more, sent the hunter over his head, where he landed on his back. The boar's tusks waved a mere hand's breadth above his face.

Zimenes lifted and swung the stone down onto the boar's head, aware that if the wet rock slipped from his grasp it might well land on Borek's face. The hunter shielded his head with his arms and rolled to the side.

The boar groaned and sank to its knees. Emboldened, Zimenes raised the stone high above his head and brought it down with all his strength. The blow did not land as squarely as the previous one, however, and broke free from his grasp, snapped one of the tusks. The boar swung his head, and the broken tusk slammed painfully into Zimenes' knee, buckled it, tripped him to the canvas. He knew he had landed on Kurk from the sound of the boy's heavy exhale.

Then the boar's bulk collapsed on top of Zimenes' feet and ankles, sending shooting pain up into his hips. He placed his arms on the thing's bloodied, rent hide, pushed with all his strength against its ribs, but it kept coming, kept rolling, covering his shins, his knees. He pushed against its spine, but still its bulk sagged down onto him until it covered his thighs. He could not move. His legs felt as though they were being flattened into parchment.

Then, over the beast's back, Prince Carlès face appeared, his visage twisted by pain and rage into a horrifying grimace, storm clouds dark above and behind him. He raised up his spear in both hands, angled it downward. Arched his back, then thrust straight down. It landed with a sticky *thunk*. He placed his foot on the ribs and wrenched the head free. Again and again, he lifted the spear in both hands and stabbed. Plunged the spear with such force that, despite the creature's massive bulk, Zimenes feared the prince might run the boar through entirely and drive the tip into his legs, or into his groin. The fearsome grimace on the prince's face made it seem as though that were his intent, to spit the beast and Zimenes both and drive the spear deep into the earth beneath them.

"Enough!" Borek roared.

Zimenes ceased his own yelling, which he only then realized he was doing. He let his jaw go slack. His ears rang. Lightning flashed above, splitting the gloom-stricken sky, then thunder cracked and rolled over them.

"Enough," Borek said.

The prince left his spear quivering in the boar's flank, staggered back out of Zimenes' view. Blood poured from the boar's gaping mouth onto the canvas, trickled from various wounds onto Zimenes' robe. The red mixed with rainwater, turned pink.

# 19

"Get this...thing...off me!"

Zimenes strained futilely to budge the boar's weighty carcass. The canvas beneath him writhed, as Kurk also struggled to free himself. Borek and Carlès pulled at the fabric, helped the sobbing boy free. Though he'd been trampled by the boar, he seemed capable of standing on his own.

"Nigredo," he said. He limped off toward the bushes.

"Help us here first." Borek placed his arm around the boy's shoulders and steered him gently back toward the boar, and Zimenes.

Together—groaning, cursing, straining—Borek, Carlès, and Kurk heaved and shoved and lifted the boar enough for Zimenes to scoot out from under the creature's massive, hairy, blood- and rain-soaked girth. The carcass fell back onto the muddy, rain-slicked canvas with a wet slap, snapping the shaft of one of the arrows that stood from his flank. Kurk set off running toward the bramble bush where Nigredo had disappeared. Carlès—eyes glistening, face flushed—joined his friend Guillem, who gave him several congratulatory claps on the back with his right hand, while still gingerly holding his left against his side.

Zimenes slowly flexed his knees, his ankles, his hips, as blood returned to his legs. He heaved a sigh of gratitude, as everything seemed to be in working order. Borek reached down his hands, helped the physician to his feet.

"Can you stand?" he asked. Then, when it became apparent that he could, "Can you walk?"

Zimenes took a few shaky steps, leaning on the hunter. He nodded.

Borek pointed toward Magda. "See to her, then."

Zimenes nodded and hobbled toward Vialle, who hunched

over her companion. His legs so wobbled and quavered at the sudden release of tension that he barely made it there, before he, too, fell to his knees on the wet turf. It was raining steadily, if not hard, but he felt thoroughly soaked with a mixture of rainwater, sweat, mud and boar's blood.

The boar had gored Magda below the knee, slicing open her calf muscle. The woman lay on her side, still curled in a ball, eyes closed, moaning. He and Vialle exchanged a glance.

"It's bad," Vialle said.

Zimenes took Vialle's hand in his and squeezed, briefly. "Heat some water. We need to clean and wrap it quickly." He rattled off a list of herbs to be added to the warming water. "A needle and thread," he added. "And clean cloths. They should be in what's left of my tent. Quickly now."

He looked at the gash, seeping blood. She had not rolled onto it; dirt had not gotten into the wound. It was fairly deep, but clean, a slice rather than a tear. Still, she had lost a lot of blood, leaving her complexion abnormally pale. Her body shivered; her teeth chattered. Her eyes remained open, but unseeing.

"He's gone, Magda," he whispered to her. "The beast is gone."

She continued to whimper. The sky brightened, and the thunder subsided, but the rain continued to fall.

While Vialle gathered medicines and equipment, he called out to Borek, and the hunter and Kurk carefully lifted and bore Magda in their arms and set her down beneath the awning that covered the cooking area. Then the men set about coaxing the fire back to strength with fresh wood and rebuilding one of the tents.

Vialle returned with the needle and thread, and she held and consoled her friend while the water and herbs came to a boil over the fire. Zimenes removed the water, brought the pot beneath the shelter, let the herbs steep and the water cool, soaked strips of clean cloth in the resulting pale tea. Vialle lit a lamp, hung it against the awning's central support post. He cleansed Magda's wound with the cloths, flushed it with the water once it had cooled sufficiently, then took the needle and thread and sewed the wound closed while rain continued to drum on the waxed canvas above them, Magda whimpering all the while. Vialle urged her to keep calm, calling her brave and good and kind and wise and every other compliment that came to her mind, it seemed. Once he had tied off the stitches, Zimenes again wiped the blood from around the wound, then took the last strips of cloth soaked in the medicinal water and bound them snug around the calf. As they dried, so would the wound; the herbs would pull any poisons left by the tusk to the surface.

Finally, he finished. The poor woman muttered and murmured incoherently and then drifted off, her head in Vialle's lap. Zimenes slowly stood, straightened his aching back, wiped the sweat from his brow with his muddy, blood-stained sleeve. He'd been so absorbed in tending to Magda that he hadn't even noticed his own injuries, but he was bruised, battered, and burnt. His legs wobbled like gelatin, his ribs and lower back felt as though they'd been tenderized with a mallet, flames had burnt the hairs from the backs of his hands and seared the flesh at his wrists and up his forearms, and even the nettle stings along his neck and ears had returned with renewed vigor. He almost had to laugh at how thoroughly pulverized he felt.

Darkness had fallen, the fire had been beaten back down by the rain, which had waned to a sparse drizzle. The men had rebuilt Magda and Vialle's tent, and were nearly finished rebuilding Carlès and Guillem's. Borek and Carlès lifted Magda, using her bedroll as a stretcher, and carried her carefully into her tent. Vialle followed after. The five men would have to share the other tent, somehow.

The ground was wet, their bedrolls damp, their clothes soaked, their feet muddy. They hadn't eaten, nor was there anything to eat aside from rations of smoked and cured venison that they were all tired of gnawing by now, and uncooked tubers and mushrooms that they recovered from the chewed-up turf. Kurk had been due to return to civilization for supplies and news on the morrow. Borek's wine skin was empty. It would be a long night.

Zimenes lowered the lamp from the stanchion and carefully walked the several treacherous paces to the place where his tent used to stand. The boar had dragged the canvas cover free from the support posts, exposing all of his possessions to the elements. His sodden bedroll would be useless. He had no dry clothes to change into. But that was hardly the worst of it.

He had taken to leaving open the sturdy wooden container that held his alembic and his specimen vials. The boar had overturned the box, punched through the lid, broken the hinges, and shattered to smithereens nearly every vial, empty or full. The powdery glass fragments glittered and glared angrily in the lamplight. He picked through the wreckage, pulled his hand back as a shard pricked his fingertip. The pain scarcely registered in his consciousness, the drop of blood that formed there remote, inconsequential.

His books were soaked, the pages swollen with water. Not far away he found the *Materia Medica*, splayed open, spine broken. A deep gouge from the boar's tusk punctured the rear board, dead center, penetrated through the last hundred or so pages. The many pressings he had interleaved within had been scattered, soaked by the rain, blown away by the wind, trampled into the mud. A number of the pages had torn from the binding as well, and been similarly crumpled, trodden, and dispersed.

He squatted, lowered the lamp to a rectangle of sodden ivory paper. He picked it up, turned it over. The Emperor, inverted. He turned the card right-side up so the Emperor sat facing him. Young Adalmund's visage—beard bushy and golden, rather than wispy and white—beamed placidly at him, his throne mud-spattered. Did not seem to be accusing him of bringing this attack upon them. Much as he would be within his rights to do so.

*She's my daughter, Zim*, he might say. *She's—*

A gentle hand on his shoulder startled him, and he lowered the card. He glanced up, saw it was her, touched his fingers to the hand on his shoulder.

"She's sleeping," Vialle said. "The bleeding seems to have ceased."

He stood up, straightened his stiff back. Her hand left his shoulder.

"What a mess," she said.

"It's all gone," he said, with a shake of his head. "All of it."

He lifted the lamp so he could see her plainly. Her emerald eyes gleamed wetly in the light. Perhaps she had been crying. Care lined her face, pinched her wan cheeks, clamped her rigid jaw. Pressed her lips tightly together.

*Her lips...*

"We brought this upon us," he said, hoarsely.

"That's nonsense," she said.

"We—" he began.

"Zim," she said. She brushed her hand against his. "We'll clean up in the morning. With the light of day."

With that, she turned and left him, walked back to her tent, disappeared within.

Nearby he found a clump of cards, a dozen or so, stuck together by rainwater and mud. He stooped and added the Emperor to these, moved off to collect more.

He crowded into the other tent with Borek, Kurk, Carlès, and Guillem. In order to fit, they would have to stretch across the width of it, alternating head to toe to head.

Borek asked Zimenes if Magda would live.

"She cannot stay here," he said. "She needs to return to civilization, where she can rest and recuperate."

"Perhaps the cloister would take her in," Guillem said.

"That would be ideal," Zimenes said. "It's close, and they should have medicinal knowledge and supplies."

Lord Guillem was in a great deal of pain. Zimenes had been so absorbed in treating Magda that he had forgotten about the young nobleman's shoulder. He inspected it, gingerly, but even in the dim lamplight he could see from the man's pale complexion and sheen of sweat that he was struggling, and would have a hard time sleeping.

"They could see to your injuries as well," he said to Guillem.

"We're all leaving, at first light," Borek said. "The camp is wrecked. Everyone is injured."

"We're quitting?" Carlès asked.

"We're going to Rotterham," Borek said. "Ten days now we've been in the woods. We're going to have a proper meal and a proper drink and a proper bath and a proper bed. For one night. And then I'm going to recruit some actual hunters from among the Champions of the Mirren, and Kurk and I shall return, set up camp deeper in the forest."

"I say—" the prince began.

"From here on out," Borek growled, cutting Carlès off, "we're doing things my way. This is my contract, entered into with your father."

The prince sat silently, sullen. Then he swung open the tent flap and stalked off into the misty darkness.

"Go cry to your sister," Borek muttered. He lifted his bald head, announced to the tent. "I'm through coddling that brat."

Guillem lay back, attempting to cradle his arm over his belly. Zimenes asked for Borek's knife, fashioned a sling for Vialle's injured suitor. Whom, he had to admit, he had come to like.

"I would stay with you," Zimenes said. "I can maintain the

camp while you and your companions hunt."

"You've proven your worth," Borek said. "It was truly fortunate we had a physician among us."

Zimenes wasn't sure he actually wished to return to the Mirrenwood. If he had a hot bath and a soft bed, he might never want to leave it. But Borek's praise brought a smile to his tired, aching, burning cheeks.

"The old lady will be missed," the hunter said. "But not her younger charge."

"The princess?" Zimenes asked.

"We'll get proper bait this time as well," Borek said.

Guillem lifted his head, as though to defend the princess's honor, as he normally would, but he let it drop back to the bedroll. It was no use arguing. They all sensed it.

Zimenes wondered if something had happened during the day, before the hunters returned to camp. But it was late, and he was exhausted. In the light of day, they would break camp and depart the Mirrenwood. Even with the wounded riding slowly they should be able to make the cloister by late afternoon, and from there it was a short ride to Rotterham.

He, too, sagged back onto the bedroll, his feet down by Guillem's head, the lord's mud-stained black boots at his.

Borek asked Kurk if he had seen to Albedo, Rubedo, and the horses, and the boy replied in the affirmative. Then he, too, wrapped his cloak tightly about him and slipped from the tent, presumably to find shelter and warmth with the hounds in their lean-to. Borek spread into the area vacated by his apprentice, though that didn't leave much more room for the physician and the nobleman.

The night dragged on agonizingly, as Guillem murmured and moaned in his sleep. Borek snored and snuffled, sounding not entirely unlike the boar that had so terrified Zimenes only a short span before. He slept fitfully, dozing and drifting off, only to snap awake at the red-eyed boar charging him down in his dreams.

Carlès did not return.

# 20

Zimenes woke with his arm flung across Lord Guillem's muddy boots. The young nobleman murmured in his sleep. It was fortunate that he would be returning to civilization. Fortunate that they all would.

Daylight flashed through the tent flap. Borek was gone. Zimenes crawled over the hunter's sleeping fur, and emerged blinking into the morning sunlight. He stretched his arms overhead—and then stopped, mid-stretch, as the heat blisters on his forearms and wrists began to crack open. The inkle—soot-stained, stiffened with mud—chafed. His back ached. His thighs felt as though the boar still lay across them, ground their flesh agonizingly into the bones supporting them. And, now that he was standing upright, his head hurt. To top it all.

The rain had stopped, but the turf remained damp, soft, chewed into muddy ruts in places, strewn with personal belongings, cooking equipment, foodstuffs, his meticulously collected and preserved herbs and flowers and specimens. His arms lowered, his shoulders sagged, breath escaped his body with a sigh.

He gingerly moved toward the place where his tent had stood. Something stabbed the sole of his bare foot, and he cried out, then hopped several times as he removed a shard of glass that had not penetrated very deeply. He picked his way forward more carefully now. He drove two of the wooden stanchions back into the softened ground to hang his clothes to dry. As he searched through the wreckage, he came across the king's hunting horn, wet but intact. He hung this around his neck.

He retrieved his knapsack, decanted a stream of water that had collected within the stiffened canvas. He removed the shears, which had already started to rust; water had blackened and swollen the leather case where he stored glass vials for transport. Within the vials, his specimens swam in water, ruined, as he hadn't had the chance to seal them with wax. He tossed the shears and the case onto the pile of useless, ruined, broken equipment, and added the soggy hat and limp jerked venison that he also pulled from the sack. At least the knapsack itself was still usable.

Nearby he found a few more of Vialle's cards, added them to the ones in his pocket. He scoured the ground for more. Found another large clump. He took these to a flat stone that had already dried in the morning sunlight, and carefully peeled the cards apart from one another, laid them out face up to dry. The pigments he'd used had been suspended in oil, rather than water, so the colors held fast, even though most of the cards were sodden and wrinkled. The reds, in particular, seemed to be flaking, for some reason. As he spread them out, he counted them. Twenty-two.

One short. He reviewed the cards again, but it quickly became clear which card he was missing: the Unicorn.

He shook his head. An ill omen. Unless he were to retrieve it.

He'd found the first cards the night before near his tent. Somehow the boar had dragged the deck from Vialle's tent to his, where most of them had landed. He returned to the remains of his tent, scoured the ground once more. Overturned his waterlogged bedroll. Perhaps the wind had taken it. He moved into the trees behind his tent. Swept aside the glistening undergrowth. Pushed further in, searching along the ground and even among the low-hanging branches.

No sign of the unicorn. Maybe it had remained in the women's tent. He returned to the camp.

Near the remnants of the fire pit, Borek, Carlès and Vialle stood huddled in conversation.

"Ah, here he is," Borek said at his approach.

The other two, brother and sister, turned toward him, then Carlès turned his head away dismissively. Vialle stepped back to allow him into their circle. Her blond hair exploded from her scalp in a frizzled, unkempt mass, individual strands kinking every which way, forming a sunlit halo. Her green eyes appeared muted, distant. Her cheeks, normally flushed, now wan and gaunt; her lips, normally plump, now pinched and drawn.

"What a mess," Zimenes said.

"I was telling our lord and lady here," Borek said, "that we must return to Rotterham. To resupply and gather reinforcements."

"Seems wise," Zimenes said with a nod.

"I'm not going anywhere," Vialle said. "Father's life is at stake."

"The camp is destroyed," Carlès said. "Guillem is grievously injured, and your chaperone is at death's door. We are in no shape to continue the hunt."

The prince taking Borek's side over Vialle surprised him. Especially after the way he had stormed out of the tent last night. He supposed that Carlès, too, simply wanted out of the Mirrenwood.

"I would also see if any news has reached Rotterham," Borek said.

"Of my father's health," Vialle said. "Or of his demise."

Borek did not react. She was simply stating what the hunter had been content to imply.

"You will not collect your bounty if you depart now," she said.

"My contract stipulates that I collect the bounty for a successful hunt," he said, voice steady, face impassive, "whether your father is alive, or not."

"Ghoulish," she said.

"I aim to see this hunt through to the end," he said. "I will claim this bounty, and this trophy."

"This is nothing more than a two-day delay, sister," Carlès said. "One day out, one day back."

"Then I shall meet you here in two days' time," she said. "Take good care of Magda, brother. See to it she receives the best of care."

"I'm not her chaperone," he said. "If you're staying, I'm staying."

"One of you must come with me," Borek said, "to recruit assistance from the Champions of the Mirren. They will only follow a member of the royal family."

"They will heed my brother," Vialle said. "I am staying. We're getting close."

"What makes you so sure?" Zimenes asked.

"I can feel it," she said. She placed her clenched fist over her heart, and her eyes gleamed with a hint of their usual avid sparkle. "In my bones. In my heart."

In their conversation by the pool, they had discussed searching for the grand tree in the tapestry, and awaiting the unicorn at night. Perhaps she saw this as her opportunity to do just that, without the other hunters lurking nearby.

Carlès rolled his eyes. "You can't stay here by yourself."

"Because I'm a defenseless little girl?"

"What's the point?" he snarled. "What can you hope to accomplish by staying behind?"

"Perhaps the unicorn will actually reveal himself, if you louts aren't here to scare him away."

Borek touched the scar on his cheek, traced it into his beard, gathered the thick hair into his hand. Considering her words.

"It would be best if one of us stayed with you," he pronounced. "For safety."

"Leave me one of the dogs."

Borek glanced over his shoulder, toward the kennel at the far edge of the clearing. The little lean-to's roof was visible, but not its occupants.

"I won't ask Kurk to part with any more of his dogs," he said. The boy had taken Nigredo's death hard. "And I need him to help bear the stretcher so we can carry the old woman out of here."

"Then...." She paused, as though going through the list of possible candidates. Magda and Guillem were out, obviously. Carlès had to go back to the forest's edge with Borek to recruit more helpers. Kurk would help with the stretcher, and the hounds would follow him.

"I shall stay," Zimenes heard himself saying. "I'll stay by the princess's side."

Carlès snorted. "You?" He cast a derisive glance in Zimenes' direction, without looking him in the eye. "She'll have to protect you more than the other way round."

He ignored the prince, kept his eyes focused on Vialle. "If you believe we are close," he said, "and you would have me along, then I shall join you."

"It is little more than an intuition," she said.

"I would follow that intuition with you," he said. "To see where it leads us."

In that moment, the slanting morning sun starkly revealed her, shorn of artifice, drained of color. A streak of dried mud by her ear. Her beauty dampened, her vitality sapped, by the previous day's defeat. Any desire he'd felt for her two days before, entranced by her radiance in the cave, had evaporated at the sight of the destruction wrought upon the camp and the hunters by the vengeful boar.

But he had known, ever since he had begun teaching her as a little girl, that she was the most brilliant, talented, determined person he knew. He still believed that. Since her return from Gothenburg, she had only confirmed in him this belief. If she had a hunch, if she had a theory, then he would follow it with her. He would follow her, and aid her, as best he could. Not because she was beautiful. Not because he desired her.

Because he believed in her.

And because he did not want to concede defeat, any more than she did.

"We will be going deeper into the Mirrenwood," she said.

"I would follow this through," he said. "To the end."

"However bitter?" she asked.

"Bitter, or sweet," he said, with his best effort at a confident smile.

She pressed her lips together, returning his forced smile with a similarly strained attempt.

"Then let us gather what supplies and foodstuffs we can salvage," she said. "And we will meet back here when we are ready."

She set off for her tent.

"Leave me your tent," Zimenes said to Borek.

"Help yourself to whatever you find in the food bins," Borek said.

The hunter clapped his hand on the prince's shoulder. "We've got some packing to do, prince."

Carlès shoulders slumped. Zimenes turned to hide the beginnings of a smirk that tugged at the corners of his mouth, and strode toward the piles of his belongings. His headache had dissipated, his legs and hips felt stronger the more he used them. He thought he had seen a pot of aloe ointment that would soothe the burns on his arms and cheeks, the itchy stings on his neck and ears.

Over his shoulder, he heard Carlès say, his tone pleading, "The two of them? By themselves?"

Almost whining.

"He's harmless," Borek replied.

The smirk vanished. If that's what they thought of him, so be it. What did he care?

He'd gathered some supplies, a change of clothes, a heavy knit jersey, and rounded up some food—smoked venison, mushrooms, parsnips. These he put in his knapsack, along with the king's hunting horn. He pulled on two pairs of socks that had largely dried in the sun, one over the other, then his boots—still damp, but drier than they had been. He also retrieved the twenty-two tarot cards. They had dried, stiffened with their wrinkles and bends. He arranged them into a deck as best he could, tucked them into a side pouch on the knapsack. Perhaps she would be glad he had preserved them.

He returned to the fire pit, sat on what remained of the retaining wall, to wait for the princess. Asked the hunter if he needed a hand loading the horses while he waited.

Borek stopped, frowned. Surprised to see him. "What are you doing here?" he asked.

"Waiting for Vialle—" he began.

Carlès laughed. "See?" he said. "Guess you're coming back with us."

Zimenes rose to his feet, tentatively. "She just...." he began. "Without me?"

"Left you by the wayside." Carlès shook his head. Waved his hand. "Let her go. High time she learned a lesson."

Borek pointed toward one of the three trails that led from camp deeper into the forest. "Go after her," he said. "Go on."

Zimenes turned his back to the men, took a few paces toward the edge of camp.

"Two days!" the hunter called after him. "We'll be back here in two days' time!"

"Two days," Zimenes shouted, with a wave.

He quickened his pace in pursuit of the princess, settled into a brisk stride.

"Vialle!"

Zimenes' voice fled from him into the trees. They whispered back to him. A rustling that, combined with the gentle swaying of the crowns above him, sounded something like laughter.

He followed the narrowing trail through the underbrush. Occasionally he came across a strand of white linen from her billowy skirts, snagged on nettles or thorns. His robe had amassed its own collection of briars and burrs.

"Vialle!"

The sunlight in the camp's clearing had warmed him, but in the shade of the woods, the damp chill returned, settled into his bones. This was going to be one of those days where he never fully warmed up, despite his exertions. Like one of those winter days he would spend in the throne room attending to the king, trying to pick his way through the maze in the tapestry, wrapping his housecoat ever more tightly about him. As he walked, the soggy hem of his robe clung to his legs.

Why wouldn't she stop, and allow him to catch up? Surely she heard him calling her. What game was she playing at now?

He thought back on the kiss he had shared with her, two days and two nights ago. The softness of her lips.

*No, not that part*, he chastised himself.

It was hard not to think of that. Impossible not to remember the physical sensation of her yielding to him. Her surrender.

He began to stiffen, even as he walked. He hated how his body betrayed him in this way.

But was it, indeed, his body betraying his mind? Or had his mind been betraying his body, all along? Just as hiking daily through the woods and gathering specimens and eating heartily had rejuvenated him, peeled away the years, so too had seeing Vialle—at his tower, in the gardens, riding horseback, singing at the campfire—and, yes, swimming naked in the pool, and standing before him, dripping, in the cave—reawakened something in him long dormant. Like one of these maple trees that he walked among, coming out of a long winter sleep. The spring sun melted the snow away and caused the sap to flow again.

*Stop. Do not dwell on the physical sensations. Use your mind. Think this through.*

What if that kiss rendered her impure? Might that one kiss disqualify her from seeing the unicorn? Prevent the unicorn from revealing himself to her?

Was it virginity that brought the unicorn from hiding? The literal interpretation of this state—yay or nay? Virgin or fallen? Unblemished or stained?

Or did it have more to do with the woman's heart? With her emotional truth? With the purity of her intentions, the chastity of her affections? The writers were never explicitly clear on this, they always simply referred to the woman as "virginal," or a "maiden." Occasionally they would describe her as being "pure of heart and of body," but perhaps this was simply a quaint euphemism adopted by the ancients, accustomed as they were to a more refined readership.

He found another white thread, yanked from her dress by a blackberry thorn. He collected this one as well. Felt like the minotaur pursuing her in this way, rolling up the skein that she unspooled behind her so she might find her way out of the labyrinth. Only she would find the thread gone.

He skipped across three exposed rocks in a quickly moving stream, continued following the faint trail. Caught sight of a footprint in the rain-soaked loam. As a dull hiss of falling water reached his ears, he recognized where he was, and slowed his pace, so as not to march over the edge of the cliff. He came to the broken arch that marked the stone steps leading down the cliff face. He stepped over the strange runes, leaned out over the sheer drop, expecting to see her white-clad figure descending the narrow stair that stretched away below, stark against the gray stone of the cliff.

But the stairs were empty.

He'd hoped to see her there, leading the way back to the waterfall. Back to the cave where they had shared that kiss. He wanted to return.

No matter how far over the edge he leaned, no matter how he craned his neck to change his angle—she had not gone that way.

He must not kiss her again. That was clear. They'd come perilously close to violating the spirit, if not the letter, of the unicorn's requirements. If their actions—or even simply their *desires*—rendered it impossible for them to lure the unicorn from hiding, then they would never cure her father. At least not with Vialle as the bait. And if they didn't cure her father, the king would almost certainly waste away, and die.

*If he hasn't already.* The thought gave him vertigo, perched on the first step of the veering staircase, at the edge of the cliff. He sat down heavily, head in his hands. Part of him wanted to weep. He was failing his friend, in so many ways.

*Think of that, you sad fool.* He slammed his fist into his knee. *She is your best friend's daughter. She is the daughter of the woman you love. She is your former pupil. A girl you've known almost since her birth. If anything is an ill omen, an augur of ill portent, it would be you kissing this girl.*

And yet. And yet. She'd wanted him to. Hadn't she? She had made that clear.

And he had wanted to kiss her. He could not deny it. Nor did he want to deny it.

Though he had to. Had to deny himself.

Didn't he?

If he did not, the king wasn't the only one who could die. He may well find his head on the chopping block. What if Carlès had spotted him? What if any one of the hunters had been watching them, from his blind? There was no law, that he was aware of, that stipulated that kissing the princess would be met with a death sentence. But the king was the king, and if he was especially displeased....

Or, if Adalmund was dead—he pounded his knee again—and the new king, young, headstrong Carlès, charged him with treason for committing an act he knew would prevent or delay his father's cure...

It hurt his hand more than his knee when he struck himself.

Then again... What if this proved to be love? What if Vialle was in love with him, and he with her? What if they became lovers, and, in due course, married? He would be untouchable then, wouldn't he? Though such a match would arouse a great deal of opposition at the castle, among the courtiers. To say the least.

But perhaps, one day—given the right circumstances—he might even become the king.

Zimenes, King of Averonne.

King Zimenes.

"Better pull your crown down out of the clouds," he scolded himself. "And your head out of your arse. If it doesn't kill you, it will certainly get you exiled."

He looked over first one shoulder, then the other. Aware that he was muttering aloud. That if someone were to overhear him, they would think him a madman.

"What of it?" he asked the forest. "What if I have gone mad?"

He shook his head ruefully, chuckled at himself. He lowered his voice: "King Zimenes."

*What a ridiculous, presumptuous fool.*

*Is that what you want? To be homeless? On the run? A hunted man? Always a nervous glance back over the road you've traveled? Simply because you weren't strong enough to rein in your own base impulses? Because you weren't man enough to lock away your carnal desires?*

The day was slipping away from them. The angle of the sun lowering, the shadows of the trees lengthening. He'd skipped breakfast and missed lunch. He unslung his knapsack and dug out a piece of stringy, dried venison, chewed on that while he ruminated.

*This is absurd,* he thought. Prince Carlès, of all people, was right. *High time she learned a lesson,* the boy had said.

*But who truly needs to learn a lesson?* he thought. *The princess? Or me?*

*She left me behind, without a word. We shared a kiss, but then she left me. Just like her mother. And yet I continue to chase after her. She doesn't want me along. She wants to go it alone.*

He stood up, stepped back from the stairs, from the cliff face. Brushed dirt and pebbles from his backside. Hefted his knapsack to his shoulders. Turned his back to the cliff, and set off back the way he had come, following his own, larger, boot prints in the mud. Back toward camp.

"Zimenes!"

The cry was faint, nearly imperceptible. He stopped. Listened.

"Zimenes!"

The tone, however, was unmistakable. A cry of fear.

# 21

He whirled. Began to run, parallel to the cliff, crashing through the underbrush. The ground took a decided downward slope, and he picked up speed, the trees a blur. On he ran, hoping he would not trip on an exposed root or a vine.

"Zimenes!" A little louder. Still ahead, but off to the right.

"Vialle!" he called, as he changed course.

He brushed aside brambles, swept apart dangling ivy with his sleeves and bare hands. He became tangled in a thicket, and had to back up, extricate himself, find another way around.

"Vialle!" he called. "I'm coming!"

The forest floor continued to slope downward. The shadows continued to lengthen. As the slope leveled off, he found himself in a different sort of forest, a place he hadn't explored before. The trees here were short, squat, bedecked with tantalizing red berries. No undergrowth grew among these trees, as their dense crowns intertwined with their neighbors' and blocked out the sun, leaving the forest floor smooth, as though swept bare. Hairy creepers wrapped around the thick trunks, tangled further in the gnarled branches, and then dangled into his face, brushed against his shoulders. Everywhere above him, the cheery red berries.

"Vialle?" he called again.

Tree-formed tunnels spread out into the shady dim ahead of him, fanning out in several directions. He had hoped to bring her back to camp by lunchtime. Now he doubted they would be able to make it back by nightfall.

"Vialle?"

Silence. Not even the rustling of leaves. The tangled boughs above him, only just out of reach, were so tightly knit together, so choked by vines, that the arched ceiling of branches and leaves could scarcely move.

Had he run too far? Had he left her behind?

He shifted his knapsack from his shoulder to his hand, rummaged within for the short paring knife he'd taken from the cooking supplies. Cursed himself for not having begged a more serious weapon from Borek. He'd meant to, but then Vialle had vanished, and the hunter had urged him to give chase...

Instead, the hunting horn took up most of the space in his knapsack, and as he shouldered the sack and began to push his way through the creepers the bouche poked into his lower back. Why on earth had he brought this cursed thing? Was he supposed to blow it if he needed help? Who remained in the Mirrenwood to come to his aid?

"Zimenes!" From directly ahead. Louder, now. He was close.

He pushed through the stiff vines and picked up his pace.

He spied her white dress through the curtains of creepers, and ran to her side. She held a bent branch, broken from a nearby tree, out in front of her. Far from a formidable weapon.

She glanced at him, then pointed deeper into the woods, into the shaded gloom. Low along the forest floor, two close-set glimmers. The eyes of a creature, watching them. It eased forward, padded silently into a thin shaft of light, revealing its bristly mane, its rolling shoulders, its gray pelt. Its lolling tongue.

A wolf. They never traveled singly. He swiveled and looked about them. Another to their right, a third to their left. She clutched his arm, but this was the arm that held the knife. A paltry weapon indeed.

A fourth wolf approached now from behind, from the direction he had come. Cutting off their path home.

Cautiously, heads turning, constantly shifting their gaze, he and Vialle retreated. They put the broad trunk of a tree at their backs.

Emboldened by their numbers and by their prey's inaction, the wolves advanced. One howled, an almost human-sounding cry that sent a chill deep into Zimenes' heart. Alerting other members of the pack that the hunt was on.

He had his own howl—though no pack of fellows to summon with it. He reached into the knapsack, pulled out the hunting horn. Raised it to his lips, filled his lungs with air and blew a blast that echoed down the tree-lined corridors.

The wolves crouched, and shrank back. Each looked toward

the others in confusion. They looked toward the lead wolf—the largest of them, the first one to reveal himself. Zimenes sucked in another deep breath and, head lowered so the horn's bell faced forward, he strode purposefully toward the lead wolf as he blew another blast. He bent forward as he went so the horn reached low and curved upward, like a boar's tusk, or the horn of the fabled rhinoceronte.

The lead wolf turned and ran back down the aisle of trees. Zimenes pursued, trumpeted another blast. Then he broke off the pursuit and returned to Vialle at the tree. The other wolves had melted away as well, following the example of their leader.

"Smart," she said. "Effective."

He'd scared them off, but how long would their fright outweigh their hunger? He still held the horn at the ready, his hands clenched the ivory tightly. He relaxed his grip, shook his head.

"What were you thinking?" he demanded. His ears still echoed with the braying of his horn. He closed the distance between the two of them. "Why did you run off like that?" He caught his breath for another blast. "You're lucky I followed you!"

"You're not my parent!"

"That doesn't mean I can't reprimand you!"

She stalked off among the trees, then hesitated. Stopped. He did not move to pursue her. Now his ears rang not with his trumpeting, but with the sudden harshness of her tone: *you're not my parent.*

She turned. Head bowed, she retraced her steps. She came to stand before him, head still lowered. She tugged the sleeve of his robe.

"I apologize," she mumbled. "I'm mad that I had to be rescued. Like a pathetic damsel."

He lifted her chin gently. She still would not look into his eyes.

"This forest will swallow us," he said, "if we don't stick together."

She lifted her eyes to his, briefly, gave a little nod that also pulled her chin from the crook of his index finger.

"They will try again," he said. "We can still make it to camp by nightfall, if we—"

"We can't turn back now," she said. "Don't you see where we are?"

He looked about them. Trees, endless trees surrounded them.

"These are yews," she said. "Judging by their size they are ancient. Each one could be thousands of years old."

He lowered the horn to his side. Finally, he could see what she saw.

"The tapestry," he said. "The ancient tree."

The weight of her stare was heavier than her fingers, still clinging to his sleeve. "Yes," she said.

"But the wolves," he said. He glanced back down the aisle he'd run through to reach her side.

"We are close to where my father saw the unicorn. I can feel it."

"We can return tomorrow. With more daylight."

"This is the place my father spoke of, when I was a child," she said. She swept the branch, held in the hand that was not clutching his sleeve, slowly about them, a gesture that took in all the nearby trees. "This is the 'dark heart of the Mirrenwood.' We have arrived."

"We can't get caught out after nightfall—"

"But we agreed," she said. She strengthened her grip on his arm. "You agreed with me that we ought to seek him at night, rather than during the day."

"Wasn't it you who said we ought not seek him at all," he said, "lest we prove ourselves unworthy?"

"We aren't hunting him," she said. "We have no weapons, no nets, no schemes. We are, simply, here."

"How do we catch him, then?"

"Maybe we aren't meant to."

The shadowy gloom among the endless rows of broad trunks, the gnarled roots that crisscrossed the barren floor, the tangle of branches that screened out the sun, the creepers that hung from the low arboreal ceiling—they all added up to something like the maze in the tapestry. Much closer than any other region of the Mirrenwood he'd visited in the past ten days.

"We can build a fire," she said. She lowered her knapsack from her shoulders. "I brought flints."

She held out her hand for his knife. Using the blade, she tore a long strip from the hem of her skirt, wrapped it around one end of the dead branch she'd been wielding. Using the flints and moss scraped from the bark of a tree, she sparked a fire, coaxed it to life, touched it to the white fabric. It took immediately, and sank its orange teeth into the wood as well. She hauled down a creeper and wrapped this around the blazing end of the torch, made a knot with it. It burned slowly, and smokily, but the flames took to the vine as well.

"We'll gather more branches as we find them," she said. "Between your horn, and my torch, we'll keep the wolves at bay."

"They have our scent," he said. "They will not be deterred for long."

"Trust me, Zim," she said.

"This is ill-advised," he said. "Your father would kill me if he found out I didn't dissuade you from this…this folly!"

"He'll never know," she said. She set off down the broad aisle where he had chased the lead wolf. "Until you tell him. After you've delivered the cure and restored him to health."

He grabbed her by the elbow, forced her to stop.

"How can you be so reckless?" he asked.

She whirled to face him. "Caution be damned!" she said, her voice strident but controlled. "This is my chance!"

"Your chance?"

"To prove myself," she said. She shook her elbow free from his grasp.

"Getting yourself killed will prove nothing."

"You wouldn't understand," she said. "How could you? You're a man. Men never have to prove anything to anybody."

She spun away and strode purposefully along the corridor of yew trees. He shook his head and set off after her, knapsack over his shoulder, horn at the ready, scanning the forest to either side.

"Truly, I have gone mad," he muttered.

The earth continued to slope down, gently. They moved slowly, their footing treacherous on the gnarled roots that broke the surface. As they brushed aside dangling lianas, a red berry or two would fall from the branches above, to roll away among the roots or be crushed underfoot.

"Don't eat the berries," he cautioned, with a glance over his shoulder.

Her lips pursed into a pout. "I'm not an idiot," she said.

He laughed. "I know," he said.

Neither of them were idiots. And yet here they were, plunging deeper into the forest, each step taking them further from camp— from safety—armed with only a horn and a torch. To follow an intuition. A hunch. A whim.

The downward slope leveled off. At each turn they followed

the broadest or clearest avenue possible while staying amongst the yews. A break in the canopy gave him a glimpse of bright sky above. He stopped and stared, blinking, surprised that night had not come on yet. The low intertwined boughs entangled with a web of vines and lianas kept the forest floor shrouded in perpetual twilight.

They came to a rivulet, a shallow channel carved into the packed earth. The water burbled over and under exposed roots. He stooped to it, cupped some into his hand. It was cool to the touch, and had a brown tinge, not muddy but clear, like tea.

"I wouldn't drink that," she said.

He smiled benignly at her.

"Sorry," she said.

They followed the water for a way, and then came to another rivulet that flowed into the first one. They stepped easily over the tributary, continued on even as tendrils of fog began to rise from the water, twist about their ankles, reach upward for their knees. Soon the low mist became so thick that they could not see their feet; Vialle had to wave the torch low to the ground in front of them to sweep the fog away so they could see the roots that otherwise might trip them up, but then the thick gray smoke from the fire lifted into their faces and caused them to cough. The hairy black creepers grew in profusion here, climbing up into the trees and then descending into curtains that they had to part—she with the torch, he with the hunting horn.

Zimenes demanded a halt. Vialle busied herself with renewing the torch, pulling down lengths of lianas and wrapping them about a sturdier branch that she broke from one of the trees. Zimenes produced the food that he had hastily grabbed from the supply before setting out after her, what seemed like an eternity ago: venison, parsnips, mushrooms. As he crunched the raw parsnips, he thought of how good they would have tasted in a stew.

"I hope Magda fares well," he said. "They ought to have arrived at the cloister by now."

"She's a tough woman," Vialle said. "I'm more concerned about Lord Guillem, to be honest."

"He merely wrenched his shoulder," Zimenes said. "He'll be fine."

"But his pride," she said. Her hungry chewing obscured any smile or other hint of emotion. "I fear it may have suffered a mortal blow."

Even as they ate, the fog thickened at their feet, obscuring the ground. Its tendrils wafted up to their waists, to their hands that held the food.

A low growl stiffened both of them. Vialle stood, lifted the blazing torch, swung it about. Yellow eyes melted back into the fog, into the dim gloom. The shadows that surrounded them had deepened, taking on an almost solid aspect. Like the fog.

And was it merely fog? The low-lying billows had taken on an ochre tint. And a sulfurous smell. He no longer liked how his food tasted, no longer had much appetite. No longer wished to rest.

"We must find high ground so we can build a proper fire," he said. "Otherwise, we will find ourselves outmatched."

He took the lead, parting the curtains of lianas, placing each foot carefully. They could not afford for either of them to twist an ankle on an exposed root, or plunge forward into one of the many rivulets that crisscrossed their path. He followed the ground up whenever possible, seeking a way out of the miasma. But each climb up led to another slope down. The trees here were larger, the exposed roots the size of branches, or even small tree trunks. The vines thick. The darkness nearly complete. The only sounds the brushing and swishing as they pushed their way through the clinging lianas, their labored exhalations, the scrabble of their feet on damp-slicked roots.

A mournful howl pierced the fog. From behind them. Answered by another, equally chilling, off to the right.

"Shit in milk," Zimenes whispered.

He checked over his shoulder. Vialle followed close behind, though her torch flickered. Wavered. Smoking more than blazing. They must stop and renew it. But the smell here, and the dampness in the air, were suffocating. He was perspiring. The roots had become so large as to necessitate skirting around them until they were sunken low enough to step over them. The trunks here were immense. Easily capable of hiding a lurking wolf.

Vialle brushed past him, breathing heavily. A wolf rushed by, its head and tail cresting the fog, and she shrieked and swept the guttering torch in its direction. Zimenes raised the horn to his lips and blew, but she interrupted the blast, jerked the horn down away from his lips.

"We may awaken something worse than wolves," she hissed.

She wrapped another creeper around her firebrand, but this

one was slow to take. A wolf darted in close. She swung the torch, and the wolf vanished into the fog.

"Come on," Zimenes said. He grabbed her wrist. "Keep moving."

They came to an enormous root. He glanced back over his shoulder, glimpsed the faint gleam of eyes in the shadows not far behind. He leaned his ribs into the root, lifted one leg up and over, then swung his other alongside, pivoted on his belly, and dropped himself to the far side.

He reached back for Vialle. A growl twisted her features into panic, and he grabbed her under her arms, and hauled her over the root. She crashed into him, and he staggered back under her weight, and they fell into the fog. She landed on top of him, forcing breath from his body.

He fought for air, inhaled greedily, sucking in a reek of rotten eggs and moldering hay.

She scrambled to her feet, reached in the fog for the torch, searching with her hands. When she stood up, branch in hand, it was extinguished. Light had nearly failed them.

He got to his feet as well. The wolves would soon find a way around. Find them defenseless.

"There!" she cried. She pointed ahead of them.

Through a screen of lianas filtered the pale gleam of fading daylight. They pushed forward, shoving aside the grasping tendrils, stubbing toes on protruding roots. They emerged from the curtain of creepers into a clearing choked with boulders.

Her hand gripped his forearm. In the center of the clearing, one immense tree towered over all others. A massive, gnarled yew whose roots curled around and, in some places, had even riven the boulders that had gathered beneath it. Its sweeping branches sprawled out to the edges of the clearing. An indigo band of horizon peeked between the crowns of the smaller trees and the lower branches of this enormous, ancient specimen. Within that thin line of pale purple, two stars burned brightly: Mercury and Venus, following the sun on its journey into the nether regions below the earth. They glanced at each other, agape, heads tilted back to take it all in.

The tree in the tapestry. This was the tree that King Adalmund had found as a boy, wandering lost in the Mirrenwood. This was where he had seen the unicorn, in his darkest hour.

She ran forward, leaping from boulder to boulder, making her way to the roots. The fog gathered thick in the spaces between the stones, but did not reach over them, left their large, rounded pates naked like islands swimming in a sea of jaundiced clouds.

He followed the princess, equally swift and sure-footed, his knees bending and straightening, cushioning his weight, propelling him from one rock to the next. *What feats wolves nipping at your heels can inspire*, he thought, as he leaped, landed, gathered himself, and ran for the next jump.

After a few such leaps they reached the central trunk, the concatenation of many smaller trunks fused into and swallowed by each other over years, over millennia, twenty trees, maybe even a hundred, slowly melded together and absorbed into one immensely wide, immeasurably strong singular column that soared above them. As broad in diameter as his tower back at the castle, and nearly twice as tall. She placed her hand on the bark, and he did the same, as they caught their breath. The wood felt warm to him, alive, though he supposed that was simply the thrum of his own pulse, the hammering of his heart, his lungs expanding and contracting like bellows in a blacksmith's forge.

They turned to survey the scene behind them. At the fringe of the boulder field stood a dozen wolves. The largest of them stood solitary on a boulder halfway between the curtain of creepers and his prey. Zimenes reached for the horn, raised it partway. Vialle touched his arm, but he did not intend to blow it just yet. The other wolves hid within the vines, under the shadows of the more ordinary yews. The lead wolf hung his head. The final glimmer of light at the horizon caught his eyes, and they burned yellow. He bared his fangs and growled at Zimenes and Vialle. But the remaining wolves whimpered, and sidled among the shadows, tentative, hesitant.

Afraid.

The lead wolf turned back toward the forest, leaped to the boulder behind him, then to another, and then he disappeared through the dark curtain of tendrils, behind which the other wolves had already vanished.

"Look." Vialle pointed down.

A curved trench between the enormous tree trunk and a boulder vanished beneath a large, twisted root. A few wisps of fog, or gas, drifted in the bottom of the narrow culvert, but up here the fog was not as thick, the air not as putrid. A smell of freshly unearthed mud pervaded here, along with a dank quality to the air, like the underside of a stone recently overturned.

She dropped down into the trench, crouched, and peered under the arch of an exposed root.

"There is room within," she said. She disappeared.

He dropped down behind her, lowered his head and shoulders, stooped at the waist, and followed the princess into the shadows beneath the tree.

# 22

He crouched and felt his way through a narrow passage, hands on cold stone.

"Vialle?" he whispered into the darkness.

"Here," came her voice from ahead.

Then his right hand touched something warm, pliable even. He removed his hand, rubbed his fingers together, and they slid over each other wetly at first, but then the stuff congealed into an oleaginous stickiness. He held his fingers to his nose: the scent was not unpleasant or powerful, only mildly musky, but close to neutral, like ambergris. He wiped his hand on his robe.

A thin sliver of light from the rising moon angled through an opening in the far side of their little under-tree cavern. As his eyes adjusted, Vialle became a hunched silhouette, rummaging in her knapsack. Sparks began to arc away into the darkness, and he crawled over what seemed to be smooth stone. Soon she was blowing gently, coaxing a wad of cotton kindling into flame among a swirling cloud of disturbed dust. Her face bloomed orange against the black. She held a candle to the small fire, and handed it to him, then lit another. They lifted their wavering lights.

The narrow passageway had opened into a small, nearly circular space. Tentatively Vialle stood up—there was enough clearance in the center for them to stand, though Zimenes remained hunched, candle in one hand, little paring knife in the other. Fuzzy tendrils descended from the ceiling, like roots seeking soil.

She turned toward him. Her eyes were black pits in the orange glow; her tousled hair a hood fringed with fire.

"The tree in the tapestry," she said. She flung herself into him, buried her face in the crook where his neck met his shoulder, forcing him to stand tall. He held his candle away from her hair.

"The wolves' sudden retreat makes me wary," he said.

She inhaled, straightened, and pulled away. Smoothed her tunic with her free hand. Her skirts, shortened for fuel, exposed her ankles, her shins, her knees even.

"We might be intruding on some creature's lair," he said. "We must investigate."

"I'll light more candles," she said.

He removed his knapsack, moved about the space while she set about touching wicks to the central flame. Dried sticks and twigs crumbled to powder under his feet. He leaned his candle into several dark crevices between boulders. Exposed roots hung low, and these hairy, branching strands brushed against his face and arm as he peered between the rocks, but they were shallow alcoves rather than passageways.

He turned back toward the center of the room. The giant yew had grown over these boulders, reached its many roots down past them into the earth, but the massive rocks had preserved this small space. On the floor, four candles burned brightly, evenly spaced around the periphery of their little underground den. She took his candle, the fifth, and knelt to place it between his feet.

She straightened. "We're safe here," she said. "Can you feel it?"

He was warm, perspiring in the close air. He removed his robe, spread it over the hard-packed dust. Laid down his knife and his horn alongside.

"Here we wait," he said. "Until daylight—"

She stepped toward him. Stepped into him. Lifted his arms to her shoulders, wrapped her arms around his waist. She looked up into his face. She did not speak.

He also had no words. There was something about the gas he had been inhaling that caught in his throat, rendered him mute. He placed his lips over hers. He meant it as a good-night kiss. As a parent might give to a child, a teacher to a pupil. A brief, benedictory kiss.

But their lips remained pressed together. Their lips pulled their bodies inexorably closer. Her arms wrapped tighter around his waist, pulled him into her, and his arms returned the pressure. He reached one hand up into the tangles of her tresses, the other he plunged down her back, to the inward curve at the small of her back, and then to the outward curve of her buttocks. He felt himself growing in strength, in vigor, in ardor. Felt his root enlarging between his legs. Becoming a tree, unfurling, stretching, standing proud, reaching for the sun, for the light, for the air. For freedom.

For so long he'd been a prisoner in his own body. For thirty-eight long years he had suppressed his desires, denied himself release, except by means of his own hand, scattering his seed over the stony, barren ground of frustration and humiliation.

"Zimenes." Her lips tickled his neck. Her breath was warm and wet as she whispered his name into his ear. "I want to feel you close to me."

"I am close."

"Closer."

He pulled her body closer to his, pressed himself against her.

"We cannot come any closer than this," he whispered.

"Yes, we can," she said.

She grabbed at his erect prick, wrapped her hand around it through his trousers. A sigh escaped from deep within him.

"It would be wrong," he said.

"Take me," she said. "Have your way with me."

*I cannot.* The words came to his mind, but he brushed them aside before they could reach his tongue. Instead: *I can, and I will.*

*What of the king? What of your friend Adalmund? Would you leave him to die?*

*There is no unicorn, and you know it. There is only you, and this woman, and this moment. United by your desire for each other.*

*What of your future?*

*It will wait for me. As it always has, and always will.*

He kissed her again. Her mouth opened fully to his, their tongues came together and melded with each other, melted over each other, turned each other over, again and again.

She pulled his tunic over his head, stroked the thickly curled hairs that tufted his bare chest. With a yank he undid the laces of her shift. She raised her arms and he lifted the frail cloth from her body, freed the buoyant globes of her breasts. The amulet that dangled between them glowed redly in the candlelight. She presented her breasts to him, to his hands, to his mouth, to his tongue. He wanted to explore every crevice of her body with his tongue, wanted to taste every part of her, even the acidic tang of her underarm, the dark thatch of hair there a tantalizing preview of that which grew in another, baser crook.

"Zimenes," she said again, and again, as he bathed her with his tongue. Her hands danced over his body.

"Vialle," he said. Another name came to his mind, unbidden. But he cast that name aside. Cast them all aside. As they had cast him aside.

"Vialle," he said again, more forcefully.

She lowered herself to the robe, pulled him down with her. She hiked her skirts up over her waist, and he pulled down her undergarments, revealing that dark place between her legs, which opened to him. She began to unlace his trousers where he knelt, and he helped her pull them down over his knees, then over his ankles. He tugged her skirts down from her hips, over her feet. He wanted her completely naked, as he was. He reached for her amulet, but she covered it with her hand.

"It remains," she said. She smiled. "As does your inkle."

He glanced at the mud and soot-stained band knotted against his wrist. His reminder. His shackle. He thought briefly of the paring knife, but her naked skin writhing against his erased any conscious thoughts.

He knelt between her legs, leaned over her, braced himself with a hand at either side. Lowered himself to her, but her hands met his chest, her elbows locked straight, sustaining him above her. Her eyes glowed darkly in the flickering orange light. They glistened wetly. She chewed her lips. Lips he wanted to kiss. He leaned forward, sank his weight against her hands, but still she kept him at bay.

"Zimenes," she whispered. "I've never done this before."

He smiled, then laughed. "Then that makes two of us," he said.

"Go slow," she sighed. She bent her elbows and lowered him onto her. "Be gentle."

He kissed her, and then he lifted himself back up and smiled down into her face.

"I make no promises," he said.

He kissed her mouth. Her chin. Her neck. Her breasts. Her belly. Her navel. Her pubis, and then lower still.

He didn't know that he had wanted to kiss her there ever since she first entered his chambers on her return from Gothenburg, a fortnight before, but it dawned on him in that moment, dawned on him that he had wanted nothing more than to slurp from that trough like a rude stable beast, wanted to do nothing more with his entire life than to explore the secrets of her folds and crevices with his tongue, with his fingers. She moaned and writhed, pitched her body side to side, and then ground her hips into his face, drove her cunt into his juice-slicked beard, his chin, his pointed tongue. He reached his hands under the round firmness of her buttocks, one globe in each palm, and lifted her like a goblet, lapped at her like a greedy peasant one moment, a kneeling supplicant the next.

She reached for him, grabbed him by his hair, hauled him on top of her. She placed her hand over him, guided him to the threshold. He pressed into her, but could not enter.

"Is this right?" he asked.

"Push," she said. Then, with a grimace, "push harder."

She cried out as her resistance gave way, and he slid into her. He pushed further, and her nails dug into his chest, pulled at the hair there. He pushed still further, pushed against the pain, his and hers. He pierced her to her core.

"Zimenes!" she cried.

He retreated, and then entered her again. Over and over, he pushed into her. Her legs splayed, her thighs gripped his sweaty flanks, and he drove his hips into hers, dug his root into her deepest profundity.

She clawed her fingernails into his shoulders now. Raked his back. His exhalation rasped in his throat, as breath came difficult in the close air, the sulfurous reek.

He looked down, and saw himself going into her, then emerging, glistening, foaming, stained crimson, and then diving home again, driving home, each buck of his hips digging a moan from deep within her.

"Zimenes," she cried. "Zim—Zim—Zim."

He felt himself melting, felt them fusing into one warm, sticky mess, as her blood seeped from her.

She grabbed the mane of his hair and slapped him in the face, forced him to look at her.

"Come..." she panted. "Come for me."

Shudderingly he spasmed over and over again, a flood that poured from the deepest place within him, into her deepest place.

He collapsed on top of her, rolled over onto his side, pulling her along with him. Their bodies pressed together. Her mouth opened, her tongue met his, in a long, broad, sloppy kiss that abandoned all pretense of restraint or sophistication. There was no need to pretend with each other, not anymore.

She caressed his beard, and he lifted his face from hers. He could not help but smile. Her eyes were moist, gleaming. He swiped the dew from her cheeks with his thumb. The candles were guttering. The moon had risen, and the silver shaft of moonlight had disappeared. Soon they would be plunged into inky darkness.

"Would it be greedy," he said, "if I asked you to do that again?"

She smiled and shook her head. "This is my gift to you," she whispered.

The candles were long since extinguished, and the faint light of dawn was stealing into their chamber when they finally stretched out over his blood-stained robe. Thoroughly spent, Zimenes lay on his back, panting. Vialle nuzzled her nose into his neck, her entire left side flung overtop his body, trembling. He ran his fingernails lightly down her naked back until her breathing came deep and easy.

He kissed her sweat-salted brow, then drifted into a deep, dreamless sleep.

# 23

A sound startled him awake. Leather scuffing rock. A murmur. Predators? The wolves? Or merely a voice in a fading dream?

He lifted his sleep-heavy head, opened his eyes. Daylight brightened their small cave. Vialle sat against the wall, near the entrance, his robe covering her.

He relaxed, relieved. The wolves had not returned.

Near his head, the inkle had fallen from his wrist, the knot burst. His dingy shackle lay broken in the dust. A final reminder, he supposed. A last stab of guilt.

Vialle's arms wrapped around her shins, held her knees tucked to her chin. She stared intently at him. Her head rocked slightly. Her green eyes wide. Her hands were knotted tightly around a small object; a leather thong dangled from her balled fists.

"Why are you sitting over there, so far away?" he tried to ask, but his throat caught, and the only word that emerged was "Why?"

Wisps of the ochre fog had crept into the room with them. He coughed in the close air. Breathing came difficult.

He said her name, but it came out strange, garbled, as though he were unfamiliar with his own lips, his own mouth.

"Zimenes," she said, strangely tentative. "I didn't—"

He placed his hands down to lift himself from the floor. Only they were hooves. Black hooves.

*Hooves.*

He shouted, but it came out ragged.

"Zimenes...." she whispered. Her lips continued to move, but her voice trailed off into nothingness.

*What is happening?*

He lifted himself to standing. To his feet. To all four feet. All four hooves. His head crashed into the ceiling. His rump backed into the rocky wall.

*What is happening to me?*

He tried to ask her this, but no words emerged. Only an insistent, "Why? Why? Why?"

He clopped toward her, head hunched, and she reflexively curled into a tight ball as he planted those hooves before her. She reached for him, placed her left hand on the inside of his right elbow. Only it was his knee, a knobby joint covered in black hair. With both hands she stroked the bristly raven hair that covered his forelegs. Her fingers so fine, so delicate, so pale. The touch so light.

"Zimenes," she said. She smiled, though tears streaked her cheeks, and her green eyes were bloodshot, rimmed with red. "I'm sorry. I never imagined—"

*Never imagined? Never imagined what? What? What am I? How is this possible?*

He spun, even as the room began to whirl on its axis about him, even as the massive tree above them seemed to sink down upon him.

"Garrimault states that deflowering the virgin, lost in the Mirrenwood—"

*A dream. Nay, a nightmare. A trick of the mind. Guilt besieging me, punishing me.*

His stamping hooves kicked into his knapsack, scattered its contents over the dusty floor. Erasing lines traced in the dust that connected blobs of white wax—one near their heads, two at their shoulders, two at their feet.

"—will bring the unicorn forth from his hiding place—"

*Soon I'll wake. Any moment now, I will be myself again. Now. Wake up, now. Now! Wake! Wake up, Zimenes, you fool!*

His right forehoof landed square on Adalmund's hunting horn, shattered it into dozens of fragments.

"—and cause him to manifest in all his magnificence."

Horrified, he lifted his hand—his hoof. Among the splintered ivory shards—a card. The twenty-third card, the missing card from Vialle's deck. The death card.

The Unicorn.

He turned to face her.

"Are you telling me you misunderstood the spell?" he demanded. Only, again, all that emerged was a horse's strangled whinny: "Why?"

He stepped toward her, awkwardly, stumblingly, his brain still unused to coordinating the movement of four legs, still reeling from the implications of what Vialle was telling him. She flinched and lowered her head to her knees, curled herself into a tiny ball, hid her face from him.

That was when he saw it, finally, in the pale light of morning that filtered into their dim cave. The extension of himself that rose from his forehead.

A long braid of bone. Three ivory strands that curved helically around each other, three braids that fused together into a slender spear that culminated in a point more than an arm's length above his head. A point so fine that it seemed to vanish. He moved his head, and the horn moved with him, inseparable, insuperable.

This space was too close. Too confining. He could not breathe.

He bowed his head, moved toward the low entrance.

"No!" she cried, rolling forward onto her knees, reaching for him. "Don't go out there! Not yet—"

He lowered his horn, his head, his shoulders, and squeezed into the narrow channel between tree and boulder, scraping his flanks, skinning his knees as he crawled toward the light, determined to breathe fresh air, determined to be free of this prison, of this woman. This woman who, somehow, did this, to him.

*What did you do to me?*

His breath came in gasps now, as the boulders compressed his ribs. He got his rear hooves under him and pushed, pushed, with all his strength, squeezing his body into a space that as a man he had crouched to fit through.

Boots landed in the trough near his head, one pair to either side. Kurk and Borek. They draped a net over his head and shoulders, though this was hardly necessary to secure him, as he was pinned in place by his own bulk and the cramped passage. He gathered his rear hooves beneath him again, and pushed, inching forward, peeling away hide at his flanks, his belly, his rump.

"Grab it," Borek grunted, indicating the horn.

Kurk reached for it, but Zimenes wrenched his head away. Borek leaped back, out of range of the sharp tip. But he kept a firm grip on the net, and now that kept Zimenes' neck bent, his head held to the side.

"Quick," Borek said to Kurk. "Now."

Kurk grasped Zimenes' horn in both his hands. In that moment, communication passed between them, nothing like the exchange of speech, but an immediate, direct communion between their souls, an instantaneous intermingling. In that moment each recognized the other for what he was. Zimenes knew Kurk to be a simple lad, devoted to animals, similarly able to commune with them, though not nearly to the intimate degree these two were sharing in that moment. Kurk, meanwhile, felt the man Zimenes imprisoned within the unicorn, straining futilely to escape, much as the creature that contained him flailed to be free of the men and the net and the stones and the tree.

"It's him," Kurk whispered, and he released the horn, even as Borek swung his broad-headed axe with both hands in a downward arc. Zimenes lowered the horn, and the axe dug viciously into a gnarled root of the yew, and stuck there.

The hunter expelled a cry of frustration, and Zimenes gave a final shove, the toes of his rear hooves threatening to snap, but then he was through, and he could breathe. The net still hung from his head and shoulders, but he could stand in the narrow trough. He turned toward Kurk, who shrank back, and kicked out toward Borek, one hoof snapping the handle of his axe, the other landing on his chest and driving him backward, knocking the wind from him. He leaped up onto the boulder.

"For Adalmund!"

Carlès was waiting there, sword raised in both hands above his head. Sunlight gleamed in the polished blade as it swung down toward Zimenes' elongated neck—

He wheeled, unthinking, to face his attacker. He moved so fast that the sword halted in its downward arc, frozen in time. He swung his horn into the flat of the blade, the jeweled quillons flashed in the sunlight as the sword spilled from Carlès' grip. It clattered over the boulders, dropped into a fog-filled gap and disappeared. Then Zimenes placed the tip of his horn against the prince's breastplate, and as he tired from the effort of moving so quickly, time returned to its normal flow, and the prince's hands—empty now—continued in their downward arc, to bounce harmlessly off Zimenes' head.

Surprise in the prince's eyes turned to shock—as the tip of his horn dug into the prince's breastplate, denting it—and then pain, as the boy's momentum carried him forward and the horn punctured metal, pierced his skin, jabbed his sternum, brought him up short. The pale blue silk of the prince's tunic, the fine gilt tracery along his leather belt filled Zimenes' vision.

When the tip of Zimenes' horn pricked the prince's flesh, it penetrated the core of his soul. As with Kurk, the prince and the physician communed. In that moment they recognized each other, profoundly—they knew and grasped at each other's souls. In that moment, Zimenes knew the prince's eternal struggle for his father's love and attention, a love and attention too often absorbed by the absence of the woman the king loved. In that moment, he knew the prince's derisive dismissal of the women around him, a defense against the anguish he'd felt when his mother left him behind— an unhealed pain that Zimenes himself knew all too well. In that moment, he understood the prince's intense jealousy of him, of the bond that knitted the physician to his father —much as it surprised him, he understood it.

And in that moment, the prince recognized Zimenes within the unicorn. And realized that the horn could punch through his breastbone and run through his heart and snuff out his life with ease. Each backed away from the other, and the connection was severed.

"You," the prince said, weakly, lifting his empty hands to his chest. Zimenes could taste the boy's fear on his broad tongue.

Suddenly exhausted from the strain of moving so quickly, and of melding with other souls, he slowly turned away from the hunters. He could see far to either side, commanding a much larger field of view than he was accustomed to, contributing to a vertiginous sense of spinning. The earth seemed to tremble beneath his feet.

*No, these are not feet. Nor are they hands. Hooves.*

He lowered his head, and shook the net free from his shoulders, his head, and finally, his horn. Unencumbered, he strode easily from one boulder to the next. He did not know where he was going, only knew that he needed to move, needed to find someplace far away from here, someplace where his head could stop swirling, his thoughts cease swimming, if only for a moment.

He had reached the edge of the clearing, the curtain of lianas hanging from the clustered yews, when he heard his name from behind, above a low roar that seemed to be emanating from the tree but that might simply be the jumbled chaos of a new consciousness. He turned his head, glanced back along his heaving flanks. Black pelt. Black mane. Long black tail.

"Zimenes!"

He turned himself around, haltingly, awkwardly. Still getting accustomed to having all four feet—hooves—on the ground. Vialle had emerged from the cave, climbed up to the rock. The enormous yew dwarfed her; she had wrapped his dingy, stained robe about her body, setting her in stark relief against the dark, shaded trunk.

"What have you done to me?" he tried to ask.

All that emerged from his mouth, however, was a repeated question: "Why? Why? Why?"

She bounded from one boulder to the next, following his course, each jump bringing her closer to him. He sidled, trying to bring his legs under his control. Still asking that question, again and again. There was no other question he could ask. No other question he wanted to ask.

Only a small gap separated them now, a fog-filled channel between the rock where she stood and the ground where he reared and stamped, whinnying.

She raised her empty hands, and he willed himself still.

"Zimenes," she cooed. "You are more beautiful than I could possibly have imagined."

He found this eminently unsatisfying. He didn't want to be beautiful. He wanted to be himself again. Zimenes, the man. The humble physician. Lying on the floor with Vialle, with his lover, with his love.

He still felt like himself, inside this strange body. Like himself— and yet, like something more. There was more to him now, he sensed it. Sensed a connection with her, with the yew, with the forest behind him. Didn't know how he had come to sense—to know—to feel—to understand all these things surrounding him. But he pushed this new consciousness to the side. He didn't *want* any of it. He wanted only to be Zimenes, the man. Making love with Vialle, the woman.

All that was gone. Forever, he felt, much as he didn't want to believe it. Much as he refused to believe it could possibly be gone forever.

"Shh," she said, "hush now." She urged him toward her. "Come, Zim."

"Why?" he asked, a single plaintive whinny.

*She had done this to him. And she had known the hunters were waiting in ambush, for him to emerge.*

He did not move, but lowered his head. She took one step

forward, empty palms extended. Her nakedness beneath his robe no longer aroused him the way it had behind the waterfall, or beneath the yew. Still, he yearned for her touch.

She stared fixedly, avidly, at his slender horn. He lowered it further, down over the gap that separated them. So she could grasp it. So their souls could...come together, and share each other. As their bodies had merged during the night.

*Could she explain this? Could she...perhaps...change him back?*

The bow creaked, then the string sang as the tension released. The fletches hissed as the arrow flew through the air toward him.

He reared back. The missile sailed beneath its target—his furiously beating heart. His front hooves waved in the air, and sent Vialle sprawling onto her backside.

Borek stood beneath the yew, nocking another of his black arrows to his bow.

Zimenes lowered his hooves to the earth, parted the creepers with his horn, pushed through them, into the maze of yew trees. The second arrow sailed past him, crashing through creepers and vines as it flew. His tired walk turned into a trot, gathered into a gallop. He ran through the trees, and his thundering hooves and swinging horn brought a rain of red berries down from the branches above.

Tears coursed from Zimenes' eyes, and cries tore from his heart—a gasping stream of unintelligible whinnies.

He ran to escape the dark heart of the Mirrenwood.

Zimenes ran to escape from himself.

# 24

He woke from a short, fitful doze, and stood quickly. He grasped immediately where he was. *What* he was.

He stood on the flat rock at the summit of the cairn of boulders where he and Vialle had first spotted the great hart. The runes at the four corners of the compass, marking the positioning of the sunrise and sunset at various times of year—he could read these letters now, their angular script oddly familiar. This place felt comfortable to him. He'd been worshipped here, an age ago, by a different tribe of people. A people more savage and yet more civilized than those who had so recently called him forth again, from the human physician named Zimenes.

His new reality. His new life.

A tear ran from his eye, down his prognathous cheek. He tasted its salt on his thick tongue. He was still capable of human emotions, such as sadness, and human reactions, such as crying. He retained his human memories, his human character. But for how long?

He longed to be human again. Would that, too, eventually dissipate?

For his new reality was like nothing he'd ever experienced before: it was magnificent.

*He* was magnificence, incarnate.

After fleeing Vialle and the hunters, he had crashed though the lianas and raced along avenues constructed by the ancient yews, his head lowered to keep his rapier-like horn from snagging in the low-swaying branches. He ran, not as fast as he knew he was capable, but still faster than he had ever run in his life—by far. Faster even than he had ever ridden on the swiftest of Adalmund's purebred chargers. The trees and the creepers whipped by in a blur, until he burst from the yews into a broader, younger forest of beeches and tulip poplars and black locusts, growing straight and tall, their trunks crowded with undergrowth.

But soon he was exhausted by his efforts, and by the strain of the change. He slowed to a plodding, head-hanging walk. At this slower pace, his flared nostrils told him immediately what trees and plants grew nearby; his twitching ears told him what creatures scampered and wriggled alongside.

As he moved among the trees, he knew immediately the names of each plant: feverfew, bloodroot, tragacanth, smartweed, sneezewort, stonecrop, lichwort, mare's tail. He knew them by these names—names he had learned as a man, in his duties as a physician. He also knew them by other, more ancient, more fitting names. Names spelled out in angular runes. He recognized immediately all their uses for man, and all their dangers. For each he comprehended a dozen more uses than those he'd learned, in his previous life, and twice the number of poisons or side-effects. He knew their uses for all the animals in the forest, and how they influenced their neighboring plants as well. This he grasped, intuitively, if he merely stopped for a moment to consider the plant, to smell it, to listen to its story, perhaps even to taste of it, a nibble with his teeth, a touch of his long tongue. What would have taken him hours of research in his library at the tower, accessible to him now in a heartbeat.

He was one with the Mirrenwood, and the Mirrenwood a part of him. Everywhere he went, the forest greeted him, spoke to him, through its scents, its sounds, subtle notes conveyed on the leaves' susurrus.

He was the luckiest man alive.

Only, he was no longer a man.

It wasn't just his improved animal senses that left him marveling as he walked. It was his horn. His power came from the braid of bone that grew from his head and tapered to a point. His horn had allowed him to mingle his soul with another. He understood Kurk and Carlès more than he ever possibly could have through a lifetime of human friendship and daily interaction. He even felt some sympathy for the prince, could understand things from the boy's perspective. Not only could he remember how he felt as an impatient nineteen-year-old boy, but when they'd come together, when they'd touched, he'd felt it, lived it, tasted it all over again.

Then there was the speed he was capable of achieving, in a

moment of dire necessity. He'd moved so fast when Carlès swung his sword at him that all movement around him had seemed to slow, to pause. Time itself had seemed to falter. But the energy he'd expended to move with such alacrity had left him drained. When Borek's arrow flew at him, not long after, he'd barely managed to evade it. Only his keen hearing and the distance between him and the hunter had allowed him to dodge, as he hadn't the energy to achieve that same blurred frenzy.

*What other powers do I have?* he wondered. *What other limits might I encounter?*

Eventually his hooves had guided him to a place that felt familiar, to both halves of him: the newborn former physician, still clinging desperately to his human memories, and a more ancient animal, with his own, long-submerged memories slowly swimming to the surface.

Awake now, after a brief, fitful sleep, he gazed south. Toward the cloister. Toward the bell tower, which he spied through the crowns of the trees.

Toward the woman he had once loved. Toward Tesse. Queen Tesse. She was there. He could sense her presence, when he cocked his ears and opened his nose. When he reached his mind in her direction. His horn, he realized, allowed him to project himself, his consciousness, in that way. When he did so, and concentrated, eyes closed, the world nearby shut from his consciousness, he could almost hear her breathing. Could almost hear her turning the pages of one of those books that he no longer required.

He was intrigued, but his human memory reminded him of his mission, his purpose for entering the Mirrenwood. His obligation as the king's royal physician. His duty to his king. To his friend, Adalmund. All it would take was a bit of his horn. A mere fragment. A figment. A sacrifice he was willing to make to save his friend's life. To grant to Vialle her father. To restore to Tesse her husband. To deliver to the nation its king.

He turned west now, faced the linden that grew at the top of the outcropping, its roots fighting for their tenuous hold on the stones that had been dragged there an age ago. Monoliths that he—or rather, another incarnation of himself, only vaguely remembered—had helped deposit there.

He charged the tree. Drove his horn into it. The slender spear pierced the wood through, with ease. He wrenched his head side to side, hoping to shear it off. But each twist and tug sent a shockwave of pain through his head, ground his teeth together, knotted his shoulders. He pulled it free, and swung it sideways, like a sword, at the trunk.

Again, a blinding pain, that drove him to his knees, scraping them on the unforgiving slab of weather-worn stone.

He reared up and smashed the thing down onto the stone, hoping to break off a piece of it. The collision rang like a blacksmith's heavy hammer on an anvil, a clang that deafened him and rang in his ears and shook him to his core. He staggered, and vomited. He searched the flat stone, then, hoping to see at least a fragment of bone, a shard of ivory. Nothing but the wind-swept stone. The slender horn—so delicate, fragile even in appearance— stood straight and true, undamaged. Not so much as a mark.

Undaunted, he reared up again, slammed the horn down onto the stone. This time the ringing in his ears drowned out all thought, lowered him to his knees, then to his flank. He lost consciousness, drifted in time and space.

*A boy.*

*A marble floor. Cold, hard marble, veined with black and green serpentines.*

*The encyclopedia he read from while he waited to be summoned from the salon for the day's lessons. Not his salon—his family was poor. His father, dead. His brothers, already in the fields, every day from first light.*

*The family that owned the mansion also owned his family, and many others besides. The boy had been chosen. Pulled from his mother to learn, while she mucked out the estate's stables. The boy showed promise, the deep voices said, high above his head.*

*A boy—and a girl.*

*The granddaughter of the man who owned it all—the salon, the mansion, the horses, the stables, the families, the fields.*

*A smile. A giggle. Fleeting touch of fingers in the hallway. Scraps of paper exchanged. Her handwriting surprised him with its crude misspellings. But each one a promise. To meet. To kiss. One day, to marry. To be free.*

*The salon again. Still a boy, though no longer small. Twice now he'd read the entire encyclopedia, across years of mornings, waiting for lessons to begin. The grandfather, stern in the mahogany chair. A formal petition for his granddaughter's hand. For the old man's blessing.*

*A smile. A word of thanks. A shake of the hand, a pat on the head. A promise.*

*And later that night, the beating. Her brothers. Her cousins. The same ones he'd taken lessons alongside. Jealous of his promise.*

*His mother, wailing.*

*A last hug. A last glance. A last cry of his name.*

*Bare feet on the dusty road. Tear-streaked face toward the rising sun. His back toward her, toward the estate, toward his entire country. To seek a new life, across the mountains, where people spoke in a harsh tongue.*

*A boy. Alone. Exiled. Outcast. Sitting beneath an olive tree, watching the sun set and refusing to cry. Clouds flaring vermilion and rose—soft, and beautiful, and forever unattainable.*

When he woke, the sun had begun its descent toward the distant mountains. Still that braided spear rose proud and perfect from his crown.

This time, standing came more slowly, required a greater effort.

Zimenes' thoughts and feelings swirled together, a mad whirlwind in stark contrast to the placid spring day surrounding him.

It was clear to him, as clear as the cloudless sky, that he must surrender his horn in order to save his friend, his king. He suspected that this would not be easy. Nor painless.

It meant returning to the one who had done this to him. She had known, she must have. He didn't want to believe—hadn't been able to believe, because he didn't believe that magic existed.

Now, obviously, he knew better.

He saw her face clearly, in his mind's eye: flushed, glistening sweatily in the wavering candlelight, loose strands of her hair plastered to her brow, trailing over her cheeks, her lidded eyes, as she panted, and moaned—and murmured. Syllables that hadn't seemed to form words, at least not words that he recognized.

Until she said, finally, *This is my gift to you.* The gift was not herself, her surrender of her body and soul to him.

No, it was something far beyond that. It was this... transformation. This revelation.

A gift, indeed. A gift, and a curse.

Maybe Vialle could figure a way to shave what she needed from his horn. If anyone could, it would be her. More importantly, she might know a way to revert him to his human form. To his old self, his old ways, his old means, his old thoughts and feelings. His old routines. His old shape.

Wonderful and powerful as he felt—magnificent as he simply *was*—still he missed familiar, comfortable old Zimenes.

He picked his way down the mossy boulders, entered the forest. Headed east, toward the camp.

# 25

The fire pit was cold, lifeless, full of ash and the charred remains of logs; the retaining wall still fragmented in the places where the boar had bulled into it. As before, only two tents remained, but much of the chaos that Zimenes recalled from his last view, just prior to chasing into the trees after Vialle, had since been retrieved and stowed. A bewildering jumble of scents hung in the air: the hunters, the horses, the hounds, the boar's bloody remains, just beginning to ripen, and bloat. At the far end of the camp, the hart's severed head still hung, forgotten, where Borek had left it days before. Flies buzzed about the gaping eye sockets, the dangling jaw.

Vialle emerged from her tent, and froze, still stooped over. Her green eyes widened as they fastened on Zimenes, as their eyes locked. Her mouth gaped as she slowly straightened.

"Zimenes," she whispered. "You've come back."

He stepped slowly over the scarred and pitted turf where they had battled the boar, crossed the dark stains where the beast's lifeblood had seeped into the earth.

She quickly glanced around the camp, then returned her gaze to him. She smoothed her tunic, her skirts. Stepped lightly toward him. He halted.

She raised her hands, open, palms toward him. To prove her defenselessness. He did not move. She came another step closer. Warily he watched her, horn upraised.

"You are so...." Her voice trailed off.

He sensed the awe in her, in that moment. The reverence. He was larger than the largest stallion she'd ever seen, thoroughly black, dipped in the inky well of a moonless, starless night, his dark coat glossy as though the sun shone bright on him, even though he stood in the shade of the tulip poplars that towered above them. Bearing an enormous spear that rose from his head, thick as a man's balled fist where it grew from his crown, tapering till it was no thicker than a finger, and then still further, a sewing needle, culminating in a point as delicate and wickedly sharp as a small-bore stitching needle.

She came another step closer, and he shied back.

"Shh, shh," she cooed. "Easy now."

She reached again. Placed her palm on his neck.

He closed his eyes. Allowed himself to feel her touch. Her caress. Indulged in the fantasy that, once again, he might be merely a man.

She let her fingers drift through his thick mane. Her hand came to rest at his shoulder.

"You want to surrender your horn to me," she whispered. "Don't you?"

He lowered his head, brought his horn down, to rest the shaft on her shoulder. Nuzzled the crook of her neck with the horn's spiraling braids. He stroked her slender throat, her ear lobe, the upward curve of the back of her head.

Her lids lowered over her green, green eyes, and she shuddered at his touch, at the horn's caress. He knew intimately the feeling of chill water that spread through her. He'd felt the same when she had pressed her dripping wet body into him in the cave behind the waterfall, eons ago.

Their minds—their spirits—their souls reached for each other, found each other. Embraced. Tentatively at first. Guarded. But he felt her love for him, and this emboldened him. The contact, once begun, proved difficult, if not impossible, to restrain.

Her unruly blond tresses cascaded down over his horn. She lifted her hand from his shoulder and wrapped her fingers around the horn. Her body quavered as its energy coursed through her. She tightened her grip, reached with her other hand as well, with both hands she traced the intertwining braids of bone.

He drew her spirit tightly to his, so she could feel the full strength of his love for her. He lowered his defenses. Revealed himself fully to her. Stood before her, naked, and unashamed.

In that moment of commingling, he sensed her drawing from him a glimpse of the power she might command were she to wrest the horn from his head. Were she able to wield it as a wand or a spear, were she able to grind it into powder for medicines or philters, were she able to brandish it as a symbol of divinely mandated authority.

—*What a gift I've given you,* she said.

—*A gift unlike anything I could have conceived as a petty, paltry human,* he agreed. *A profound connection with every living thing.*

—*It's incredible,* she said. He was aware of her marveling at the things he knew. At the power he possessed. *It's magnificent.*

He understood, now, how small his love for her had been. How small any human's love for another is, even at its strongest, its most unconditional: the love of a mother for her child. Even then, this "love" was nothing compared to the love he now bore for all of creation. The same love that drove creation to continue, over and over, an endless cycle of birth, and death, and rebirth.

—*I sought after love,* he said. *And instead was granted enlightenment. But, in giving me this gift, you took from me the one thing I truly wanted.*

—*What was that?*

—*You,* he said. He'd been so happy—so ecstatic—when she had pulled him into her, when she had given herself to him, surrendered herself to his petty, pitiful, eminently human love. *You were all I wanted.*

—*But this....* Her mind drifted through the expanse of his consciousness. *This is so much more.*

The human part of him would throw all this knowledge and power away, if he could only be that man again standing with his love, naked, so that they might come together again in that sweet sexual embrace.

He loved her for this gift, and yet he hated her for it.

—*You needed me to believe in your love,* he said, *for your enchantment to work.*

She could not behold him naked, could not partake of his new, enlightened consciousness, without also revealing herself to him. He saw her plainly now. No longer blinded by her feelings for him, or his for her.

*Strange,* he thought. He had never seen this quality in her before, neither as a child, nor as a woman. He certainly hadn't expected to find this in her now: fear.

She feared him.

Was it just the horn that frightened her? Perhaps.

Had vengeance been his intent, though, she would be dead.

They both understood that. Still, she feared him.

There was something else, though. Something even beyond the fear. There was a thing within her that burned even brighter than the love she'd harbored for him ever since she was a little girl, and he, her tutor, guiding her into the ways of the world, into the endless corridors of learning.

Something she wished to hide from him. Something she had tried to bury deep within the recesses of her mind. Something she had tried to lock away with arcane incantations, to camouflage with occult formulas.

She swiftly retracted her hands. But it was too late. She'd tried to keep her heart hidden, but she could not withstand him.

He reared back, tugged his horn free from her hair.

She stumbled back from him. He searched through his memory of her consciousness, rapidly receding from him, as she regained her balance, both on her feet and within her mind.

Saving her father had always been merely a means, not an end in itself. A means to prove her usefulness to Adalmund. A means to earn his love, and to earn her freedom. The freedom to decide her own fate, to claim her own destiny, to write her own history. A freedom the men in her life had always taken for granted.

The thing that burned even brighter than her love for him, the thing that drove her to weave her enchantment around him and through him, was her ambition. In the end, she could not keep this a secret from him. When she grasped his horn—when she touched his soul—she could no longer keep any secrets from him.

Sounds of men running alerted him to Borek, Kurk and Carlès approaching long before they reached the camp. He whinnied and reared back, faced toward the place where they would emerge.

Soon she, too, heard the men. She moved to stand between the unicorn and the hunters, raised her hands. The men fanned out, Borek with an arrow loosely crossing his bow, Carlès with his sword in hand, Kurk with the two hounds straining at their leashes, barking and slavering.

"Stand down!" she called to them. "Hold your ground! He has come of his own volition to render his horn unto us!"

She glanced over her shoulder at him. He could still nod his head, and snort.

She cupped his whiskered chin. She released him, simply said, "come." She guided him toward the canopy where Magda had prepared their suppers. Toward the log sawed crosswise. She plucked a carving knife from the wood.

At the sight of the knife in her hand, he shied back.

She raised her other hand, her empty hand.

"Not all of it, Master Zimenes," she whispered. "Merely some shavings. Just enough to make the medicine."

He willed himself still, lowered the horn within her reach. Very slowly, she laid the flat of the blade against his horn. Angled it ever so slightly, as though to peel the skin from an apple. She scraped the blade against the rough ivory braid, and the steel snapped with a spark and a crack that startled them both.

She gaped at him. He hadn't even felt the steel bite into the horn, hadn't felt anything before the blade gave way, curled like a dried autumnal leaf.

She laughed. "Impressive," she said.

Zimenes turned toward the hunters' tent, lowered his horn to point at a heavy broadsword that hung in its scabbard from the tent frame.

She came to stand beside him, lifted her eyebrows. "You want me to try with that?"

He touched the pommel with the tip of his horn. She pulled the sword free from its velvet lining with a silken hiss.

He backed away from her, strode over to the bisected tree trunk, and laid his horn across the surface. She stepped back, and he drew the horn back as well, so that only a hand or two at the tip of the horn rested flat on the block, waist-high. He watched her as she touched the blade to his horn where she would attempt to cut it, at the narrowest part, near the tip, barely thicker here than a finger.

"You're certain?" she asked.

He blinked at her, then snorted, pawed the earth with the hoof of his right foreleg. He was sure. He would give this part of him to save the king's life.

Hoping, praying, wishing blindly that the entire thing might shatter, that freeing himself of this accursed horn would revert him back to his familiar human form.

The princess raised the sword above her head, in both hands, and swung it down.

The explosion knocked Vialle onto her back, and sent Zimenes reeling from the block, staggering through the camp. Borek dropped the bow and clapped his hands to his ears, stumbled senseless into the clearing; Kurk moaned and writhed on the ground; Carlès sank to his knees. The dogs bayed, and the horses whinnied, bucked and chomped at their tethers. Zimenes' cry of pain spoke directly to them, his cousins, while it deafened the humans and the dogs and sent birds up into the air from every tree in earshot.

Zimenes vomited, coughed blood. Collapsed. Lolled onto his side. Closed his eyes. As he did, a flash of Vialle's mind and soul returned to him…he reached for it, as avidly as the man Zimenes had once reached for her body, but her consciousness, already distant, further receded and vanished, even as his own slipped away from him.

When he opened his eyes, the tall tulip poplar crowns swayed above, scraping the low clouds. All of their flowers, every single one of each tree's hundreds of pale yellow and green goblets, had bloomed, opened, and fallen at the sound of that thunderclap. The last stragglers still drifted down to earth, burying him and Vialle and Borek and Kurk and Carlès and the tents and the chopping block beneath their tulip-like bursts.

He cast his eyes along his spear. It remained intact. As though untouched. He got to his knees, and then slowly, achingly, stood. Vialle moaned and turned over. His hooves prodded aside the tulip poplars' flowers, exposing fragments of shattered, even warped steel.

There was only one way to remove the horn from his head. He'd known it all along, but he hadn't wanted to admit it to himself, he supposed. Hadn't been ready to acknowledge the fact.

The only way to prise that spear from his head, the only way to get the ingredient that would save her father, would be to kill him. Only then would the horn come free.

Vialle shook her head and moaned. Borek began to crawl through the flowers, shedding them from his broad back and shoulders as he went. He still clutched his arrow. He crawled toward his bow.

Zimenes turned from Vialle and staggered into the trees. He could barely muster a trot. He heard the bowstring tensing behind him, even as the thunderclap rolled back to him from the distant Mjolnur Mountains at the very limit of the Mirrenwood. Suddenly a pain blossomed in his rump. He craned his neck to look over his shoulder; a black shaft rose from his hindquarters, on the left side. The feathered end described a small circle in the air with each step he took.

The hunter had shot him. He'd been so tired and disoriented that he hadn't been able to move from the arrow's path. Hadn't even had time to react.

Borek nocked another black arrow to the bow. Zimenes turned and fought to move his hooves into a gallop, tried to stretch his legs, but it was no use. There was little underbrush here to impede him, and yet he felt like he was walking in water, water up to his shoulders, walking in a deep river with a strong current pushing against him. Threatening to drag him under the surface and drown him.

This arrow whistled close by; the arrowhead sliced painfully across his flank but did not stick.

Still, he staggered on, lather now foaming at his chin, his shoulders, his withers.

A third arrow *thunked* into a tree behind him. Finally, even at his agonizing pace, he'd put enough distance and enough trees between him and the hunter to shield him.

They would be after him, though. Sooner or later. Their work was not done. Nor was his.

# 26

He limped through the forest. Blood trickled steadily down his left hindquarter, dripped from his fetlock. He knew he would have to remove the arrow soon, somehow. But he wanted to put more distance between himself and the hunters. He knew they would be after him. And he was leaving an easy trail to follow.

He found himself back in the glade, where Vialle had patiently awaited the unicorn, braiding wildflowers together into crowns. The runes carved into the overgrown stones underfoot spoke to him of a fallen henge, built by a people who had lived in the Mirrenwood, in harmony with the forest, long before the kingdom of Averonne had laid claim to it.

He eased himself down into the flowers, to keep his rump immobile while he reached for the arrow shaft with his mouth. He managed to wrap his tongue around the feathered dowel, enough to bring it into his teeth, as though it were a carrot offered to a horse as a reward for good behavior. He bit down, carefully, not wanting to chomp through the wood, and began to pull. The movement wrenched the arrowhead within his hindquarter, and the pain made him cry out, and release his hold. Blood had dried around the wound, but now it flowed freely again, spilling across the sway of his back, given his contorted position.

Again, he reached with his tongue, again he secured the now saliva-slicked shaft between his teeth. Determined not to let loose his prey a second time, he closed his eyes and pulled. With a snap, it was free! But opening his eyes confirmed his worst fear: the head had broken from the shaft, and remained partially buried in his flesh. He could see the threaded socket protruding from the gash in his pelt. Much as he strained and twisted his spine, he could not reach the steel with any part of his mouth. He flopped back into the grass, lathered, panting, almost delirious with pain.

Then it occurred to him: the horn. He raised his head, twisted his neck. He pushed the horn through a portion of his pelt, and then into the arrowhead. At first the head slipped away among the folds of his flesh, but then he tensed his muscles, held the intruder in place, and shoved the tip of the horn through the steel. Then, slowly, gently, he lifted his head, raised his horn. The head came with it. Confident he held it secure—and sick from the pain—he flipped his head with one deft motion that freed the arrowhead from his body and sent it flying into the air. It landed in the trees behind him. He splayed out over the flowers, legs akimbo, exhausted.

After a time, he roused himself, walked to the stream, and entered it. It was too shallow to wash his wound, however, so he pushed against the current, lowered his head and ducked in under the spatterdock. He emerged near the pool where he had seen Vialle bathing. Here the water was clear and deep and cold. He submerged his rump, and at first it burned like an iron was being pressed against it, but then the chill began to numb that area. After sitting for a while, he moved to the waterfall, and stood beneath the cascade, let the water drum over his entire body, let it wash away the blood and any impurities the hunter's arrowhead may have left behind.

He caught a strange scent. A whiff of something.

He pushed through the waterfall, into the cave. Dimmer than he recalled, now that the sun no longer angled in off the surface of the pool. He shook water from his coat, mane and tail. Here the odor, while still faint, was stronger. It was...almost nothing. Little more than a wafting. A swirling. He opened his nostrils.

There: the smell of a tree that lightning had recently split open. Of a storm brewing on the horizon. Of rust just beginning to take hold on iron.

The remnants of an enchantment. Or an attempt at one.

The smell dissipated, but as it did, he could feel the blood at his wound drying, his flesh knitting together. He was healing. The magical energy was drawn to him, or he was drawing on it, pulling it into his body. Channeling it, somehow. Through the horn.

He heard horses. The hunters were close—the steady crashing and thrumming of the waterfall had masked their approach. He could not let them trap him here, in this cave with no exit. The magic was gone now, and he was still tired. He would not be able to evade multiple arrows—and he knew Borek was a deadly shot.

Instead of leaping through the fall back into the pool, he exited the cave through the gap between the wall and the water, clipped nimbly along the ledge where he and Vialle had sat and talked while they watched the sun lowering in the sky. After their kiss.

"There!" Carlès cried.

Zimenes tried to run, and found that he could. His hindquarter still ached, the wound was still open, but he felt rejuvenated, from bathing in the water and then in the ethereal remains of whatever spell Vialle had tried to cast. The summons? Had she tried to transform him there, even, on that sunny afternoon? Only he had resisted?

An arrow hissed toward him, but he knew instantly from the sound that it would impact the slate behind him, as indeed it did.

He reached the narrow stairs, and scampered up them, at a pace he never would've dared as a human. Let Borek and Carlès dare try to follow him on their pack horses. The horses would refuse. Soon he would leave them far behind.

At the summit, he saw a thread from Vialle's white skirts, snagged on a briar thorn. He turned to follow the path he had taken when he'd been pursuing Vialle. *Yesterday*, he thought. *It was only yesterday.*

He shook that self-pitying thought from his mind. He had an idea.

He followed a familiar smell, only to realize he was following his own scent, the scent that Zimenes as a man had left in his wake. The trail led him to the yew forest. At the border he hesitated. Reminded of the wolves, the tangled roots, the poisonous berries, the noxious gas.

But beyond all that, which he knew to be no real obstacle to him at all, now: the memory of what had happened there, beneath the great ancient yew. The memory of Vialle. And of his transformation. He did not need another reminder.

His still-smarting wound pricked him like a spur, goaded him forward. He knew the magic would be strong there.

And it was. He could nearly see it swirling around the base of the tree, vaporous hints of archaic runes, breaking and reforming among the ochre gas that emanated from vents hidden among the boulders.

He picked his way across the rocks. Came to stand at the base of the tree.

Now he could feel the magic surrounding him, the way Vialle had claimed to. Or, perhaps, the way she was able to. Perhaps she was more attuned than he ever was, whether through innate ability or training he could not imagine.

The enchantment's currents still eddied and swirled here, the odor a melancholy effluvium that seared his sensitive nostrils. Now that he was among her spell's residue he could see its architectonic remnants, a once-harmonious palace of glass that could be glimpsed only if he kept moving about the base of the tree, to catch the sun glancing against its panes at the proper angle. And so, he stalked among that swirling, shifting, wraith-like edifice, calling its fragments down from the branches of the trees, digging its debris up from the gnarled roots at his hooves, pulling these figments in through his horn and further into his body, extruding the poisons, knitting his flesh, stitching his pelt, drying his blood. Healing his wound.

When he was done, night had fallen, and he lay down on the largest of the boulders, and rested his bearded chin on his forelegs. Images of her giving herself to him, surrendering herself to him completely, festered and suppurated and oozed through his soul, reminding him of what was slipping from him: his humanity.

Would he truly never walk through the woods with her again? Would they never read each other's futures in the cards again? Would he never sit opposite her, the way they used to when she was his pupil and he her tutor?

Could it be true that he would never lie with her again? After finally realizing the meaning of love, reciprocated? Their physical union had fused them as closely together, had been every bit as meaningful to him, as when their souls intertwined, through his horn.

To be given a glimpse of that paradise, only to be cast down from it, forever. Into this existence that was, in its way, far greater. Into an ability to love that far exceeded that petty, conditional, scheming love that he had known as a man. But that wasn't what he wanted. He wanted Vialle. Still.

Despite this havoc she had wreaked upon him.

Her surprise had seemed genuine. Her apology sincere.

But what did he know? He was a novice in these matters. She'd been a step ahead of him all along.

And she'd been right. About magic. He was the proof.

How would he ever return to his human self? How could he ever become Zimenes again? If the only way to remove the horn was to sacrifice himself?

—*Give her the horn,* he thought. *Give her the cure for her father's malady. The key to her own salvation.*

—*Then she will have won,* a part of him whispered. Angry. Betrayed. Selfish. Jealous. Vindictive. The human part.

—*She deserves to win, if you must call it that,* the newer consciousness replied, calmly. *She took the principles and the truths that you instilled in her as a girl, and she built upon this foundation. She followed learning where it led, into the darkest depths, up to the highest peaks. Much further than you were willing, or able. She did what she had to do to save her father. And, in the process, she changed you.*

—*Changed me irrevocably. Into a monster.*

—*She gave you this gift, Zimenes. This enlightenment. This magnificence.*

If he were to do this, his sacrifice would reunite his best friend, Adalmund, with his true love, Tesse.

—*True love?* The human part of him snickered. Sneered. *You deserted Tesse at the first temptation. Some devotion. Some love.*

—*Don't you see, though? You had devoted yourself to a memory. To a fantasy. To an absence.*

—*Even so, I loved her,* the human within insisted. *Had I remained faithful to that love, this never would've happened.*

—*Would that have been a good thing? To stay stuck, for the handful of years left to you, as Zimenes the royal physician? You came to the Mirrenwood for a reason. You followed Vialle to this tree for a reason. You sought change. You sought the unicorn.*

—*I had no idea it would be so…drastic. So radical.*

—*We never do, Zim.*

First Mercury, then Venus followed the sun below the glowing horizon. No magic could heal that deeper, inner wound. No magic could soothe those darker, more sinister doubts.

His body—and then finally, shudderingly, his soul—relaxed into sleep.

# 27

He woke with the dawn, and the zephyr. The wound on his rump had closed, but was still raw, the flesh not yet solidified into a scar. The magic surrounding the ancient tree had dissipated, left nothing more than a taste of dew on his tongue, a faint shimmer in the air.

His head clear, and his heart light, he knew what he must do.

He would surrender himself. His sacrifice would reunite the family. Would make the entire kingdom whole again.

But he would not give himself to Vialle. No—he had a better solution. Instead, he would complete the legend of the unicorn. The creature that rescued the lost and starving boy in the Mirrenwood would now present himself, not to his daughter, but to his estranged wife. A gift to the exiled queen, to render unto the dying king, to save his life. To bring them back together in a loving embrace.

The symmetry of it appealed to him.

Thus, he would expiate himself, atone for abandoning his true love, for succumbing to temptation. His sacrifice would prove his love. To Tesse, to Adalmund. To the world.

*—Thus, you would also deny Vialle her victory*, the unicorn part of him whispered. *Hand it to her mother instead.*

*—A part of us is still human*, the human part of him reminded himself. *If some of that pettiness remains, so be it.*

He set off at a relaxed pace through the Mirrenwood—*his* Mirrenwood—letting his hooves guide his way.

When he emerged from the trees, an ivy-covered wall blocked his path. He'd reached the cloister. Queen Tesse sat in the gardens, on the far side of that wall. He could smell her. Hear her. *Sense* her.

Seeing her again, he hoped, would help him accept his cruel

fate. Confirm him in his decision. Now he was truly ready for her blessing, as he undertook this next—this final—stage of his strange journey.

He called out her name. It emerged as a whinny, of course. Her breath caught in her throat. Her head lifted, the lace fringe of her veil slid back over the silk tunic covering her breasts, her shoulders.

He whinnied again. Pages crinkled as a book softly closed. She rose from the lawn where she sat. Bent blades of grass slowly straightened.

He snorted, and stamped his hoof. He followed her footsteps along the way, till they both came to a disused wooden door, nearly hidden by streamers of ivy. The shiny leaves gleamed in the morning sun. She placed her hand on the latch—on Zimenes' side, the iron handle lowered ever so slightly—but did not turn it. They listened to each other breathing. Each wondering what they would see when that door finally opened.

He backed away, so as not to frighten her, and so he could take her all in at once.

The latch turned from horizontal to vertical. The door swung outward, then was arrested by the vines. A pale hand pulled them down. A foot, bare, stepped on the lower ones, pushed them down. The door swung open the rest of the way, and she walked through.

*Tesse.*

She lifted her veil to see him more clearly, to ensure that this was no trick of her eyes. Her blond hair showed gray strands at her temples; faint wrinkles radiated from the corners of her eyes, gently creased her cheeks. Cloistering herself away had not rendered her immune to the passage of time, nor to the sorrows of the world. Still her beauty struck him dumb.

One hand went to her open mouth, as though to catch an emerging prayer. The other hand reached out, tremulously, toward him. She wanted to touch him. She could not help herself. The human part of him found her astonishment gratifying. Her shock, and her desire. He was beautiful, he knew. He shook his head, unfurled his mane. His black pelt lustrous and radiant in the morning light. The prismatic tip of his ivory braid caught and refracted the sun's rays, split them into little rainbows that danced upon the shimmering ivy leaves.

Her eyes filled with recognition, and surprise. Her lips formed an "O" that mouthed the word "you."

She took a step in his direction, both hands outstretched now. Her cheeks dimpled into a tentative smile. She blinked, and tears fell from her disbelieving eyes, ran down her incredulous cheeks. He could smell their salt, could taste them on his tongue.

He wanted nothing more than to lick those tears away. To tell her that he was here, now. That everything would be—

"Can it be?" she whispered. "Can it be true?"

He nodded his head. His only way of communicating.

Emboldened, she came closer now.

"Have you come"—she hesitated as she searched for the words—"to give me your horn?"

He bowed his head, lowered the horn between them. Aware of its infinitesimally sharp point. Then lifted it again.

"To cure...Adalmund?"

He nodded again. Her hands lifted toward his face.

He wanted nothing more than to embrace her soul. To finally learn what she felt for him, now, and all those years ago. To relive her last night in the castle, when she came to his tower, from her perspective. To learn her most intimate desires. Even though it was too late for him to fulfill any of them.

She reached for his horn.

He wanted her to know that within the fantastical creature that stood before her, he—Zimenes—strained to break free. Surely then she would see—

She would see how it was that he became the unicorn.

She would see him, with her daughter, behind the waterfall. Beneath the yew tree. She would relive it all, with him, through him. As him.

"NO!" he snorted.

He reared up, swung his forelegs in the air, loomed over her. She could never touch his horn, so long as it was attached to his head. So long as he was alive.

He found himself bellowing at her. He yelled at her for leaving him. Yelled at her for being a coward. For not following her heart. For not being strong enough to either embrace him or tell him to cease, to leave her in peace. Berating her for being so pure. So sanctimonious, to use her daughter's word.

Of course, she could understand none of this. And now the human part of him found her wide-eyed terror gratifying.

—*You realize*, the non-human part of him whispered, *that*

*everything you just said is merely a mirror of how you feel about your own behavior.*

—*Shit in milk, I know!* Zimenes screamed at himself. *We are one and the same! I know, I know, I know!*

It all came out, to the queen's ears, as "Why? Why? Why?"

She turned and ran, through the door, back into the gardens. She hauled the door closed behind her, sending severed leaves fluttering to the grass.

He lowered his forehooves to the ground. Snorted, panted, caught his breath. The sudden eruption of these very human passions had taken him by surprise. Seeing her had brought the human part of him to the fore.

In one bound he cleared the wall, landed softly on the far side, in freshly planted rows of tender mint and sage and oregano shoots. In the center of the quadrangle a small marble fountain burbled, ringed by a grassy lawn.

She whirled from the door to face him. She gathered her skirts and ran toward the portico, toward the interior of the cloister. He easily intercepted her, lowered the horn into her path, backed her away from her goal. While keeping it far from her reach.

"I'm not going to hurt you," he tried to say, but it came out as a series of snorts.

She retreated, her feet dirtying themselves in freshly tilled planting beds. Soon her back pressed into the ivy-covered wall. She could retreat no further.

Her widened hazel eyes reflected his enormous, horse-like face back to him. She lowered her eyelids.

"Please," she whispered. She raised her hands together in front of her, as though in prayer.

Around her exposed wrist looped an inkle. A slim band, a simple design: alternating diagonal stripes of white and yellow, shot through with emerald green. The green of her daughter's eyes.

Abashed, he backed away from the queen.

A commotion at the door startled them both. Shook them from their stances: she pressed against the wall, hands clasped in front of her, tears pushing through her tightly squeezed eyelids; he with his head raised, the spear of his horn pointing toward the sky, nostrils flared, staring fixedly at her with a mix of love and compassion and jealousy and hatred, the man within pulled to the fore by these human emotions.

He no longer wanted Tesse to see him like this. When he had glimpsed himself in her eyes, he had seen himself as she saw him: as a monster, looming over her, backing her to the wall, leering lasciviously.

He no longer wanted to be like this. Split between two lives, in this unfamiliar body.

Vialle burst through the door that her mother had been trying to reach, and ran along the colonnade, vaulted the low wall into the garden. Breathing hard, strands of her hair stuck to her brow, others flying wild. An older woman followed after her, making apologies for interrupting the queen's meditation, but when she saw Zimenes, she merely muttered, "oh" and shrank back to the threshold.

He felt strangely naked, even though of course, as an animal, he wore no clothes. He felt as though his petty self and all his pitiful secrets were on display, exposed for all the world to see.

"Mother," Vialle acknowledged Tesse briskly, then turned to Zimenes. She had come to the cloister looking for him. Expecting to find him there, even. Still a step ahead.

"They're coming," she said. He knew who she meant.

She crossed the lawn and came to stand in front of him. Paused briefly to catch her breath.

"You need to run," she said. "Now."

"But Vialle," Tesse said. She separated herself from the wall. The veil had fallen from her head. "He has come to give us his horn."

"Yes, Mother," Vialle said. "But this is a gift we cannot accept."

"Why ever not?" The queen picked her way uneasily through the overturned soil, lifting her skirts. "Your father—"

"Because this—" Vialle began. She inhaled deeply. "This is Zimenes."

The queen stopped. Frowned. "Zimenes?" she asked. "What are you saying, girl?"

"He—" she began, faltered. "He changed."

Zimenes snorted and reared back on his hind legs. As he did, Tesse and Vialle both instinctively recoiled, shielding their faces with her arms.

He was yelling at Vialle. *I did not change. You changed me.*

He reared up again, swung his forelegs in the air. Yelled at her for doing this to him. For abandoning him in this place. For using him to further her own ambitions.

"I made a mistake!" Vialle said.

She extended her hands, stepped closer to him, urged him with her open palms to lower himself to all fours. To calm himself. She locked eyes with him, and he found a certain solace in her eyes, green as the soft grass that he stood upon.

"I caused this," she said. "But I will find a solution."

"But—" Tesse lowered her arms as well, straightened her hunched shoulders. Stepped onto the lawn. "But he *is* the solution."

Vialle waved her mother silent.

"I was not the only one to guess where you would go," she said to Zimenes. "Borek and Carlès are not far behind, and only because they stopped to gather the Champions of the Mirren from the gatehouse."

Zimenes nodded, lowered his head. Then sank down to his knees, flopped onto his flank. Stretched himself out over the turf.

# 28

"No!" Vialle cried. "Don't you understand? They're coming!"
He had no desire to flee. No desire to remain the unicorn, wandering the Mirrenwood, an exile from humanity. An outcast. Let the hunters come, and find him here, ready.

*Let her have her victory,* he thought. His horn would give Vialle the key to cure her father, to heal the wound between her parents. And to carve her own destiny in the world. Her own life. A life where she would not have to marry for political purposes, or listen to the dictates of any husband, for any reason.

Let her purchase her freedom, with his horn. She had brought it into the world, after all. The horn was hers as much as his.

Vialle leaped over him, fell to her knees at his back, tried to shove him upright, as though she could possibly lift his bulk. Her hands pressed futilely against his spine, but still, he did not budge. He flicked his tail at her as though she were a bothersome biting fly.

"You said we need the unicorn's horn," Tesse said, "to cure your father."

"Yes!" Vialle said.

"If indeed this be Zimenes," Tesse said, "then he has come to give it to us."

"But they'll have to kill him," Vialle said. He could taste the tears welling up in her eyes. "We can't just remove a part of it. We already tried."

She knee-walked closer to Zimenes' head now, spoke into his ear, as though he were hard of hearing and that was why he wasn't doing as she asked.

"They're going to kill you," she said. "Don't you understand?"

He flicked his ear against her damp cheek, craned his long neck to stare into her eyes. He tried to smile, but wasn't sure whether that would produce a grimace or a grin on his long face.

"Come on, you stubborn mule!" she said. Again, she placed her hands on his shoulders, and pushed. "Move!"

Then, in a more tender register: "Please. Zimenes. I'm begging you. We'll find a way to reverse this. But I need more time. *We* need more time."

"But—your father," Tesse said.

"Enough, Mother!" Vialle said. "I don't care about him!"

"How can you say that, child?"

"Did he care what I wanted when he sent me off to that horrid school? Did he care what I wanted when he offered me to any of these dolts? It's my life! Mine!"

"Always so headstrong," Tesse said, with a faint smile. As she knelt alongside Zimenes and her daughter, she dabbed tears from her eyes with her kerchief. "We will sit with our friend, while he meets his fate."

"It's not fate!" Vialle said. "He can decide! He is free to choose!"

"And he has chosen," Tesse said. Zimenes nodded in agreement. "See? He has always been such a devoted friend to our family," her mother said.

Zimenes turned toward Vialle, even though he could say nothing to her to put her at ease.

Vialle looked past him, though. She raised her hand in warning.

"This is so noble of you," Tesse whispered in his ear. "I would give you my blessing again."

"Mother!" Vialle cried. "No!"

In that moment, Queen Tesse wrapped her hands around the slender spire that grew from Zimenes' head. The horn that he had brought to render unto her, to save her husband's life.

Her whispered words echoed in his brain as a new consciousness joined him there, as their souls came together in a more intimate way than ever their bodies had, than ever their minds dreamed possible.

Tesse knew Zimenes, and he knew her.

He recognized a love there, but a broader love, a deeper love— not a carnal love. A love like the one he now had for the forest, for all the plants and creatures of the Mirrenwood. She did not need his "gift" of enlightenment—she'd already found it, on her own, painstakingly, over the years of seclusion.

There ought to be another word. Something other than "love."

This word we use for what we feel for a father, or a mother—for a teacher, or a pupil—for a benevolent king, or a queen—for a lifelong friend. For all living things. For our own life, for our gods and for our ancestors. How can we possibly use this same word for our lover? A useless, meaningless word, in the end.

He knew, though, her deepest feelings for her husband. For his friend. His king. The man whose life he was trying to save. Knew the guilt and the anguish that had led her to leave Adalmund, to exile herself. The feeling that she had betrayed his trust, the feeling that she could not trust herself around Zimenes. The feeling that she deserved to be alone, and unloved, because she had indeed, loved Zimenes—for a time, long ago—almost as he had loved her.

But not in the same measure. She'd sought him out that winter night, all those years ago, because she wanted to feel desired, wanted to feel a man's embrace, in the long absence of the man she truly wanted. But he had quailed. He'd failed her. Failed himself. And she had realized, even as he held her in his arms, that he wasn't worth tearing apart her marriage, tearing apart the kingdom.

He wasn't worth her love.

So, she had departed to the cloister, punishing herself for her emotional betrayal, to await her husband's summons. But that summons never came, and she took that as a sign that she had failed him.

In turn—though he tried—he could not hide from her what he'd done with her daughter, and what her daughter had done with him. She knew how he lusted for Vialle, now, rather than her. And she was present with them, behind the waterfall, as he gazed at Vialle's naked, dripping body, golden in the reflected sunlight. With them, as well, in the dim orange glimmer beneath the yew tree, in the dark heart of the Mirrenwood.

Shock. Betrayal. Jealousy. Anger.

The meditative tranquility of her consciousness roiled and churned and frothed now, as though Zimenes had hurled a boulder into that placid pond. She released the horn, and raised her hands to her mouth.

*Always such a devoted friend to our family.*

Her words echoed in his mind, now freed from her soul's presence.

His ears were drawn to the world outside the garden walls, where men's heavy boots rumbled down the footpath from the bridge to the cloister. The greaves and breastplates of the Champions clanked and clattered.

*—I wasn't worth it,* he thought. *Wasn't worth her love. Wasn't worth her sacrifice.*

*—Then what makes her worth yours?*

Curiously, he didn't know whether this last thought was the human within him—petty, vindictive, conditional—or the unicorn: analytical, dispassionate. Aloof to the affairs and concerns of humans.

The men's boots pounded over flagstones now, interrupted by a conversation between Borek and the matron of the cloister, in tones too low for even his acute hearing to discern the words. More footfalls cushioned by grass as men fanned out to either side of the cloister, to surround the garden walls, to enter through other doors and gates.

He lifted himself to sitting, hindlegs still splayed, forelegs gathered under him, head lifted, horn raised.

"Zimenes, please," Vialle said.

*We need more time,* she had said. *We'll find a way to reverse this,* she had said.

He didn't need her to grasp his horn to hear the concern in her voice, to see the love in her eyes.

She had made a mistake. She was young. Naive. Unaware of the transformative power of her magic. Of her love.

He didn't need their souls to meld again to know that when their bodies came together and clung to each other in that cave beneath the yew, their passion had bonded them. Branded them.

"They're here," she whispered into his ear.

Borek pushed through the door, followed by Carlès and Kurk. Borek knelt behind the low wall of the colonnade, and the other two followed his lead. Three knights entered through the gate that Tesse had opened, two through another gate at the rear of the garden, and two more scaled the low wall covered in thick ivy and swung themselves over the top, dropped down into the planters, their boots crushing tender young shoots striving for the sun.

"Hold!" Borek called.

He stood, nocked a black arrow loosely to his bowstring, but did not pull it taut.

Tesse rose to her feet, raised her hands.

"Gentlemen of the Mirren!" she said. "The unicorn has

returned—to give us his horn!"

"No!" Vialle flung herself overtop Zimenes, draped her body over his.

# 29

Queen Tesse leaned over and grabbed her daughter by her thick blond tresses.

"Remove your body from that foul beast!" the queen cried, as she dragged Vialle, shrieking, from Zimenes' back.

Vialle tore herself from her mother's grasp, flung herself across Zimenes' body again, shielding him from any attack, even as the knights spread out along the wall, brandishing their swords and spears, their eyes fixed on the wondrous creature at the center of the garden.

"It's Zimenes!" Vialle said.

Her mother pursued her, reached for her again. Leaned over her and hissed at her daughter, "I know who he is—and I know what he is. Believe me, girl—this is no more than he deserves."

"No!" Vialle screamed, even as her mother dragged her from his body once again, wrapped her arms around her daughter.

"You had no way of knowing," Tesse said, as she wrestled to keep Vialle pinioned tightly to her breast.

"This is Zimenes, Mother," Vialle said through clenched teeth as she struggled. "There has to be another way."

Zimenes gathered his feet beneath him and stood to face his attacker. His executioner. Borek stepped from behind the column, sighted along the length of his nocked arrow.

"You were young," Tesse said. "And naive."

Borek's steely arrowhead settled over Zimenes' exposed breast. The bowstring tensed.

"Just as I was when he seduced me."

Time slowed around him. A bead of sweat formed on Borek's bald pate, right at the place where the scar began its run down the side of the man's face. The bowstring had nearly reached maximum tension; in an instant Borek would loose the arrow, send it flying straight and true into Zimenes' heart.

"He is a monster now," Tesse said, her voice little more than that of a gnat in his ear, "because he *always was* a monster."

No—not always. Zimenes was still in there, somewhere. He wasn't dead yet.

And he knew who he truly loved, and who loved him in return.

Borek's arrow quivered, that bead of sweat broke and began its course down the scar's channel.

Zimenes charged. He crossed the garden and buried his horn into Borek's heart so quickly that he essentially materialized there, his hooves in a patch of mint planted at the fringe of the yard. His neck leaned over the low colonnade wall, his horn projected from Borek's back.

The arrow limply twirled from the hunter's suddenly slack bowstring, stuck harmlessly into the turf. The hunter's blood dripped scarlet from the horn's ivory braids.

The blur of speed exhilarated him. He lifted Borek, still momentarily alive, off his feet. Zimenes walked backward, brought his trophy from the colonnade into the light of the sun, for all to see.

As he did, unicorn and hunter embraced each other's soul, even as Borek's punctured heart ceased pumping the blood and bile and phlegm throughout his organs, even as his last breath fled from his lungs. Zimenes glimpsed the many creatures, mundane and monstrous, that this man had killed over his life's span, and he felt no pity for having taken the hunter's life in turn. He knew that Borek felt no remorse either: a fell beast he'd been hunting had vanquished him, finally. He'd hesitated—halted for the briefest moment to admire the creature he knew he must slay—and thus, in that momentary delay, had met his master.

Borek's soul clasped his—fervently, devoutly—and then their spirits untwined, and Borek's slipped away, unravelling into the abyss.

Zimenes lowered his head, allowed the hunter to slide from his horn. He laid the dead man gently down on the grass.

Kurk grabbed the sword from stunned Carlès' hand. The boy vaulted the low wall, clenched the pommel in both hands and raised the blade high as he ran at Zimenes.

Zimenes' efforts had left him exhausted. Communicating with Tesse, the blink-of-an-eye charge at Borek—these required a supreme effort and focus that left him drained and spent. Kurk leaped at him, slashed at him, and he stepped back over Borek's body, barely backpedaled out of range.

Kurk paused, and knelt, and closed the hunter's lifeless eyes. Then he stood, his face wrenched and overwrought. No sounds emerged from his mouth, but the tears streamed silently down his cheeks. He came at Zimenes.

He dodged the first wild swing, then the second, the lad coming closer each time. Kurk was crying so much for the death of his beloved master that his tears obscured his vision. His shoulders and torso shook so much that it weakened his swings. He sidestepped another lunge.

For Zimenes, even in his exhausted state, it would be a trivial thing to kill Kurk. He didn't want to, though. He was just a boy, in mourning for his father, or for the man whom he had adopted as his father. The human within remembered genuinely liking Kurk. Zimenes had found him quite interesting in those moments when the two had walked alongside each other in the woods, or the morning when the two of them had constructed frames for the tents.

Still Kurk came at him, bawling, sputtering curses, having found his lungs and his voice. Anger and a thirst for revenge began to overtake the initial shock and heartache of seeing his master spitted on Zimenes' horn. Kurk hacked and backed Zimenes into the center of the yard, and the knights pressed forward, their weapons at the ready, giving him less room to maneuver and dodge. The gore-encrusted horn on his head no longer felt like a slender spire, but instead seemed a thing as heavy and clumsy as a blacksmith's anvil.

Kurk raised the sword above his head, in both hands, and swung it down.

Zimenes swung up his horn to parry the strike, met the arcing blade in mid-stroke. The thunderclap blasted the sword from Kurk's hand, knocked the boy to the turf, caused the surrounding knights to drop their weapons and cover their ringing ears.

Zimenes turned toward the center of the yard. Toward the fountain. Toward Vialle, and Tesse.

The queen clutched at Vialle, put her own body in between Zimenes and her daughter.

"You'll not take her from me again," she spat. She held Vialle behind her, her chest thrust forward, her body her only defense against the cruel, heartless, murderous monster that she now believed Zimenes to be.

Zimenes, head heavy, limbs tired, slowly crossed the lawn. The broad toes of his hooves dragged over the turf.

He came to stand in front of the woman he once loved, who hid the woman he now loved from him.

"Mother, this was all my fault," Vialle begged.

"You think you worked your magic on him?" Tesse said. She had gleaned that much from Zimenes' memory. "He played you for a fool, my girl. And I should know, because he did the same to me."

"Kill him!" Carlès shouted from the colonnade. "Kill that hideous creature!"

The knights tried to gather their senses. They stooped clumsily to retrieve their weapons.

"You were under his spell the entire time," Tesse whispered. "He knew how vulnerable you were."

"We dare not strike the queen!" called one of the Champions.

Zimenes looked past Tesse, much as the queen tried to hold his eyes in her fierce, regal glare. She tightened her grip on Vialle, moved them backward, toward the fountain, burbling merrily away.

He sought out Vialle's green, green eyes, found them. Saw the fear. The hesitation. The doubt.

"Don't worry, my child," Tesse said, defiant. "I won't let him hurt you again."

*I will not give my life,* he thought. *Not for these people. Not for anyone. There is a destiny for me yet, beyond these walls. A new life awaits me there. My life awaits.*

He lifted his head, and walked past them. He had extended his invitation. He would not compel her to join him. Could not do so, whether he wished or no. He was not her king, nor her husband— he was not even a man. Nor would he ever be any of those things, ever again.

He was, simply, Zimenes. And the time had come for him to leave.

"Kill him!" Carlès shouted, voice ragged.

Zimenes put the women behind him, and readied himself for a final run at the wall. He was tired from his exertions, but he should still be able to clear it—

A weight landed on his back.

Arms wrapped around his neck. Thighs clenched his flanks.

A cheek pressed against his ear. Whispered: "go."

"For Adalmund!" Carlès cried. "For my father!"

"Sire! We dare not!" a Champion replied. "The princess!"

Zimenes reared back slightly, careful not to fling his passenger from his back, but wishing to make sure she held him tightly. She gripped him with her entire body.

"I don't care!" the prince yelled. "I want that thing dead!"

Zimenes charged toward the wall, even as the knights rushed toward him, a thicket of steely edges and sharp points. A last burst of speed, of energy—he drew on deep reserves within the horn, and he flew past their thrusts, skipped over their hacks at his legs, and leapt.

He cleared the wall, and landed on the far side. Vialle's teeth clacked in her mouth, the air rushed from her lungs, but still she held tight. He stopped, gathered himself, turned his head toward her, stretched out on her belly along his spine.

"Don't worry about me," she panted. "Just go. Run!"

The knights spilled through the gate, ran at them with their spears and their swords. He moved from walk to canter to trot, and soon the men's stubby pairs of legs were no match for his long, graceful gallop.

He plunged into the trees, and soon left the Champions far behind, a distant clamor and clatter. A final shriek of frustration from the prince echoed after them, but soon that too was lost in their wake, and it was just the two of them, Zimenes and his rider, Vialle, plunging through the trees.

He slowed to a walk. Still, she kept her arms tight around his shoulders, her hands clasped at his chest, her thighs around his flanks. She pressed her cheek against his neck. He needed to rest, but he didn't wish to disturb their closeness. Didn't want to lower her from his back. Not yet.

The Lady of the Mirrenwood opened herself to her children, enveloped them in her dappled light and sweet, swirling breath, enclosed them in her welcoming arms.

It wasn't forever. He knew that.

It was for now. And that was enough.

# About the Author

Born in Australia, raised a Mennonite in the heart of Amish country, educated at Harvard University, Andrew Hallman now lives in Philadelphia where he works in the rare book trade. MIRRENWOOD is his debut novel, and the first in a projected series. Please visit andrewhallman.com to be kept apprised of future releases.

## Acknowledgments

The author would like to thank Richard Curtis for his invaluable editorial aid and tireless efforts; Daniel Sheinberg for his keen insight; and a special thanks to James Rahn and all the wonderful writers and readers of Rittenhouse Writers Group who helped with early portions of the manuscript.

Curious about other Crossroad Press books?
Stop by our site:
http://store.crossroadpress.com
We offer quality writing
in digital, audio, and print formats.